“Do you … **?”**

Sarah eyed hi… torial grin spread, brin… view. “Truth be told,” s… adore it. I learned from my cousin’s dancing master. God bless Lady Jersey for bringing it back from Vienna. It is truly the only dance worth dancing.”

Malcolm felt his own grin spreading. He held out his hand. “In that case, will you do me the honor?”

She stared at his hand as if he offered her a snake. “You are asking me to dance?”

“I am asking you to waltz,” he corrected her. “Turn about is fair play, after all. Well?”

She stared at him a moment longer, as if weighing the repercussions. Then she laid her hand firmly in his.

“I would be delighted,” she told him, and he pulled her into his arms and out onto the floor.

It was the finest waltz he had ever danced. From the moment he held her womanly frame against him, the ballroom receded to a soft gray blur, like a mist around them. She was attuned to his every movement, reacting seconds before he even knew he had prompted her to do so. She moved so gracefully that it heightened the feeling they were dancing on air. He gazed down into those witch’s eyes, now a deep blue, and wondered whether he was under a spell he would ever care to break.

Anne Prestwick would only laugh at him. Her charming husband had presented Malcolm with the Incomparable Miss Compton, and Malcolm found he much preferred her chaperon.

Other Books by Regina Scott

THE UNFLAPPABLE MISS FAIRCHILD

THE TWELVE DAYS OF CHRISTMAS

"SWEETER THAN CANDY" in A MATCH FOR MOTHER

THE BLUESTOCKING ON HIS KNEE

"A PLACE BY THE FIRE" in MISTLETOE KITTENS

CATCH OF THE SEASON

A DANGEROUS DALLIANCE

THE MARQUIS'S KISS

"THE JUNE BRIDE CONSPIRACY" in HIS BLUSHING BRIDE

Published by Zebra Books

And look for THE IRREDEEMABLE MISS RENFIELD coming December 2001

THE INCOMPARABLE MISS COMPTON

REGINA SCOTT

ZEBRA BOOKS
Kensington Publishing Corp.
http://www.zebrabooks.com

ZEBRA BOOKS are published by

Kensington Publishing Corp.
850 Third Avenue
New York, NY 10022

First Printing: August 2001
10 9 8 7 6 5 4 3 2 1

Printed in the United States of America

To the Incomparable Miss Kristin Manke,
for her friendship, her advice, and her professionalism.

And to the intelligent and fortunate Mr. Richard May,
who had the good sense to recognize an
Incomparable when he saw one.

ONE

"Are we agreed, gentlemen?" Malcolm, Viscount Breckonridge, glanced around the table in the library of his London town house. He met the gaze of each of the peers who had joined him that evening. The older Walcott was eager; the jowls on his long face nearly quivered in anticipation. Yarmouth was cautious; he chewed his full lower lip like a nervous schoolgirl. Wells, by far the youngest, exhibited his usual studied boredom; he leaned back in his chair, a difficult feat when one considered that the chair was of stiff mahogany like the table and Wells was tall and angular. Yet, despite their posturing, Malcolm knew he had them. He squared his shoulders and leaned forward, holding their gazes until he saw commitment.

"Agreed," they chorused, then Walcott and Yarmouth grinned at each other. Wells merely nodded.

Walcott rose and offered Malcolm his hand. "I don't know how you do it, Breckonridge. However intractable we are, you find a way to make peace."

"Frightens us into it," Yarmouth ventured, although his tone was admiring. "Shouldn't like to cross anyone the size of Lord Breckonridge, by your leave."

"There are dockworkers with Lord Breckonridge's height and reach," Wells drawled. "I don't fear them."

"Nor should you fear me," Malcolm joked. "Gentlemen, you must know I live to serve."

Walcott chuckled, a deep sound that rumbled through the dusty library. "And serve you do. I would have thought this act was dead before it saw the floor of Parliament."

"An act worth penning is an act worth saving," Malcolm replied as he shook the earl's hand. He had to hide his smile of triumph. They must none of them know the many moments he had doubted, the many hours he had spent devising strategies to win them over. "May I get you gentlemen anything? Dinner? A glass of brandy? My carriage home?"

Walcott waved him off even as Wells and Yarmouth pushed back their chairs to rise. "I must be going," Lord Walcott replied, making his slow, ponderous way toward the door. "My lady is expecting to go to the theater this evening."

The more dapper Yarmouth shook his head in obvious pity. "Shame, that. You'll miss all the excitement. Almack's, don't you know. Blasted lottery of sorts. Who would have thought she could pull it off? See you shortly, Breckonridge."

Malcolm froze in the act of opening the door, but recovered quickly by turning the movement into a bow of acknowledgment as they filed past him into the marble-tiled hall. Shortly? Had he forgotten a meeting? The Prime Minister, Lord Liverpool, had promised him there would be no session tonight so that he could bring these last three recalcitrant peers into agreement. But Viscount Yarmouth had said Almack's. Had Malcolm lost track of the day again? No, it couldn't be Wednesday, when the lady patronesses held the subscription balls for which Almack's was famous. Parliament was expected to vote on the return to the gold standard Wednesday, and they had only just begun discussing it yesterday.

"Or do you plan to be fashionably late again?" Wells quipped with his usual dry humor. "You may yet earn Lady Prestwick's wrath."

The ball! Anne would have his head if he didn't go. One of the things he admired about Lady Anne Prestwick was that she never raised a fuss, never so much as raised her voice. Yet he'd seen her silences drive people to repentance. He never thought he'd be one of them. He smiled politely and escorted his colleagues to the door, offering additional congratulations, promising to see them shortly. Only when the door was shut safely behind them did he bolt for the stairs.

The clock on the mantel in his bedchamber informed him it was a quarter to three, but that couldn't be right. He had evidently forgotten to wind it again. He kicked off his shoes and began shucking off his trousers. The dressing room door opened, and his valet Appleby stepped to his side to assist him with the tailored coat.

"How late am I?" Malcolm growled.

"It is a quarter after nine," his valet replied. "The ball in your honor started over a half hour ago."

"Leave the vest then," Malcolm barked. "I'll have to go as I am."

Appleby said nothing, but the set of his thin lips told Malcolm the valet disapproved of his wearing the navy striped waistcoat with his evening black. An unobtrusive fellow with sandy brown hair, prominent front teeth, and a slight build, Appleby had been part of Malcolm's inheritance when he ascended to the title after his older cousin died. Malcolm had never felt particularly fond of the fellow, although he could have said the same about any of the servants in the town house, in fact, of any of the servants on any of his estates across England. As long as the house functioned and he had clothes and food when he needed them, he generally let his staff go their way as he went his.

The problem was, of course, that the house did not appear to be functioning. His dinners, when he bothered to come home for them, were tasteless. His library was a cluttered mess. The house echoed with neglect. Someone needed to get his life in order, and he certainly didn't have time to do it. All the more reason for this ball, even if the thought of courting made him shudder.

Appleby silently produced a black velvet evening cloak, and Malcolm swung it around his shoulders. He paused to glance in the gilded mirror over the dressing table. Although a thin layer of dust coated the surface, there was no mistaking the gentleman who looked back. As leader of the moderate Whigs, he was a well-known sight. His usual hunting grounds in the halls of Parliament swarmed with prey and predator, and he relished the verbal games that allowed him to tell which was which. But tonight it would not be his fellow lords who sought his time. Tonight he would be the prey, and the predators would be closing for the kill.

He could not shake the feeling of impending doom as he rode in his carriage to the assembly rooms on King Street. How his peers in the House of Lords would laugh if they knew that he detested what he was about to do. Malcolm, Viscount Breckonridge, the gilded tongue, the intimidating countenance, the tireless diplomat, balking at persuading a woman to marry him. Truth be known, it wasn't the persuading that concerned him. It was the time that persuasion would take away from his career. He must have been mad to agree to this.

Climbing the stairs of the building to the main salon, he could hear the strains of dance music. The ball was apparently in full swing. Still, it was probably too much to hope he might slip in unobtrusively and make his apologies to Anne. He handed his cloak to a waiting servant at the top of the stairs and took a deep breath, stepping through the arched entryway. Lord, it was worse than he had thought.

The ball was a tremendous squeeze. He was not arrogant enough to suppose it was all because of him. Lord Chas Prestwick had been known for outrageous stunts such as betting his best friend he could not somersault from one end of Hyde Park to the other. Even though he had ascended to the title of Earl of Prestwick and married the quiet Anne Fairchild, many in society doubted he'd changed his stripes. They had no doubt come hoping for some excitement. He could see one of the stern-faced lady patronesses of Almack's even now, watching his friend Lord Prestwick with narrowed eyes as he did the pretty with his lovely wife on the dance floor. Lady Jersey looked sure he would disgrace the reputation of her famed hall. What did she expect, that he would suddenly leap up to catch the crystal chandelier overhead? She obviously didn't know Anne well.

It was not every young society matron who chose to rent Almack's to host her first ball. The hallowed hall was draped with streamers of multicolored satin, like the tail of a peacock. Fresh beeswax candles glittered in the sconces next to the busts of prominent Greeks. The polished floor gleamed, where he could see it beneath the crush of the crowd. Even the sharp-tongued Lady Jersey could find no fault, he was sure.

But he could. Despite his silence on the matter, word had evidently gotten out that Lord Breckonridge sought a bride. What had Yarmouth called it, a lottery? Even now heads were turning to gaze at him, eyes were lighting, ladies were simpering.

He was done for.

But he would go down with honor. Head high, he attempted to stroll around a group of young ladies, all of whom giggled madly as he approached. Detouring to his right, he was forced to sidestep another young lady who gazed at him imploringly all the while dropping a curtsy that revealed far too much of her bosom. Across the expanse of floor, he could see the dance ending, and Lady Prestwick smiling at her handsome husband. Surely she would expect him to present himself immediately. He tried another detour.

"Good evening, my lord." The rotund Lady Renderly put herself neatly in his path so that he was forced to stop to keep from ramming the purple ostrich plume in her turban up his nose. She did not bother to drop him a curtsy, but merely thrust a young lady toward him. "I believe you know my daughter Elspeth?"

He bowed and smiled at the blushing girl gowned in white. "A pleasure to see you again, Lady Elspeth. Your father speaks of you often." *In loud, lamenting tones,* he refused to add as the girl blinked vapid blue eyes at him. Three Seasons on the ton, and the Renderly chit had yet to find a fellow willing to accept her considerable dowry over the dubious honor of being related to her mother. He could not find it in himself to change her luck. "If you'll excuse me, ladies, I must pay my respects to Lady Prestwick."

"I am much put out," Lady Renderly replied in booming tones that set those in the immediate vicinity to staring. "We were promised an interview, and we've barely had a moment of your time."

Malcolm would have liked to have her put out—out of the ballroom, out of London, preferably out of the country. But Lord Renderly was a staunch supporter of the Whig party, and Malcolm could not bring himself to alienate even a single member of the struggling minority.

"I shall be delighted to call on you and your charming daughter next week," he promised.

Lady Renderly smiled triumphantly, like a cat handed a bowl of cream. "How delightful," she purred. "Send round your card anytime, my lord. We will be at home. Come, Elspeth."

Malcolm bowed and moved around them. Unfortunately, the way between him and Anne was still thronged with hazards. To his right below the gallery that held the musicians, a group of young ladies caught his gaze and whispered behind rapidly beating fans. To his left on the large dance floor, a woman he remembered meeting at a ball earlier in the Season took a turn with another fellow, but her knowing smile was all for Malcolm. Straight ahead near a draped alcove holding a bust of Diana, another aristocratic mama bore down on him with no less than three young ladies in tow. There was nothing for it. He squared his broad shoulders, put on the frown that made the Commons quake, and strode as fast as he dared for the gentlemen's retiring room.

Once through the padded doors, however, he could only shake his head. Was the only way to survive this evening to pretend a weak bowel? A man who managed estates from one end of England to the other should not have this kind of difficulty arranging his life. Neither should that same gentleman, who was a few years from a cabinet post and in line for the prime ministry itself, have trouble making decisions. Malcolm had an unerring sense when a bill was ill-fated. This ball smacked of failure.

"Regretting you agreed to let Anne stage this rout?" Chas asked, stepping into the room.

Malcolm greeted him with a handshake. "I can't blame your lovely wife," he replied after they had exchanged pleasantries. "It seemed like a sensible idea at the time. Rather efficient, actually—bring all the eligible young ladies under one roof and let me take my pick. Unfortunately, picking a bride isn't as easy as choosing a horse at Tattersalls. The horses don't look at your legs or demand your undivided attention."

"What did you expect?" Chas countered. "You may be a famous orator and statesman, Malcolm, but the London ladies will want to make sure you're as great a catch as they hope."

Malcolm frowned but it only made Chas grin. He shook his head. Anne Prestwick wasn't the only one in the family who was unflappable, he was beginning to learn. In truth, he hadn't known what to expect when Prestwick had succeeded to the title. Unlike his dour older brother, Prestwick was quick-witted and clever-tongued. He was also tall, blond, and handsome, turning ladies' heads wherever he went. Unfortunately, the fellow's reputation for wildness had preceded him and he had taken his seat in Parliament under a flurry of ill-bred whispers.

"If he tries climbing the gallery the way he did in Covent Garden two years ago," Lord Sidmouth, the Home Secretary, had murmured behind his hand to Malcolm, "I'll not be surprised."

"If he does, I'll have him horsewhipped," Malcolm had countered. But though there were times Malcolm caught the fellow grinning with eyes alight with unholy glee over some bizarre statement made by a somber politician, Chas had never disrupted Parliament. In fact, he was far more attentive than most of the other young lords. Before Malcolm knew it, they seemed to have developed a friendship based on the unlikely political coin of honesty. He could not cheapen the friendship by hiding his feelings now.

"I doubt I can live up to my own reputation," he replied. "I have no intention of spending hours flattering a woman's vanity to win her hand. I believe marriage is a partnership no different from a business venture. And I know what I need in a partner. I need someone who will manage my home efficiently. More, I need someone who'll listen to my positions and find the flaw in my logic. Someone who'll correct the turn of phrase in my speeches so my words will be memorable. Someone who'll tell me when I'm about to make an ass of myself."

Chas clapped him on the shoulder. "Malcolm, old chap, if you attempt to say that to any of the young ladies in there, you *will* make an ass of yourself. You've just described a very efficient personal secretary. Where's the romance, the fire, the passion?"

"Do you honestly believe in that rubbish?" Malcolm countered. When Chas bristled, he held up a hand in surrender. "All right, all right, I see that you do. But Prestwick, you're young. I feel a great deal older than you."

"Well, you're hardly aged enough to stick your spoon in the wall just yet," Chas replied. "You're in the pink of health. You nearly put me away with that right of yours at Gentleman Jackson's the other day. And that mane of devil's black hair of yours has but a few strands of gray."

"A few more than I'd like," Malcolm grumbled. "Don't try to make me appear youthful, my lad. At thirty and eight, I'm well aware that I need an heir, and a wife who will be an asset to my career, not a hindrance. But I tell you, Prestwick, when I consider marrying one of those simpering misses out there, I feel ancient. Every time I bow I expect to hear my bones creak."

At that moment the door creaked open. Both Chas and Malcolm turned to eye the dandy in the lemon-yellow coat who attempted to enter. One look at Malcolm's frown sent him scurrying back into the ballroom. Chas shook his head.

"You can't hide in here all night, Malcolm. Is there anything else Anne should know about your requirements? Should the lady be tall or short? Fair or dark? Willowy or voluptuous? Anne will not rest until she has found you a bride."

Malcolm knew that for the truth. In the first year of their marriage, Lady Prestwick had managed to find a husband for each of her two widowed aunts. It was her success in marrying off the elder of her aunts, the crusty Lady Agatha Crawford, that had made Malcolm believe she might be similarly adept at pairing him up.

"I am not so arrogant as to think I can dictate the

lady's hair and eye color," he informed the young earl. "Though, mind you, I'd like the lady to be neat and simple. She must also be sensible. My real love is politics. Any woman who marries me must accept that."

Chas shook his head. "You sound cold, Malcolm. But I've seen the fire in you when you're out on that floor debating for something you believe in. Do you really intend to share that heart only with your work?"

"Did I hear something about heart?" Rupert Wells strolled through the door to the gentlemen's retiring room, dark head high, face bland. Malcolm knew him well enough to see the light in those heavy-lidded gray eyes. "Do not tell me you've succumbed already, my lord?" Wells drawled.

Malcolm inclined his head in acknowledgment. "Good evening again, Wells. Enjoying the ball?"

"Tolerably," Wells pronounced, moving to eye his reflection in the looking glass affixed to one wall. He must have decided his evening black was acceptable, for he turned quickly to meet Malcolm's gaze once more. "And you?"

"Something seems to have disagreed with my lord Breckonridge's disposition," Chas quipped, making an easy excuse for their prolonged visit to the retiring room. "I'm sure he'll return to the ball shortly."

"I should hope so," Wells replied. "The young ladies appear to be getting restive. We wouldn't want a riot, would we?"

"You give me too much credit," Malcolm told him. "By the way, thank you for your assistance this afternoon. The act won't come up for a vote until next session at this rate, but I appreciate your support. We appear to have a majority now."

Chas raised an eyebrow. "Both the Tories and the Whigs in agreement? You *are* a miracle worker, Wells."

The young man inclined his head. "You are too kind, my lords. I hope you finish your discussions soon. Barrington is bouncing up and down from foot to foot outside the door. If he doesn't have a moment in here soon, he'll likely make a further spectacle of himself."

"Tell him I won't eat him," Malcolm growled. "And assure Lady Prestwick we'll be out shortly."

"Always your servant, my lord." Wells bowed again and quit the room.

Chas shook his head. "I'm not sure why you trust him, Malcolm," he said as the door creaked open and the bright-coated Barrington put in a pale face. Malcolm waved him in and the fellow scurried to the screen in the corner to make use of the chamber pot provided there.

Malcolm stood silently until the fellow had scurried out again. Then he sighed. "Young Wells deserves a chance that he likely won't get unless I sponsor him. I knew his father. Thank God, Wells appears to be made of stronger stuff. He could have a brilliant career ahead of him if he'd learn to let his passions show more often."

"Ha!" Chas proclaimed. "This from a man who doesn't consider love important in a marriage."

"You're an idealist, Prestwick," Malcolm replied with a sigh. "A well-meaning one, I'll grant you, but an idealist nonetheless. My life is politics, and politics is compromise."

"Or perhaps learning what you're willing to compromise and what you're not," Chas quipped. "Very well, then. I'll tease you no more on the matter. I can't make the same claim about Anne. She'll be disappointed if you don't find someone of worth after all this effort. Perhaps if you were to spend a bit more time with each lady, you might be able to form a more accurate assessment."

"I've never needed time to form an accurate assessment of character before," Malcolm countered.

"Perhaps you could try putting them at ease by dancing."

"If a woman is so timid she cannot speak until we dance, she can hardly be the woman I seek," Malcolm pointed out. "Besides, I abhor these tedious country airs. God bless Sally Jersey for bringing home the waltz from Vienna. Almost makes me forgive her Tory tendencies."

"High praise indeed," Chas acknowledged. "Well, Malcolm, I don't know what to do for you. I only know that if we don't return soon, Anne will likely sally in here to get us."

Malcolm sighed. "Very well. Let us not disappoint your unflappable bride. Lead on."

They exited the room and stepped back into the press of the ballroom. However, no one seemed to notice. Indeed, all eyes were turned toward the entrance to the room, where a young lady stood framed in the archway. Her golden curls tumbled back from a perfectly oval face of translucent cream. Her curves in the demure violet gown were willowy. She held herself with the command of a duchess. Malcolm raised an eyebrow, intrigued.

Chas grinned. "Perfect. Here's a lady for you, old man. Allow me to introduce you to the belle of the Season, the Incomparable Miss Persephone Compton."

TWO

Sarah Compton was halfway across the main salon at Almack's when she realized her cousin Persephone wasn't following. Keeping her head elegantly high and fully prepared to ride to the rescue as the stern-faced chaperon, she turned to see who was detaining the girl this time. Persy had gone on and on about this event ever since Lady Prestwick had sent them an invitation. Nothing Sarah had said could dissuade her from attending, even though gossip had it that the ball had been set up for the sole purpose of finding a bride for Viscount Breckonridge, the famous orator. Even Norrie agreed that Lord Breckonridge would surely want a more mature bride than the seventeen-year-old Persephone. Norrie had been Countess of Wenworth for over three years now and could be counted upon to know how things were done in the fashionable world. Even if she were somehow wrong, Sarah could not imagine what Persy would find to even *say* to a man like Lord Breckonridge. Yet, her cousin had been determined. Sarah somehow doubted the girl would turn faint-hearted now.

She need not have worried. It was plain to her that Persy was merely making the most of the moment, standing framed in the entryway to allow everyone to get a good look at her. Her cascading golden curls caught the light of the crystal chandeliers overhead. The simply cut silk ball gown, a violet that matched her almond-shaped eyes, flowed over the curves of her willowy body. Her rosebud lips were curved in a smile of welcome, as if she were pleased to see everyone in the room. She was a delight to behold for anyone looking.

And they were looking. Ladies whispered behind their fans, casting her covetous glances. Gentlemen young and old raised their quizzing glasses or straightened their cravats. Several elbowed their way closer to the entrance, obviously hoping to be the first to make her acquaintance. Though she was used to the reaction her cousin caused, Sarah shook her head and walked back to the girl's side.

"That's quite enough, Persy," she murmured, linking arms with the girl and smiling charmingly. "Another minute and you'll have them drooling."

Persy smiled in obvious satisfaction, and Sarah was able to lead her away from the door. "I am a bit of a sight, aren't I?" the girl whispered with a gossamer giggle. "Do you see Lord Breckonridge? Does he look interested?"

Sarah refused to make a further spectacle by glancing about for the gentleman Persy had come to impress. The safest thing she could do was to greet their hostess and find Norrie in all this crowd. Together they surely could keep an eye on Persephone before she incited a riot.

"I have no idea whether he saw you," she told her cousin, steering her expertly through the groups of gossiping gallants. "As I have only seen his caricature in *The Times,* I cannot be sure I'd recognize him if I *did* see him. Come along now, and pay your respects to Lady Prestwick."

Persy's pretty mouth set into a petulant pout, and Sarah wondered whether she had been too forceful in her wording. One could never be certain how Persy would react to suggestions. Sometimes the girl seemed eager to please, sometimes she acquiesced graciously, and, more frequently of late, she stamped her foot and tossed her head, refusing to budge while her normally creamy complexion turned an unbecoming shade of red. Fortunately, as they drew near to where the ivory-gowned Lady Prestwick was standing with a regal older woman in deep green, Persephone's lovely face broke into a charming smile.

"Lady Prestwick," she gushed when their hostess had offered a smile and the other woman had paused in her conversation to eye the girl and Sarah appraisingly. "I just had to thank you for inviting me. This is the most wonderful ball of the Season!"

Sarah wasn't sure how their hostess would take such effusions, but Anne, Countess of Prestwick, only smiled more deeply. No bigger than Persephone, the young countess had skin just as creamy, although her hair was a straight midnight black to Persy's golden curls.

"A very kind person," Norrie had said when Sarah had asked her about the woman. "Prestwick Park is not far from Wenworth Place. I am told that Lady Prestwick is so sweet as to have attained the status of angel in the eyes of her tenants and staff."

As Lady Prestwick turned to Sarah, she could well believe that. Her gray eyes were somehow warm, her demeanor comfortingly capable. Despite the fact that Sarah knew she looked far less charming than her cousin in the navy silk gown that befitted a chaperon, Lady Prestwick's smile was just as welcoming to her as it had been to Persephone. "How nice to see you as well, Miss Compton," she said in her quiet voice. "The dancing has only just started. Shall I find you both a partner?"

"No need for that," a smooth male voice intoned behind them. "I should be delighted to accompany Miss Persephone for the next dance."

Sarah turned to look up at the chestnut-haired Duke of Reddington, who stood tall and splendid in his evening black. His gaze on her cousin was positively worshipful. Sarah hid her smile of triumph under a graceful curtsy, which Persy mimicked.

"Your Grace is too kind," Persephone murmured. Sarah rose in time to see the girl glide off on the duke's muscular arm.

Lady Prestwick sighed. "Well, I suppose Lord Breckonridge is doomed to disappointment where your cousin is concerned, Miss Compton. The duke appears to be quicker to act."

The older woman at her side sniffed through her long nose. Sarah realized she must be Anne's recently remarried aunt, Lady Agatha Wincamp, whom Norrie had mentioned with a shudder. "He appears besotted," the woman clipped in a sharp-edged voice that could not fail to sound critical. "I thought your cousin was going to accept that count, Miss Compton."

"Count Rogan was called away suddenly," Sarah replied, trying to block the memory of the count's angered face when Persy had sent him packing for refusing to carry her parasol in the park. The girl had claimed she could not possibly marry a fellow so insufficiently devoted. Rogan had retired to the country to nurse his wounded pride.

"What a shame. And how is your aunt?" Lady Prestwick asked pleasantly.

"I understand she could not come up for her daughter's ball," Lady Wincamp put in, affixing Sarah with a glare that somehow implied Sarah was at fault in the matter. "She must have been looking forward to that since the chit was born."

"Nothing would have pleased her more than to be here," Sarah informed the woman. "Unfortunately, our family physician counseled otherwise." That was only the truth. Aunt Belle had talked of little else than Persy's come-out for months, even with the girl away for the last year at a fancy finishing school in London.

"Your cousin does not seem distressed by the matter," observed Lady Wincamp, pointing her nose toward the dancers. Sarah could not argue that fact either. Persy had barely registered a yawn when she was told her mother had to spend the spring and summer in bed. At the moment, she was capering through the steps of a lively country dance as if she hadn't a care in the world, which, Sarah reflected, she hadn't. Even when the duke was forced to take the hands of the other pretty dark-haired lady in his set, he could not seem to keep from glancing at Persephone. The other fellow in the set was ogling her so intently that he forgot to accept his partner back from the duke and had to be nudged by the frustrated woman. He stammered an apology, but somehow it appeared as if he were apologizing to Persephone, and not his partner.

"I'm sure your aunt's mind was eased knowing you were here with Persephone," Lady Prestwick said, bringing Sarah's attention back to the conversation at hand. Lady Prestwick's obvious sincerity warmed Sarah's heart, and she found herself smiling.

"You are apparently devoted to the girl," Lady Wincamp put in. "I imagine you won't know what to do with yourself once she's wed."

Sarah kept her smile in place from long practice. There was no reason for anyone to know that she was not the devoted older spinster everyone believed her to be. She was relieved when another couple presented themselves to Lady Prestwick and her formidable aunt just then so that Sarah might go in search of Norrie.

In truth, she reflected as she circled the dance floor, watchful for her friend, she had once doted on Persephone. Yet, she was sure that there were those who would doubt that. There was such a difference in their ages and circumstances. She had been twelve when her cousin had been born, shortly before Sarah's parents had died in a carriage accident. Sarah had long ago walled off the pain that came with remembering that dark time. She had been plucked from a loving home and thrust into the guardianship of her mother's younger sister, Persephone's mother Bella. Aunt Belle had had little time for Sarah, unfortunately, for Persephone, her only child, was rather sickly. Before Sarah could even accustom herself to her loss, she had been sent to the Barnsley School for Young Ladies in far-off Somerset. It wasn't until Sarah's disappointing come-out six years later that she had spent any time with her aunt.

The dance continued, with some of the dancers showing signs of fatigue. The gentleman dancing next to the duke was fanning himself with one gloved hand and his partner's dark curls were wilting down one side of her reddening cheek. Persy, however, looked as dewy and fresh as the moment she had entered the set, pausing to flutter her thick lashes up at the duke, who barely remembered it was time to turn. No, Sarah was nothing like her cousin. She had never mastered this art of pretending to give her heart.

"So she's settled on the duke, has she?"

Sarah turned to find her friend beside her. Eleanor, Countess of Wenworth, was a tall, elegant creature with silky light brown tresses and speaking deep blue eyes. Her Mexican blue gown was square cut across her slender bosom, draping in sweeping folds to the white satin underskirt peeking out near her slippered feet. The only child of a long-dead soldier, she had been the charity case of the Barnsley School, kept on by a scholarship from the Darby family, who held the Wenworth title. Against all odds, she had met and married the second son, Justinian Darby, becoming his countess when he ascended to the title. Although she was two years Sarah's senior, Sarah was grateful that she had befriended her when Sarah had arrived at the school. They had been friends ever since.

"Thank goodness you found me," she told Norrie now. "I was about to give up hope in this crowd."

Norrie smiled. "I feared I wouldn't find you either, but then I remembered I merely had to find the largest knot of gentlemen, and there I would find Persephone. And where I find Persephone, I shortly find you."

"Only until she accepts the duke," Sarah promised her.

"And then you will accept that position I have offered to lead our Dame School?" Norrie prompted.

Sarah nodded. "With great relief. I would have left Suffolk sooner if I hadn't been worried for Aunt Belle. But the physician says she will be up and about by fall. Besides, I know you will understand me, Norrie, when I say I'm heartily sick of having to be grateful for everything I own. Gratitude is a lovely thing when you know the gift is given in love. But when it's given out of pity or a sense of duty, I cannot abide it. It becomes a weight, a burden. I have far too many burdens right now."

Norrie reached out a gloved hand to squeeze hers. "I understand completely. You will remember how Miss Martingale was wont to remind me, and anyone else who would listen, that we must remember our places. I have come to believe that we must each find what that place is, and not let others dictate it to us. But I must disagree with you that you have had to receive too many gifts of duty. Surely your aunt owed you more than that one aborted Season years ago."

Sarah shook her head, watching as the dance ended and the duke requested another. Persephone hesitated only a moment, glancing back over her shoulder as if to find Sarah. More likely she wanted to see who else was in line to partner her. *Accept, accept,* Sarah willed in her mind. To her relief, her cousin shrugged a slender shoulder and laid her hand on the duke's arm. Sarah took a deep breath as the music started again.

"I think Aunt Belle did me more of a favor than she knew," she confided to Norrie, continuing to watch her cousin. "I hated the Season back then. It is only bearable now because I am firmly on the shelf at nearly thirty. London and all its pleasures seemed huge and terrifying at eighteen. The people I met seemed far more intelligent and polished than I could ever hope to be. I was fumble-footed and tongue-tied, and the gentlemen fled from me in disgust."

"Somehow I doubt that," Norrie replied. "I would

rather believe that your aunt pressured you to leave. I'm sure she missed Persephone. From your letters, I take it she feared for the girl's very life. To this day she cannot remember that your cousin is safely grown."

"You didn't know Persy when she was little," Sarah reminded her. "My cousin was tiny and fragile, like a fairy child with her huge violet eyes and blond hair. She seemed fated to catch every chill. She could not even look at a field of hay without convulsing in a fit of sneezing. Her first attempt to mount a pony, and a very small, spiritless one at that, resulted in a broken arm. A single bite of strawberry raised angry red welts. Uncle Harold had no idea how to respond to her, and Aunt Belle was constantly having hysterics from worrying."

"And so Sarah came to the rescue," Norrie guessed. "I know your tender heart, Sarah, for all you try to hide it from the world. Besides, you are far sturdier than your cousin, both in body and in spirit. You tried not to brag in your letters, but it was clear to me that you were the one managing the household. You were the one who took the night watch when Persy lay with a fever. You administered the vile-tasting medicine when Persy refused it from all others. You entertained her when she was once again confined to her bed for days. And you were the one to convince your aunt that the girl should receive tutoring so that she could learn to be a proper young lady."

"I was so pleased when Aunt Belle agreed to send her to London to school," Sarah mused with a smile. "She missed so much, Norrie, not being with her peers. I knew it was the right thing to do."

"And now she shall have her day," Norrie replied, turning her gaze to the dance. "And you shall have yours, Sarah. You cannot tell me you didn't enjoy this last year when you could do more than be Persy's shadow."

Sarah felt her smile deepen. "Yes, I enjoyed working at the Dame School in our parish. I know I enjoyed being with Persy when she was young, but I find I like children in general. They have such inquisitive minds. And they ask the most fascinating questions. They make me think beyond myself."

"You should have children of your own," Norrie told her sternly. "I warn you, Sarah. Should you take that position at our school, I will be merciless in bringing forth gentlemen to petition for your hand."

Sarah shuddered theatrically. "And they will likely all be old, fat, lecherous widowers with a dozen children at their feet. No, thank you. I do not give my heart so easily. Besides, if I am to spend my life caring for other people's children, I'd rather have my independence."

Norrie shook her head. "I have much better taste, I assure you, than to try to pair you with some flatulent farmer. But you will soon find that, if you allow me to spirit you away to Wenworth Place."

"If only Persy could be settled," Sarah replied with a sigh. "There is no dispute she is the reigning belle of the ton, as I predicted. You should see the mountain of cards we receive daily, inviting her to ride, to dance, to attend the opera, play, or musicale. Lovelorn swains crowd our sitting room; flowers from admirers choke the entryway. She is infamous."

"And becoming more so," Norrie remarked. "How many offers has she refused now?"

Sarah sighed again. "Three besides Count Rogan. She claimed the Marquis of Atwich was too old and stodgy. She threw away Lord Sómbly because he only had twenty thousand pounds per annum. And she rejected the Russian ambassador because she was certain no one would ever see her in St. Petersburg."

"Well, the duke is hardly old or stodgy," Norrie countered. "He is rumored to be worth fifty thousand pounds per annum. I will grant you he prefers his estates to town, but surely he will come up for the Season each year. She must accept him."

"I wish I could be certain of that," Sarah replied. "She needs to marry well, Norrie. Aunt Belle will suffocate her, and her father hasn't much use for single females at home. He all but told me to look for a position while I was here in London, as he cannot be expected to care for me indefinitely."

"Nipfarthing," Norrie complained. "As if your keep cost him anything, the way he worked you as a servant."

"Be that as it may," Sarah replied sternly, although her heart was warmed by her friend's loyalty, "Persy must wed. What we need to find is a gentleman who is handsome, charming, and wealthy enough for Persy's taste, but sensible enough to curb her tendency toward self-absorption. Given Persy's girlish nature, he had also better be kind and not too intelligent. To my mind, the duke is perfect."

Norrie bit back a smile at that. Sarah watched His Grace bow to her cousin as the dance ended. The warm smile and glow in his eyes told her he was besotted, like nearly every other man in the room. While Persy did not look nearly so delighted, still the girl had to be mindful of the opportunity the duke presented. If only the girl would settle on the fellow!

It was then she noticed a handsome blond fellow

moving toward the parting dancers. He was accompanied by an imposing gentleman with hair nearly as black as Lady Prestwick's, although much less tidy.

"Who is that?" Sarah asked with a frown, watching as his long legs strode across the polished floor.

Norrie frowned as well, following her gaze. "The charming blonde is Lord Prestwick, our host. And the dark-haired brute beside him is, if I am not mistaken, Lord Breckonridge."

"Really?" Sarah looked closer, noting the powerful build, the determined carriage. "He looks more like the town bully than the orator I fancied. I've read reprints of his speeches in *The Times*. He's quite brilliant. What on earth could he want with Persephone?"

Norrie shook her head. "What do any of them want with Persy?"

Sarah started. "You don't honestly think he could be interested in courting her?"

"I doubt he wants her to vote on an act of Parliament," Norrie countered.

Sarah watched her cousin dip a graceful curtsy as Breckonridge bowed over her hand. He certainly did seem to be taking an interest. And Persy was simpering.

"But he cannot be serious," Sarah protested. "She couldn't be more than a bon bon to him. He'd have her for lunch and still be hungry."

"Perhaps the gentleman is fond of bon bons," Norrie said darkly.

She seemed to have the right of it, for the gentleman in question was now smiling over something Persephone had said. The duke beside her was glowering. Lord Prestwick was grinning. Sarah felt a chill crawl up her spine.

"Do you think Lord Breckonridge could possibly be the man Persy needs, Norrie?" she asked.

"I wish I knew," Norrie replied. "Justinian has only spoken of him a few times, mostly in regards to some doing in Parliament. From what little I know, he appears to be a good man at heart, loyal to his party. Yet, he is a determined man, used to power. He appears to be absolutely devoted to his career. Persy would never take first place in his affections."

Sarah's eyes widened. "Persy, take second place? The match is doomed."

"Yet if she dallies with him," Norrie pointed out, "she may lose her chance with the oh-so-eligible duke."

Sarah knew the signs by now. Already Persy had turned so that the duke was behind her, as if she had dismissed him. Her warm smile was all for Breckonridge. The duke had paled.

"I must stop this," she murmured to Norrie.

"Sarah to the rescue," Norrie muttered, but Sarah was already hurrying across the ballroom. Couples were once more lining up for the next set. She must stop Breckonridge before he took the floor with her cousin. Ahead of her, Persy was tittering and batting her lashes to effect. Lord Prestwick was regarding her, bemused, and the duke's jaw was a tense line. Malcolm Breckonridge wore the slightest of frowns, but he bent his dark head closer as if to hear what Persy was saying.

Sarah stepped boldly up to the group and laid her hand on Lord Breckonridge's arm. Beneath the black evening coat, she could feel the hard muscle. She swallowed.

"My lord," she said overbrightly.

Malcolm turned to face her and she found herself

being regarded by eyes nearly as black as his hair. Up close, his face was as strong as his carriage. He was a handsome man, she decided, watching the play of light and shadow across the craggy planes. The black hair held a hint of silver at the temples, but the gleam in his dark eyes belied any lessening of youthful energy. Power, held firmly in check, seemed to coil through him like heat from a carefully banked fire. He would never be noted for the tragic glory of Lord Byron or the quiet command of Wellington. No, this man would be a silent power, more subtle, more deadly. She had a feeling that he carried his thoughts deep, and woe betide the one who made him display his passions openly. She forced a smile to remain on her face.

"I'm so sorry to keep you waiting, my lord," she warbled, while Persephone frowned at her and the duke and Lord Prestwick eyed her curiously. "I am ready for that dance you promised me."

She held her breath as Breckonridge's sharp eyes narrowed. His gaze raked her from top to bottom and despite herself, she felt her color heightening. Just as she thought he would give her the cut direct for her audacity, he snapped a bow.

"Your servant, madam," he intoned.

Her hand still on his arm, her pulse pounding in her ears, she let him lead her out onto the floor.

THREE

Malcolm watched the woman on his arm with a mixture of annoyance and amusement as they formed part of a set for a country line dance. As blatant as she had been, he should have depressed her notions immediately. Yet something about her intrigued him. For one thing, she was considerably older than most of the ladies who had sought his interest. While her dark blue dress with its modest neck was neither fast nor fashionable, he wondered fleetingly whether she might be a doxy. She had the curves to put a French courtesan to shame. Yet, surely Anne Prestwick would never allow anyone less than a lady to enter her ballroom. No, there must be some other explanation.

She looked a bit embarrassed by his scrutiny as she took her place across from him, her porcelain complexion tinted a charming pink. She kept her head high as if to deny her embarrassment, but as he took her hands to start the dance, he found that they trembled in his grip. Others would have hastened to put her at ease, but he was too used to putting his enemies in their places, he supposed, to let her off easily. Accordingly, he said nothing as they moved through the figure of the dance, even when the motions brought them close enough that conversation might be expected. She likewise said nothing for the first few turns, giving him ample opportunity to look his fill.

What he saw only intrigued him all the more. She was a tall woman, standing almost eye to eye with him, yet her hands were small and delicate. Her hair was the color of honey and just as thick. It was knotted at the back of her head to allow a tantalizing curl to hang over one shoulder. As they crossed the set, his gaze held hers. With surprise, he found it impossible to tell the color of her eyes. It was very much like looking in some imagined crystal ball—gray, blue, and green swirled in various shades in equal measure, pulling him into the depths. As he was forced to break the spell, he noticed that her eyes tended to tilt up at the outside corners, enhancing the impression that there was something mysterious about them. Otherwise, she had a pleasant face, round-cheeked and generous-lipped. She carried herself well, even under the present circumstances, as if sustained by some inner strength. He caught her gazing back at him again and wondered what she saw.

He had never considered himself handsome, but he was aware he was considered striking. He was also aware he was fully capable of intimidating people. That would have been a curse to many, but he had found the trait useful. Still, it didn't seem to be helping him learn the reason this woman had brazened her way into a dance with him. He could not see her as the conniving debutante. He took her hands again for a promenade and surreptitiously squeezed the left hand. He could feel no ring beneath the silk of her long gloves; certainly none was visible outside. She was unmarried then, and not a wife seeking support for a law her husband wanted to enact. He'd met those types before as well. Could she be someone's sister or cousin, then?

He decided to give her his best smile in hopes of fostering conspiracy, but she only gave him back the tightest of responses, her pink lips barely curling. The dance parted them for a moment, and he found himself losing patience. It seemed after her initial bout of bravery that she was as timid as the others who had attempted to attract his interest that night.

"You have nothing to say to me, then, madam?" he demanded as the dance once more sent them past each other, shoulder to shoulder. As she took her place opposite him, her expressive eyes widened at his gruff tone. He waited for her to pretend he had actually asked her to dance, to say anything that would give him some idea of her game. She merely allowed the gentleman of the second couple in their set to take her hand and lead her out, as the dance demanded. When he approached the lady of the second couple to do the same, he could not help but notice that she quailed under the frown that had evidently formed on his face. He managed a grimace that would have to pass for a smile and found himself back opposite the mysterious lady. He was rather glad to see that they had reached the end of the line of dancers and would be standing out for a round.

"Forgive my impertinence, my lord," she said as they waited to rejoin the set. Her voice was deep for a woman, seductive, surprising, and his mind tumbled once more to the doxy theory. "I must thank you for not giving me away. It was most kind of you."

"I hope you plan to reward my kindness with an explanation," he replied. She blushed again, and he found the effect even more charming. Was she some kind of sorceress that he could not focus on his intended interrogation?

"I shall try, my lord," she said. "You had just been introduced to Persephone Compton, I believe?"

He frowned, toying with the idea that she was bent on usurping the lady in his affections. As he had not had time to form any affections, and she was not in the lady's league in looks, he threw the idea off as preposterous. "Lord Prestwick had performed the introduction as you arrived," he confirmed.

"May I ask why you wished to be made known to her?" she persisted.

His frown deepened. That ought to have been enough to cause the most ardent campaigner to desist, but she did not seem to be affected by it. "I am not in the habit of discussing my affairs with strangers, madam," he said quellingly.

She gazed at him. "I imagine you must get them to vote your way out of sheer intimidation," she said wonderingly. Surprised, he could not think of an answer. Malcolm Breckonridge, speechless. His peers would laugh themselves sick. He was so appalled that the moment of silence stretched. As the dance ended, she dropped a curtsy, and he remembered himself and bowed.

"Your servant, madam," he managed. "I wish you luck."

She laid a hand on his arm. "I fear I have been forward. Would you take a turn about the room with me, my lord, so that I might explain myself further?"

Malcolm stared at her. He had given her a set down calculated in look and manner to quell the most pretentious upstart and she remained focused on her purpose. Could she be the woman he sought? She certainly had the courage to stand up to him. One could not have asked for a more queenly consort. It was too much to hope that she be intelligent as well. He decided it only made sense to investigate further.

"Very well, madam," he replied, offering her his arm. They began a slow promenade about the room. He had never paid much attention to Almack's, remembering only that sofas were spaced around the room for those who wished to watch the dancing. He paid the people ogling him less attention now, focusing on the woman on his arm. She strolled beside him, offering an occasional smile to other couples similarly engaged, and glancing every so often toward the next set of dancers, which included the Incomparable Miss Compton, now partnering Lord Rupert Wells. They would have made a striking couple, except that she was pouting and he looked bored by the whole affair. The Duke of Reddington, Malcolm did notice, looked on from the edge of the dance floor with ill-disguised annoyance. He had thought when Prestwick had introduced him to Miss Persephone that the usually suave and sophisticated Reddington was besotted. He felt nothing but pity for the fellow.

"I should start by introducing myself," she said when he had begun to wonder whether she would be silent after all. "I am Miss Sarah Compton, Persephone's cousin and her chaperon for the Season."

Disappointment shot through him again. She was after a favor after all. "I see. You accosted me for the sole purpose of furthering your cousin's case."

"Not in the slightest," she assured him fervently.

Malcolm frowned. "Is it my intentions you question, then? I assure you, madam, they are strictly honorable."

"Oh, dear," she said with a sigh. As he looked at her in surprise, she hurried on. "That is, I'm sorry to hear you have intentions, my lord. You would never suit."

"Indeed," he replied, glancing at the gossamer young lady on the dance floor with more interest than he had felt earlier. "May I say, madam, that you came to that conclusion on remarkably little evidence."

"Not at all, my lord," she corrected him, obviously warming to her argument. "I have read and heard a great deal about you. You are obviously a gentleman of mature years, with a thriving career and every expectation of a glorious future. You will want a wife who can help make that future a reality, someone with intelligence, breeding, and a great dollop of common sense. My cousin is beautiful, cultured, and well-read, completely self-absorbed, and utterly lacking in common sense. She would attempt to lead you a merry dance, as she does the youth who cluster about her. You would see through her shortly. I merely save you that time."

He stared at her for the third time that night. "Thank you, Miss Compton," was all he could think to say. She smiled at him, revealing dimples on either side of her generous mouth, and making her eyes appear the color of a southern sea at sunrise.

"You are most welcome, Lord Breckonridge," she replied. "If we are in agreement, I shall take my leave of you."

He had no choice but to bow, still stunned by her logic, her intuition, and her honesty. "Your servant, madam."

She dropped a curtsy and started to go. Out of the corner of his eye, he caught a movement. To his left,

Prestwick was motioning frantically toward Sarah. The dance on the floor was ending, rather soon he thought, and he heard the musicians begin the strains of a waltz. He found himself smiling. Hadn't he always said Prestwick was a clever fellow?

"Miss Compton," he began. She turned to him. "How do you feel about the waltz?"

"I have yet to give Persephone permission to dance it," she said primly, casting a quick glance to the floor, where indeed her charge was suffering herself to be led away.

"Do you find it so wicked?" Malcolm asked, waiting for her to confirm his fears.

She eyed him for a moment, then a conspiratorial grin spread, bringing her dimples once more into view. "Truth be told," she replied, "I adore it. I learned from my cousin's dancing master. God bless Lady Jersey for bringing it back from Vienna. It is truly the only dance worth dancing."

He felt his own grin spreading. He held out his hand. "In that case, will you do me the honor?"

She stared at his hand as if he had offered her a snake. "You are asking me to dance?"

"I am asking you to waltz," he corrected her. "Turnabout is fair play, after all. Well?"

She stared at him a moment longer, as if weighing the repercussions. Then she laid her hand firmly in his.

"I would be delighted," she told him, and he pulled her into his arms and out onto the floor.

It was the finest waltz he had ever danced. From the moment he held her womanly frame against him, the ballroom receded to a soft gray blur, like a mist around them. She was attuned to his every movement, was reacting seconds before he even knew he had prompted her to do so. She moved so gracefully that it heightened the feeling they were dancing on air. He gazed down into those witch's eyes, now a deep blue, and wondered whether he was under a spell he would ever care to break.

Anne Prestwick would only laugh at him. Her charming husband had presented him with the Incomparable Miss Compton, and he found he much preferred her chaperon.

FOUR

It was the finest waltz she could have imagined. From the moment he put his strong arm about her waist, the ballroom receded to a soft gray blur, like a mist around them. Any fear scattered in the warmth of his gaze. She was attuned to his every movement, was reacting seconds before she even felt his hand move. So light was his touch that it heightened the feeling they were dancing on air.

Gazing up into his eyes, darker than night, Sarah wondered whether she was bewitched. How on earth had she ended up dancing the waltz, of all things, with the most eligible bachelor in London, at a ball designed to find him his bride? Every unmarried female in the room must envy her at the moment. It was like something out of a fairy tale.

But that sense of wonder quickly disappeared as he continued to dance her about the floor. In fact, everything disappeared, until there was only the music, his powerful body so close to her own, those very black eyes, and his hand upon her back, guiding her in slow circles. This was no dream, but reality, and the reality was more potent than anything she could have imagined. Something deep inside her warned that this bliss could not last, but she ignored it. She wanted only to give herself up to the moment, enjoy for once being the center of someone's universe, let her heart free of the confines she placed on it. This moment was hers and hers alone.

It seemed forever and only seconds when the music drew to a close. She gradually became aware of another noise rising above the beating of her heart. It was applause. Lord Breckonridge was bowing over her hand, and most of the other dancers were clapping for them. Small wonder she had felt alone on the dance floor. The others had stopped to watch the more practiced couple execute the steps. She felt herself flush, a heat that only sharpened as Breckonridge brought her hand to his lips in tribute. The gentle pressure was nearly her undoing. But far worse was the sight over his left shoulder.

Persephone stood staring at her, pale-faced. Her rosebud lips were compressed in a sharp line. Whether she was shocked by Sarah's behavior or furious that it had eclipsed her own, Sarah couldn't be sure. Either way, it did not bode well for the remainder of the evening. She had seen such looks on her cousin's face before and knew the storms that usually followed.

"Now, that was something, Miss Compton," Lord Prestwick declared, appearing at her elbow. She managed to murmur her thanks, keeping an eye on Persephone, who was once more partially hidden by her throng of admirers. No doubt they would hasten to assure her that Persephone was the true belle of the ball. Sarah squared her shoulders.

"And Breckonridge," his lordship was continuing, "I didn't know you had it in you."

"It's all in one's partner," Malcolm said, waving off the praise. Sarah could feel him eying her as if he'd noticed a change in her, and she fought to smile back at him, even as her heart retreated to safety. He did not seem encouraged. Indeed, his frown reappeared. Sarah managed to keep the smile on her face, although she was certain it was strained.

"And humility as well!" Prestwick proclaimed. "Miss Compton, those of us in the Lords who must deal with this curmudgeon daily would be indebted if you would continue to exert such a good influence." He moved back a step as Malcolm shot him a dark glance. Sarah wasn't fooled. There was obviously camaraderie between the two. "And perhaps you could start now. There's a late supper being spread in the next room. Why don't you show her in, old fellow?"

Malcolm glared at him for a moment, then he turned to Sarah. "I have monopolized your attention too long, I fear, Miss Compton," he said gallantly. For once, he seemed unable to meet her gaze. Her heart sank. He was dismissing her. Obviously, the dance had not affected him as it had her. She should have expected that. Doubtless he would be regretting it soon enough.

"Thank you for your time, my lord," she replied, curtsying.

She rose to find him eying her speculatingly. Her heart began to beat unaccountably faster. "Is there something else, my lord?"

"I suppose," he said with such casualness that she could not imagine what would follow, "that it would be an imposition to ask you to have supper with me?"

Sarah stared at him. There was a quick flash in his dark eyes that looked suspiciously like yearning, only to be covered by a brightness she was certain was false. Oh, how she longed to disagree with him, to accept his hesitant offer. Never had a gentleman seemed so perfect, so right. There would be no need for Norrie to trot out her farmers, flatulent or otherwise. Yet her gaze was drawn across the room, where even now she could see the duke murmuring something to Persephone, who stood woodenly with two bright spots on her otherwise pale cheeks. She shook her head.

"I'm sorry, my lord," she murmured. "I have my duty. Besides, you would not want to set tongues a-wagging. Two dances and supper? There will be gossip."

There was no mistaking the fire that sprang to those dark eyes. "Let them gossip," he growled, seizing one of her hands. "Have supper with me. We must talk."

Sarah felt as if it were her heart he held in his iron grip. Never had any of the few young men who had called on her in her aborted Season moved her the way this man did. Really, she scolded herself, it was too much to think that she could enter into a love match when she was already an acknowledged spinster. Her responsibility lay with Persephone. So why was she having such a hard time saying no?

"I regret, my lord," she managed with just the right degree of propriety, "that I cannot. I must see to Persephone."

His brow cleared. "Ah, of course, your cousin. Well, invite the chit to join us."

Sarah was torn between gratitude and chagrin. Having had the gentleman to herself for some all-too-short minutes, she hardly wanted to share him with her cousin now. On the other hand, the only way to get a few more of those precious minutes was to do just that. She dropped another curtsy. "You are too kind, my lord. I'm sure Persephone would be delighted to join us."

He nodded and released her so she could cross the

room. Persephone's face did not brighten as she approached. Indeed, her cousin's lovely eyes narrowed until she resembled some kind of spiteful elf. Lord Reddington had left, and her cousin's other admirers looked none too happy at the moment. Sarah stepped to the girl's side even as Norrie appeared behind her.

"Lord Breckonridge has asked us to join him for supper," she explained, hearing herself sound breathless.

"Then of course you must go," Norrie insisted eagerly. "You need not take Persephone. She can join Lord Wenworth and me."

But Persephone's face had cleared. "How splendid," she declared in her musical voice. "Of course I would be delighted to join you, Sarah. I can be your chaperon for once. Pray excuse me, everyone."

The gentlemen uttered a chorus of regret, some more forceful than others, imploring her to relent and go with one of them. She waved a hand airily.

"I must go," she said firmly. "My cousin needs me. I should be delighted to take up our conversation at a later time. You will wait, won't you?"

Immediately they were her faithful servants. Sarah shook her head while Norrie tried to hide a smile. They all bound her cousin with promises for dances later, and, with Norrie's help, Sarah managed to extract her and bring her to the waiting Malcolm. Persephone dropped a curtsy, and Malcolm bowed. Persephone dimpled, and Malcolm smiled charmingly. Persephone blushed, and he offered her his arm. Sarah wanted to scream in vexation, until he offered her his other arm. The look he gave her took her breath away. He stepped forward, and the three of them went in to supper.

Lady Prestwick had a buffet served in a salon behind the ballroom. Sarah was pleased to find that, in addition to the traditional lobster cakes and champagne, the tables held any number of sliced meats and cheese, canapes and crudites, and her own downfall, sweetmeats, jellies, and creams. Lord Breckonridge gallantly began to fill a plate for her, but when she saw how little he was putting on it, she gently removed it from his hand.

"I'm not a debutante, my lord," she reminded him with a smile, selecting several of the tarts and pastries. "I do not need to eat like a bird to impress the eligibles."

"No, madam, you do not," he replied, and she found herself blushing at the approving tone.

"Sarah seems to have no trouble keeping her figure," Persephone commented beside them, being much more fussy in her selection. "I, however, must work continually."

"Somehow, Miss Persephone," Breckonridge murmured, "I doubt that as well."

Persy colored nicely as he led them to a nearby table.

As they were seated, Sarah couldn't help noticing the curious gazes being cast in their direction. Lady Renderly was regarding them with narrowed eyes, and her daughter looked bilious. Lady Wincamp was frowning from across the room. Sarah caught Lady Prestwick's gaze, and their hostess smiled encouragingly. Still, it was discomposing. She was quite used to having everyone stare at Persy. It was quite another thing to find them staring at her.

But perhaps they were staring at her dinner companion instead. Apparently it wasn't often that the great Lord Breckonridge stayed to dinner, let alone in a lady's company. Malcolm looked more comfortable with the notoriety than she did. His occasional glance about the room was merely accompanied by a nod to an old acquaintance or other. Only once did he frown, and that was when the particularly handsome young man who had danced with Persephone earlier paused in the doorway to eye their trio in a brooding manner reminiscent of the dark poet Lord Byron.

"So tell me, Miss Compton," Malcolm said after they had eaten for a few minutes. "Are you a Tory or a Whig?"

She frowned, considering the matter. For anyone else, the question would simply be part of polite conversation. For him, it surely held greater significance.

"In truth, I vacillate," she admitted. "I admire the fiscal responsibility of the Tories, but it seems to me that the Whigs have a better understanding of the people's problems. I would be hard-pressed to align myself in one camp or the other."

His dark eyes glittered, and he leaned forward. "I feel the same way, some days, but those who call themselves Tory tend to be far too conservative for my tastes. How closely do you follow politics, Miss Compton?"

Sarah toyed with the shrimp on her plate. His tone was becoming more intense. She had not had such questioning since leaving the Barnsley School for Young Ladies. "I try to keep abreast, my lord. I read voraciously. We get *The Times, The London Gazette, The Morning Chronicle,* and *The Courier* in Suffolk, though they are several days old by the time I see them."

"My father reads them before we do," Persy put in for explanation. Sarah smiled at her, pleased her cousin would be so friendly when the conversation must bore her. Persephone was watching Malcolm, who in truth seemed to suddenly remember she was at their table.

"Do you read the papers as well, then, Miss Persephone?" he asked. Sarah tried not to frown. His tone had gone from pointed to polite. Indeed, there was a definite edge of kindness, although she tried to tell herself it was more of a fatherly tone than that of a friend.

Persephone answered readily enough. "Certainly, my lord, although I am not as well-read as Sarah. She even reads *The Political Register* when she can find a copy."

Sarah suddenly found the custard she had tried too thick in her mouth and almost choked. She managed to swallow the lump in her throat as Malcolm glanced at her with upraised brow. His brows were particularly thick and rough, she noted, with a few silver hairs like ribbon in a horse's mane. She was certain such a look turned his opponents into as useless a blob as her custard. Certainly she felt her hands tremble.

"Aren't William Cobbett's controversies a little inflammatory for a gently reared lady?" he asked.

She stiffened. "I find Mr. Cobbett's writing intelligent and thought-provoking," she told him. "It is a welcome counterpoint to the more conservative reporting in the other papers."

He barked out a laugh and she felt herself color. "With that I quite agree," he said. "What did you think of him likening Brighton Pavilion to the Kremlin?"

"As I have seen neither palace, I have no point of comparison," Sarah replied, starting to relax in the debate. "However, I find it unconscionable of the prince to spend money on another palace while our country labors with too high prices and too many people without work."

He nodded in obvious approval. "Well said. I wish I could back you for a seat in the Commons, Miss Compton. We could use someone with your ability to read and analyze."

Sarah was astonished by his praise, but before she could respond, Persephone spoke up again. "Sarah has little to do but read and analyze, my lord," she said. Sarah somehow thought that was supposed to be praise as well, but the description at the least made her sound boring and at the worst downright lazy.

"I have a few other interests, Persy," she reminded her cousin.

"Oh?" He was certainly able to invest that word with a great deal of significance, Sarah thought as her comfort with the conversation diminished once more.

"Tell him how well you ride, Sarah," Persy encouraged brightly before proceeding to do it for her. "She rides like an angel, my lord."

"One does not generally think of angels being particularly adept on horseback," he replied. She could hear the amusement in his voice, but it only served to make her more uncomfortable.

Persy giggled. "No, I suppose not. Very well, then, she rides like a captain of the cavalry."

Sarah grimaced.

Malcolm chuckled. "Some cavalry officers are less useful riders, but I think I understand your analogy. What else?"

"Really, my lord," Sarah started, but Persy was obviously too pleased to have his attention to be stopped so easily.

"She grows and distills herbs," Persy said proudly.

"She can make the most marvelous potions, my lord. I vow she is better than an apothecary. She can cure most any disease."

The ability had been a necessity, given her cousin's real ailments and her aunt's imagined ones. Still, she could hardly tell him that. "I merely dabble with useful remedies, Cousin," she said. "Now, could we please find a more interesting topic?"

"I'm finding the topic quite informative," Malcolm told her. The twinkle in his eyes belied his serious tone. "Particularly the way Miss Persephone discusses it. What else, my dear?"

Persephone preened even as Sarah bit back a retort. "Well," her cousin said, lowering her voice conspiratorially, "she collects rocks."

Sarah wanted to scream.

"Rocks?" Even Lord Breckonridge had a difficult time making that sound fascinating.

"Truly," Persephone assured him. "Tell him, Sarah."

Sarah had no intention of gratifying either of them with an explanation of her old schoolgirl habits. "I collect rocks, my lord," she said sternly. "Now, Persephone, drink your champagne before it grows flat."

Persephone frowned at her matronly manner, but reached for her crystal flute just the same.

Malcolm leaned closer to Sarah, forcing her to lean back to keep from touching him. "And if I grow too bold," he asked quietly, "will you order me to drink champagne as well, Miss Compton?"

"No," she replied. "I'll simply tell you to take yourself off."

He threw back his head and laughed. The couples seated nearest them turned to stare, and Sarah felt herself blushing again.

"Really, Sarah," Persephone scolded. "She doesn't mean that, my lord."

"Somehow I doubt that, Miss Persephone," he replied. "I have a feeling your cousin says only what she means, a trait I find admirable. However, since she insists on finding this topic tiresome, perhaps we should try another. What are your interests, Miss Persephone?"

Sarah should have been pleased to have his attention off her, but somehow his easy defection rankled. Her cousin obviously saw nothing wrong with it, straightening under his regard even as her face composed in satisfaction.

"I play the piano, sing, embroider, and paint with watercolors," she said with obvious pride.

"Worthy activities," he intoned. "Ones I believe expected of any young lady for her Season."

Was it her wounded pride that made her hear boredom in his tone? Persephone evidently didn't hear it, for she sighed dramatically.

"Quite expected," she admitted. "But I fear I have had little time to practice of late. I regret we have been too busy since coming to London."

"So I understand," he replied with a small smile. "How does it feel to be a complete success?"

Sarah watched as her cousin's delicate skin turned a becoming rose.

"Oh, I would not term my success complete, my lord," she demurred, lowering her gaze. "After all, I am not yet engaged."

Sarah raised an eyebrow on the obviously leading comment, but Malcolm only shrugged.

"That will be remedied shortly, I'm sure," he replied. "And do I understand that you are acting as her chaperon, Miss Compton? Isn't that a great deal of responsibility for one so young?"

While it was nice to be considered young, Sarah could not help but be annoyed by his once-more censorious tone.

"Sarah is very used to responsibility, my lord," Persy answered loyally for her. "She serves as chatelaine at our home in Suffolk. My mother has been ill since Christmas, and before I came to London I was not always in the best of health. I'm sure my family would not know how to go on without Sarah to help us."

"That may be a bit strong," Sarah put in hastily, not yet ready to be martyred. "My aunt and uncle were kind enough to take me in when my parents died. I am more than happy to repay them any way I can, including helping Persephone with her Season."

"Commendable," he intoned. "Though I would have thought someone older and more formidable would be a better choice."

Now Sarah frowned at him. For a gentleman who had demanded her hand at supper like some impassioned lover, he was certainly going out of his way to find fault. Again, Persephone answered for her.

"Oh, Sarah can be quite formidable, my lord," she assured him earnestly. Sarah wondered whether that was something so very praiseworthy. "She has been known to frighten off inappropriate gentlemen with only a look."

"Indeed," Malcolm murmured, clearly doubting the truth of the statement.

"Indeed," Sarah intoned, scowling at him. To her surprise, he cracked a smile. She colored, lowering her gaze in confusion once more to her still loaded plate.

In defiance, she speared an apricot tart and popped it whole into her mouth.

"Oh, indeed," Persephone chorused. "I feel very grateful for her care. It is so very important for young women such as myself to have someone older and wiser to guide us in our choices."

Sarah tried not to frown. Was that really how her cousin felt? She had the feeling that Persephone wanted nothing more than to escape her sensible advice. She cast a glance up at her cousin, but the girl was gazing wistfully at Lord Breckonridge with such longing that Sarah wondered how the fellow didn't expire on the spot. Lord Breckonridge, however, was digging into his own food with gusto. Catching her gaze on him, he winked conspiratorially. Sarah instantly dropped her gaze to the lobster patty below.

"Well, it appears you could not do better than your cousin for advice, Miss Persephone," Malcolm said after a short while. "She strikes me as most levelheaded."

"Very levelheaded," Persy agreed readily. "She is steadfast in her loyalty and unswerving in her service."

Sarah nearly gagged on a sweetmeat. Persy made her sound like the family spaniel! Glancing up again, she found both of them beaming at her. She smiled self-consciously.

"You are too kind, Cousin," she managed. "Now, perhaps I might provide a bit of that unswerving service. I hear the music continuing in the ballroom, so surely you are missing a dance. If you are finished, we should go. Doubtless Lord Breckonridge has better things to do all evening than entertain us."

"On the contrary," he replied readily. "I find that I am the one being entertained."

Sarah glared at him. Persephone gave her gossamer giggle.

"Oh, my lord," she said, "you tease us terribly. I vow I do not know when I have had a more gentlemanly escort."

He inclined his head in a bow of acknowledgment of her praise, but somehow, Sarah did not think he was pleased. He turned to her. "Are you ready to return to the ballroom, then, Miss Compton?"

Sarah glanced longingly at the remaining desserts on her plate. But, looking up, she saw that only a few of the guests had availed themselves of the food. Apparently they had expected the stale cakes and weak lemonade that was usually served at Almack's. In the meantime, the duke had been left to his own devices, and the wiles of the hundred or so young ladies present. Indeed, most of the people in the room with them were gentlemen. Several, including the Byronic fellow in black, still lounged near the door, most casting glances at Persephone. The only group of young ladies cast similarly longing looks in Malcolm's direction. Sarah felt caught between two fires, and very likely to be burned in the process.

"Yes, I believe I am," she replied with a sigh.

He rose. "Then allow me to escort you. I will then take my leave."

"Oh, must you?" Persephone begged, rising in a rustle of silk. "We have enjoyed your company, haven't we, Sarah?"

He was watching her again. In truth, there had been moments when she intensely enjoyed his company. Now, however, she scarcely knew what to think.

"We have kept Lord Breckonridge to ourselves long enough, Persy," she said, head high. "Thank you, my lord, for your time."

He bowed to each of them. "Ladies, my pleasure. May I ask one more favor?"

"Anything, my lord," Persy breathed.

He said nothing, watching Sarah. His dark eyes were hooded, but she could feel his tension. She could not imagine what could be so important to him, but she nodded as her heart began to beat more rapidly once again.

"If I may call on you later in the week? I would like to further our acquaintance."

Further their acquaintance? Sarah felt the blood rush to her face. She cast a quick glance at her cousin, who was staring, wide-eyed. She glanced back at Malcolm, but he was still watching her. For a moment she had the insane idea that he was holding his breath.

"Certainly, my lord," she proclaimed. "It would be our pleasure."

He bowed again, but not before she sighted a smile of triumph. Her gaze followed him from the room. Then she turned to meet Persy's stare.

"We did it, Sarah," she breathed. "We won the prize."

Sarah swallowed, nerves tingling. "Nonsense, Persy. I can't think what you mean."

"The ball, silly," Persy replied. "All these ladies, vying for the attentions of the prince among men. Only we caught him first." She smiled dreamily as her entourage closed around her once more. Like a princess in a fairy tale, she was whisked back to the ball on a cloud of murmured praise.

Sarah followed more slowly, wondering. They did

indeed seem to have attracted the interest of the handsome prince.

But was it the princess or her lady-in-waiting whom he fancied?

FIVE

Sarah wasn't the only one asking the question. Malcolm was not a little surprised to find an excessive amount of interest in his behavior at the ball. To his mind, he had been rather blatant in his attentions. Indeed, had he shown as much interest in an act introduced to Parliament as he had shown in Miss Compton, his opponents would have had no doubt as to how he intended to vote. Yet he had not even quit Almack's before he was questioned on his intentions.

The first person was Prestwick.

"Very nice," he complimented Malcolm as he exited the refreshment room. His position near the door left no doubt that he had been lying in wait.

Malcolm raised an eyebrow. "I beg your pardon?"

Chas shook his head. "Come, Malcolm, I know a ploy when I see one. God knows, I've run them often enough. I merely wished to express my appreciation at your subtlety. For a moment, even *I* thought you were interested in the elder Miss Compton."

"And now you think otherwise?" Malcolm asked with a frown.

Chas chuckled. "Of course. Oh, I'll grant you Miss Compton is handsome in a sturdy sort of way. But she cannot hold a candle to her cousin."

"There we quite agree," Malcolm replied. "Prestwick, I am surprised at you. A man who could recognize the depth of character of your fine wife should have better sense. Miss Persephone is a delightful young lady, I'm sure, but she'll take a great deal of maturing before she can be the woman I need. From what I can tell of her cousin, however, Miss Compton is very nearly perfect."

Now Chas raised an eyebrow. "I stand corrected. Well done, Malcolm. I see you hold to your principles even in the face of very real temptation. Very well, then. I'll say no more on the matter. Miss Compton it is. I wish you the best of luck."

"Luck?" Malcolm snorted. "Luck has very little to do with it. The lady appears to possess certain characteristics I require. I need to confirm those characteristics and then I need to determine what I have that would make her find me similarly attractive."

"Besides money, position, and questionable charm?" Chas quipped.

"Precisely," Malcolm replied. "Tell me, what do you know of her?"

Chas rubbed his chin thoughtfully. "Not a great deal, I suppose. I believe someone said she had a short Season herself some years ago. She stands as guardian dragon to the fair princess Persephone, and they come from Suffolk." He shrugged. "Rather pitiful collection of facts. Try asking your valet."

"My valet?" Malcolm frowned. "What the devil would my valet know about Miss Compton?"

"A very great deal," Chas informed him. "Surely you know the network our servants have. How else do you think gossip flies so quickly through this city? My butler Rames has been invaluable to me. He's saved my skin from a vengeful relative more times than I care to admit. I'd wager your man would be similarly helpful if you ask."

"Perhaps," Malcolm allowed. "I'll consider the matter. First, I need to make my regrets to your lovely wife."

"Allow me the pleasure of joining you," Chas replied. They strolled across the ballroom to where Anne was visiting with a number of the young ladies in attendance. As they approached, Malcolm saw that visiting was not the right word. Instead, Anne was carefully pointing out young gentlemen to whom she might introduce the ladies. Conversation ceased immediately as Malcolm and Chas approached. Lips curled into smiles and fans began to beat rapidly. Malcolm swept her a bow.

"Dear Lady Prestwick, I must take my leave of you."

He could feel the stilling of the wind as the fans halted.

"Always a delight, my lord," Lady Prestwick replied with a deep curtsy. "And will you tell me one thing before you leave?"

He straightened, feeling the heat of a dozen gazes on his face. "Anything you desire," he replied magnanimously, although he feared having to answer before such a company.

"Did you enjoy the ball?" she asked blandly.

He grinned at her. There was a teasing light in those gray eyes, a light for him and her husband alone. *God bless the woman,* he thought. "I enjoyed it immensely," he replied.

She smiled. "Then I am well pleased. Will we see you for dinner next week?"

"With a certainty," he agreed. Bowing again, he

quit the room, thinking that Chas Prestwick was a lucky man.

It remained to be seen whether Malcolm would be similarly fortunate.

Someone else wondered about Malcolm's choice of bride, but he was too sure of himself to ask. Besides, asking might betray his interest. Rupert Wells had learned to hide any interest behind a thick mask of ennui. As long as no one knew he was interested, no one could take away what he cared about. It was a tool that stood him in good stead in Parliament.

Unfortunately, Breckonridge was conversant in the use of the tool as well. Anyone else watching him would have been hard pressed to tell which of the ladies he fancied. True, he'd danced twice with the elder Miss Compton, but, by the looks that had flitted across her face at supper, she was not entirely pleased by his attentions. *Her* face, at least, was as open as the betting books at White's. She was at best confused and at worst embarrassed by the entire evening. And while she was somewhat attractive for an older woman, she was no comparison to her cousin.

He allowed himself a smile as he strode home in the night from Almack's. Breckonridge was no fool. A man with a beautiful wife could command loyalties. Surely he was after the Incomparable Miss Compton. If Rupert had found her a bit shallow and vacuous, that did not signify. He'd seen the way she toyed with her admirers. She had a natural gift for manipulation, a gift only enhanced by her beauty. She'd make an excellent wife for a rising politician. Breckonridge was more transparent than the man thought. Perhaps Rupert had him at last.

His long fingers tightened on the handle of his ebony walking stick. Breckonridge had provided him with one difficulty after another. The man was well respected, though Rupert liked to remind himself that the respect was only because of the fellow's size and prowess. If the members of Parliament knew him as Rupert did, they would have turned their backs on him years ago. That, of course, was another problem. Breckonridge was a master at dissembling. No one truly knew him. And one could never quite catch him being uncivil to anyone. They all thought him a jolly good fellow.

Rupert, however, knew him for a black-hearted devil, and he would not rest until all of London knew it as well. With any luck, the Incomparable Miss Compton would help him in achieving his goal. If not, he'd find another use for her. If he could not expose Breckonridge, at least he could make the man pay. It did indeed look as if his luck was turning.

His smile deepened as he disappeared into the darkness of London.

By the time Malcolm's carriage pulled up before his town house in Grosvenor Square, he had his campaign planned. There were any number of ways to learn a person's background in London. He had thought he had used them all over the years. A few discreet inquiries could go a long way to determining whether Miss Compton was all she seemed. He would start in the morning.

He had to admit, however, that he was enheartened.

From the first he had found her attractive, with her witch's eyes and seductive curves. It was a pleasure to learn that she had intelligence and fire as well. From what her cousin had said, she apparently had experience in household management. She was certainly familiar with the London social scene, having to chaperon her cousin through it. She seemed of sturdy stock; the dancing had not winded her. Perhaps that would bode well for her success in childbearing. She was not a conservative Tory, but neither was she a radical Whig. She knew something of politics and governance. He could find nothing that would deter him from pursuing her acquaintance further.

Except the fact that she collected rocks.

He smiled, remembering her set down. There was a story there; he was certain of it. Perhaps he could get her to reveal it the next time they met. She would not divulge it easily, that much was clear. Sarah was a strong-willed woman, exactly what he needed. He looked forward to persuading her of that fact.

Appleby was just turning down his bedclothes when he entered the room. Malcolm started to wave him out, then remembered Chas's advice. He eyed the fellow appraisingly as his valet went to stir the coals of the fire. The red glow from the black marble fireplace cast a somber look to the fellow's narrow face. Of course, it took very little to make Appleby look somber. All Malcolm had to do was pick the wrong coat.

"Is something amiss, my lord?" the man asked in his slow, quiet voice as he straightened and caught Malcolm watching him.

"Do you mix much with other servants, Appleby?" Malcolm asked.

His valet's eyebrows rose at the personal question,

and Malcolm realized it was probably the first of its kind. "I'm not certain what you mean, my lord," he murmured.

Malcolm prowled over to the bed, debating how much effort to put into the questioning. He didn't want to alienate the fellow—he had little time to hire a valet and train him to work as Malcolm preferred, which was quickly and silently. On the other hand, having another avenue to learn about his fellow Parliamentarians would be very helpful. One never knew what obscure fact could win an argument. He had gotten Lord Wincamp to vote against the Corn Laws by pointing out their potential effects on badgers, which happened to be on the fellow's ancestral shield.

"Lord Prestwick informs me," he said carefully, keeping his gaze on the gold-shot green bed hangings, which appeared to need a thorough cleaning, "that his valet entertains him with stories from other servants and their masters. I note that you do not do so with me."

He could hear the frown in his man's voice. "I never had the impression my lord enjoyed stories. In fact, I rather had the impression my lord would prefer I not speak at all."

"Certainly you may speak," Malcolm told him, feeling annoyed for no reason he could name. "Particularly if you had something useful to speak about."

Glancing up, he saw Appleby's brow clear. "Useful? I see. My lord would perhaps like tips on fashion or personal hygiene?"

"My lord would not," Malcolm snapped. "I'm no fashion leader like Brummell."

"You certainly aren't," Appleby agreed with a sigh.

Malcolm frowned. "Was that a comment on my dress, Appleby?"

Appleby frowned as well. "Certainly not, my lord. However, may I point out that my lord did just indicate that he prefer I speak? Perhaps my lord would prefer to return to our usual silence?"

Malcolm took a deep breath and prayed for patience. The bed hangings would not be cleaned until he had a wife to oversee the household. There would be no wife unless he exerted himself to find one. And Sarah Compton was the most likely candidate.

"Appleby," he said carefully, "I understand that there is a chain of servants who bandy information about their masters and associates. What I am trying to ascertain is whether you are connected to this chain and whether you would be willing to pass information from it to me when asked."

"I see," his valet intoned. "You would like me to relay gossip. I generally try to avoid gossip as it is always overblown and frequently dead wrong. So, I would say this would be an addition to my duties, and I do not think I could add to my duties without expectation of an increase in pay."

Malcolm cocked his head, amused despite himself. He would not have thought the fellow held such scruples, or that he held them so cheaply. "I imagine additional remuneration can be arranged for the right information," he allowed.

Appleby inclined his head. "Always your servant, my lord."

"Very well," Malcolm agreed. "See what you can find out about Miss Sarah Compton, late of Suffolk."

Appleby stared off toward the far end of the room, for all the world like some gypsy going into a supposed trance. "Miss Sarah Compton," he mused, voice echoing oddly. "Yes, of course, Miss Compton."

"You know her?" Malcolm frowned.

"It's possible," Appleby intoned. "Yes, quite possible. Elegant female, chaperoning the Incomparable Miss Persephone Compton?"

"Yes, deuce take it," Malcolm admitted, "the very one. Speak up, man. What have you heard?"

Appleby blinked and focused his bleary blue eyes on his master. "Why, nothing. Nothing at all. But perhaps I can remedy that by the time you awake in the morning."

"See that you do," Malcolm growled, thoroughly put out with the fellow. "I expect a full report at breakfast."

"Your servant, my lord," Appleby replied, starting to bow himself out.

Malcolm held up a hand to stop him. "And, Appleby, I don't think I need to remind you that you are not to relay information about me without asking first."

Appleby froze halfway up from his bow. "You would give me permission to gossip about you?"

"If it suited my purpose," Malcolm explained. "It might be an expedient way to let a colleague know of my opinions without advertising them, or humbling him. However, in all other circumstances, I expect you to be silent about my doings."

"Will not the other servants see this as a difficulty, my lord?" Appleby asked, licking his lips as he slowly straightened. "I imagine I shall have to pay in some way for their confidences."

"I pay no one to stand as betrayer," Malcolm informed him, scowling at the very thought. "Understand me well, Appleby. If servants are talking of their own free will, I see nothing wrong in listening. In fact, it appears to be expected that you will relay it to me. However, I do not want to offer any inducement to them to tell tales on their masters. That betrays a trust. Do you understand?"

Appleby nodded. "I believe so, my lord. If you need nothing else, then?"

Malcolm waved him out, then shook his head. He could not help feeling that Appleby would prove singularly unskilled at this game. The man would likely be as hesitant in gathering information as he was in dressing Malcolm. Just in case, Malcolm would send a few pointed notes to others from whom he had previously learned much. With any luck, he would soon know just how qualified Sarah Compton was for his purposes.

He could hardly wait.

SIX

Sarah wasn't certain what time they left Lady Prestwick's ball. The night seemed to stop the moment Viscount Breckonridge left, the time slowing, the people dulling. She watched the gentlemen flatter her cousin as if from a distance. She barely noticed that several others had joined the throng, including the brooding gentleman who had watched them from the doorway at dinner. Even the renewed attentions of the Duke of Reddington failed to pique her interest. The world had somehow shrunk and with it her enjoyment. She had no idea what spell Lord Breckonridge had woven over her, but she could hardly wait to go home.

Even Norrie remarked on her change of attitude. "Sarah, this isn't like you," she protested when repeated questions had failed to get Sarah to answer in more than a monosyllable. "You've spent well over an hour in the gentleman's company. Give over, my girl. What do you think of him?"

Sarah rubbed her temple. "I think I shall have a headache for the first time in my life," she murmured crossly. "I shall have to go home and brew a potion of feverfew leaves. Aunt Belle claims that always works wonders for her."

She looked up to find Norrie regarding her with narrowed eyes. Sarah threw up her hands. "Honestly,

Norrie, I don't know what to think about Lord Breckonridge. There were moments in his company that were delightful beyond words, and moments that drove me to distraction."

"Distraction, eh," Norrie mused. "That could be auspicious or disastrous. I suppose the important thing is his intent. Did he ask to call on you?"

"He did," Sarah admitted, still marveling at the fact. "Though truth be told he asked in such a way that I cannot be sure he did not include Persephone in the request."

Norrie's face fell. "Well, that is a leveler. I can see why you're confused. Let us just hope the gentleman is more obvious when he visits. Would you like to go home? I can take up Persephone with us. It will only take a moment to pry Justinian away from the discussion of literature he is no doubt finding so fascinating."

Sarah shook her head. "You are kind, but I have my duty. I just hope this evening ends soon."

Unfortunately, her cousin obviously felt otherwise.

"What a lovely evening," Persephone remarked hours later when they at last rode home in the family carriage. "Lady Prestwick puts on the best attractions. I vow there will not be another ball to rival this all Season."

"It was interesting," Sarah allowed, stifling a yawn. "Though in truth I still am not sure what to make of it. But one thing I do know. You are quite a success, Persy. You should be pleased."

The girl lowered her head demurely, but not before Sarah saw her smile widen in triumph. "Thank you, Cousin Sarah," she said quietly. "I am pleased that people seem to like me. The duke was even attentive."

"Wonderfully so," Sarah agreed, but her mind immediately conjured up the image of a raven-haired gentleman who had danced attendance on her instead. She forced her attention back to the matter at hand. "I hope His Grace will come calling this week."

"Oh, very likely," Persephone replied. She gave a gossamer giggle that echoed against the hard wood panels and made it sound as if an entire family of pixies had been let loose in the vehicle. "Can you see his face when I refuse him? He will be beside himself."

Sarah blinked, feeling suddenly at sea. "Refuse him? Why would you refuse him?"

Persephone giggled again, and this time the sound sent a chill through Sarah.

"Because I've found someone better, of course. You do want me to make the best match possible, don't you, Sarah?"

"Of course," Sarah said with a frown. "But I was under the impression that the duke was the best of your suitors. He is wealthy, he is titled, he is handsome and charming, and he is besotted. What more do you want?"

"Power?" Persy said thoughtfully, elfin head cocked so that her golden ringlets tickled her dainty chin. "Position? Influence?"

Sarah stared at her. It had never dawned on her that her frail cousin would crave such things. But the interest in her voice could not be denied. "And you don't think you'll have those things as the Duchess of Reddington?"

Even in the dark, Sarah could see that Persy had made a face. "Doubtful," she replied. "Everyone says the duke is somewhat of a recluse. He spends most of the year at his hunting lodge in York of all places. I am not convinced I can persuade him to stay in London. And I refuse to waste away in the country."

"I imagine even London would cloy after a time," Sarah told her. "It swelters here in the summer and oppresses with fog in the winter. Besides, wouldn't you miss the quiet of home? We haven't been here three months and I miss it already. Why would anyone want to live here all year long?"

Persy shook her head. "That is just one of the differences between us, Cousin," she said with a sniff of superiority. "You do not mind being hidden away. I should hate it."

"It does not follow that you must therefore hate the duke," Sarah pointed out, ignoring the slight. "He seems a fine gentleman to me."

"If you like him so much," Persy replied airily, "then perhaps you should marry him."

"Perhaps I should," Sarah snapped. Then she bristled despite herself as Persy laughed.

"Oh, Sarah, you are so good at distracting me," she said as if she had done nothing wrong. "I remember how you'd make a game of taking that horrid medicine. 'Pretend you're the stable, Persy. Here comes the horse, a fine strawberry roan. He's so tired, he needs to rest. Open up and let him in.' "

It was so hard to stay angry at the girl, even when she needed a dressing down. Sarah smiled at the memory. "I remember. You were very good to open up. I tasted that stuff once. It was quite nasty."

"Completely abhorrent," Persy agreed. "Unfortunately, I'm no longer that child, Sarah. You can't get me to accept someone with a pretty story. If I don't wish to marry the duke, I won't."

Sarah held back a sigh of vexation. "I cannot force

you to marry, Persy. Nor would I even if I could. But you must marry eventually. Do you want to end up like me?"

It was a dire threat and an empty one. They both knew that Persy would never countenance being an old maid. Besides, there were simply too many men willing to marry her to allow her to remain single against her will. Persy merely eyed her contemptuously before turning her face to the window in dismissal. Sarah let the sigh slip out.

She was still perplexed when she retired to bed two hours later, after making sure their butler, Mr. Timmons, had settled the house for the night. Mr. Timmons was nearing retirement. Indeed, his replacement was practicing at the Compton home while Sarah and Persephone visited London. Sarah had worked with him too many years to let the fellow shoulder all the burden of running the household. Besides, all the servants were used to bringing her their problems. Aunt Belle was too preoccupied with Persy, and Uncle Harold felt managing servants was woman's work.

"Bless you, miss," Timmons had said to her tonight when she'd finished locking up for him. "One more trip up those stairs would have done me in."

Though Sarah was just as tired, she had only smiled into his wrinkled face. Patting him on a frail shoulder, she had sent him off to his room in the corner of the basement for a well-deserved rest.

Unfortunately, she still had one more task before she could say her prayers and retire for the night, and she was far less sure she wanted to handle it. Every night she wrote to her aunt and uncle, although she posted the packet of letters only once a week. In the letters she reported how Percy was doing, which beau was the current favorite, and what places they had visited. She wasn't certain what to tell them tonight. "Persy refuses to marry and I wish I could escape," seemed spiteful and ungrateful. Perhaps she should try in the morning. Maybe by then she could think of something better.

The thought of collapsing in her quiet bedchamber had never been more appealing. She could not say that Aunt Belle and Uncle Harold stinted in their material support of her, for all Uncle Harold bemoaned the cost. She had lovely clothes, even if they were all drab, dark colors that befitted her spinster status. She had a beautifully appointed room here in London as well as in Suffolk, both done in blues and golds, with bed, writing desk, comfortable chair, and marble fireplace. They were no more hers than any other guest bedchamber. When she moved to the cottage that Norrie said stood next to the Dame School at Wenworth Place, she had already planned to use her meager inheritance to purchase paintings for the walls and porcelain vases and figurines to place on the mantel. Her home would look like Sarah Compton lived there.

Unfortunately, she was not to be left alone that night. While Persy had her own maid (a young lady named Lucy who was as nearly puffed up in consequence as her mistress), Sarah was long used to fending for herself. She was therefore surprised to find Lucy turning down the bedclothes on her blue-hung four-poster bed when she entered her room.

"Miss Persy thought you might have a need for my services, Miss Sarah," she explained with a bob of a curtsy. A tiny black-haired girl a year younger than Persephone, she nevertheless had cultivated a reputation for being a knowing one. Still, Sarah was glad for the help for once. It was obvious Persephone was trying to make amends.

"Some help with my buttons would be very welcome," Sarah acknowledged, turning so the girl could apply deft fingers to the task of unhooking the blue silk gown.

"Let me help you with your nightdress as well," the little maid admonished as she finished with the gown. She bustled to the dresser and opened the drawers until she found a white lawn gown. In the meantime, Sarah pulled off her dress and chemise and loosened her stays. Before she could have counted to ten, Lucy had her in the nightdress and perched before the dressing table, where she took down and brushed out Sarah's long, thick, straight hair.

"I could crimp this for you," Lucy offered, letting the strands run through her fingers. "We could set up the curls real easy. It would draw attention to your speaking eyes."

Sarah caught herself wondering how Malcolm Breckonridge would react to her hair in curls around her face. Letting Lucy apply the hot crimping irons to her locks would definitely be worth it if she won that look of warmth again when he called.

If he called.

"I could help you in other ways as well," Lucy continued, watching her in the mirror. "I was told I have a lovely hand. Perhaps I could help you with your correspondence, like to Mr. Compton."

Sarah stiffened, then turned to confront the maid. "Is that what this is all about? Persy's afraid I'll write to her father about her behavior. She sent you to stop me."

"Oh, no, mum," Lucy protested, green eyes wide. "Heavens no, mum. Why would you think so?"

Sarah stood. "Perhaps because Persy's never seen fit to share your services with me before. Nor have you ever seemed so eager to help. Good night, Lucy. You may tell your mistress that I will keep my own counsel, thank you very much. And if I want my hair crimped, I can jolly well do it myself, like I do everything else."

The maid ducked out, and Sarah stalked to the bed and climbed in. Lucy was new to the household, having only arrived when Persephone was graduated from school. The maid could not know how easily Persy manipulated people. Sarah would have to mention Lucy's behavior to Timmons. The rest of the staff was immune to Persy's tantrums and tearful entreaties. If Sarah wanted to keep the household running smoothly, she would have to find a way to teach Lucy to think for herself. Once one stood up to Persy, her cousin often stopped attempting to manipulate.

She plumped the goose feather pillow and lay down her head. Did anyone stop to wonder about the woman who made sure Persephone's life ran smoothly? If others knew the story of her background, she was certain they would believe she must harbor a deep resentment of her cousin. Persy had been given all the attention, while Sarah had worked harder than most nursemaids. Yet, she could not regret her time away from London. In the quiet of the Suffolk countryside, she knew she had grown from a timid, gawkish teenager to a self-confident woman. Ministering to Persephone had taught her patience and presence of mind. As she read to pass the time, she learned things she might never have known. With no one to talk to on her lonely night vigils, she had learned to fill her mind with her own thoughts and to listen for the thoughts of God. She had also learned to analyze what she read by firelight and form her own opinions. Hadn't Lord Breckonridge praised her for that tonight?

And there she was again, thinking of him. Small wonder he was a force in Parliament. He had certainly mesmerized her. She could not remember his thick black hair without wondering how it would feel to run her fingers through it. She could not consider his strength without thinking about how it felt to be held in his arms. She could not ponder their conversation without savoring the deep rumble of his laughter when she'd been witty or audacious. Was she therefore lost?

She sat up and pounded down the pillow, then threw herself flat once more. That was quite enough. She was not some ape leader, some graceless, faceless spinster to feel grateful for a moment of his time. She might be nearly penniless, but she had a purpose and a future. She would focus on that and let Malcolm Breckonridge be hanged. She just had to get Persy married first. Surely she could accomplish that.

She was not so confident the next day. As usual, the knocker sounded repeatedly throughout the afternoon, and by the time the duke arrived at four, Persy was surrounded by no less than six suitors, all trying to outdo one another for her favors. Though two had already overstayed their welcome by an hour, none showed the least inclination to leave. The duke had engaged Sarah in fifteen minutes of meaningless conversation and taken himself off in high dudgeon. Persy didn't even notice.

Nor was she repentant when Sarah pointed out the problem that evening at dinner before a theater outing with Norrie and her husband.

"He will value me all the more if he knows I am popular," Persy assured her calmly. "Have we heard any word from Lord Breckonridge?"

Sarah started at the name. Indeed, she had started at every knock at the door that afternoon, only to sag with disappointment when each caller was only another of Persy's admirers. *Silly woman,* she had scolded herself for her yearnings. He probably wasn't coming anyway. And even if he was, it was only the day after the ball. It was much too much to think he would appear so soon. True, Persy's admirers seldom let twenty-four hours go by before rushing to renew the acquaintance, but Lord Breckonridge was hardly a lovesick swain.

"I have heard nothing," Sarah told her cousin.

Persy sighed, fussing with the skirt of her lavender lustring dress. "Perhaps he was not interested after all."

"I'm sure we are the least of his worries," Sarah replied, feeling as if she were trying to convince herself rather than her cousin. "He has a country to run, after all. You cannot expect him to dance attendance on a woman who is not even a close friend."

"I suppose not," Persy replied. Her tone was so subdued that Sarah could not help but be touched. Perhaps if Persy could care about Sarah's potential suitor, all was not lost with the girl.

No sooner had the thought crossed her mind than Sarah cringed inwardly. She had to stop this nonsense at once. She could not get her hopes up that Malcolm Breckonridge might court her. She was long past the age of whispered secrets and longing glances across crowded ballrooms. She had other plans for her future, and Lord Breckonridge would surely be looking for a woman with more social connections, anyway, certainly not a reclusive spinster from the back of beyond. He must have another reason to call.

But if he called on Persephone, she thought she would cheerfully be sick all over her cousin's fashionable gown.

SEVEN

Appleby was tight-mouthed as he dressed Malcolm the morning after Lady Prestwick's ball.

"I take it the gossip was less than useful," Malcolm probed.

"I regret to say, my lord," his valet intoned, "that Miss Sarah Compton is a singularly uninteresting female."

Malcolm chuckled. "I did not find her so. You learned nothing then?"

"Nothing of import," Appleby replied with a dour face. "Her servants adore her. Her neighbors find her a model of decorum. She is virtuous, hardworking, and loyal to her family. She has a select group of acquaintances, including the Countess of Wenworth. I could not find a crumb of gossip associated with her name, my lord, outside of the fact that she is nearly thirty years of age and unmarried. I have failed."

"Not in the slightest," Malcolm assured him with a grin. "You've told me exactly what I wished to know. There will be something extra in your pocket this month. Keep up the good work."

Malcolm would have thought it was the first time he'd praised the fellow by the sly grin Appleby effected. As Malcolm went down to breakfast, however, he had to own that it probably *was* the first time he'd ever praised the fellow.

So, Sarah Compton's servants adored her. He did not know whether that was good or bad. It might mean that she was too generous or too lax in her demands on them. On the other hand, it might mean that she ran an orderly household in which they were proud to work. He caught himself wondering how his servants liked him. He glanced at the footman who was pouring his coffee, but his face must not have been sufficiently composed, for the poor fellow's hand began shaking and he was forced to set the pot down and back trembling from the room.

God, how he needed a capable wife.

As the morning progressed, he began to think more and more that Sarah Compton could be that wife. Reports from his other sources trickled in throughout the day as he worked with his fellow Parliamentarians. From the snippets of information, he learned that Sarah was an orphan and a graduate of the Barnsley School for Young Ladies in Somerset. Her family was an old and reputable one. Her only known relatives were the aunt and uncle who would be Miss Persephone's parents. She had apparently made a brief appearance on the social scene some eleven years ago, only to mysteriously disappear. It was not until he spoke late in the afternoon with burly Micky McGaffin, a Bow Street runner who was not above an extra quid in his pocket, that anyone was willing to hazard a guess why.

"Any number of reasons a lady runs off quiet like," the redheaded runner offered as he ambled beside Malcolm in a quiet corner of Hyde Park where they were unlikely to be observed. "Money troubles, family troubles, suitor troubles."

"From what I can learn," Malcolm replied, "her

aunt and uncle are rather wealthy, her parents were long dead by the time of her Season, and her list of suitors is remarkably short."

"That only leaves one thing, then, in my mind," McGaffin said. He paused to spit as if to lengthen the silence. "She went and got herself in the family way."

Malcolm jerked to a stop. He seized the surprised fellow by the front of his coat and lifted him off the ground. "If you ever sully Miss Compton's name in my presence again, I won't be accountable for my actions. Do I make myself clear?"

McGaffin's blue eyes bulged from their reddened sockets. "Perfectly clear, yer lordship. No disrespect intended. Lots of very fine ladies find theirselves in trouble that way."

"Not Miss Compton, I assure you," Malcolm replied, releasing him so quickly the fellow stumbled. "There must be another reason. I suggest you find it."

McGaffin bowed. "Right away, me lord."

Watching him hurry away, Malcolm shook his head. He had never before felt a murderous rage rush over him like that. It was as if something deep inside him refused to believe anything bad about the woman. More, something was quite furious that anyone would even *think* anything bad about her. He shook his head again. No doubt he had been working too hard lately. But with the people free from last year's Gagging Acts that had banned public meetings, and the rising talk of Parliamentary reform, he feared the Tories would move to enact stricter laws against free speech. The fools in the Commons only made things worse with their cries for radical change. If he could only get both sides to see reason. The more that comments were suppressed, the more dangerous they became. Yet, the harder he focused on his work, the less time he could devote to other thoughts, such as the very interesting Miss Compton.

He did, of course, have another call to make. He had promised Lady Renderly a visit, however unpleasant that prospect appeared. It was nearly as bad as he had feared, with the woman complaining on a variety of subjects while her poor daughter sat chewing her narrow lower lip. Malcolm tried to remain polite, but when the subject of Miss Compton came up, he was once more hard-pressed to keep his temper.

"I told Elspeth you had no interest in that wheyfaced spinster," Lady Renderly proclaimed. "And I knew you'd see through the Compton chit in a minute. She isn't nearly as pretty as they say. Poor bloodlines."

"I hadn't noticed," Malcolm managed, trying to think of a way to leave before he disgraced his reputation of civility.

"You should notice," she scolded. "Do you want your children sullied? Timidity, sir. It runs in their veins. Look at the elder Miss Compton. Scared of her own shadow."

Malcolm frowned. He could not help but glance at Elspeth, who lowered her gaze with a blush. "Reticence would appear to be a congenial trait," he offered. He thought he saw a brief smile flash across the girl's face, but her mother reached out to rap his knuckles with the gold edge of her quizzing glass. Malcolm had to fight the impulse to strike back.

"I'm speaking of cowardice, if you please," Lady Renderly informed him. "There is a difference, sir. Miss Sarah Compton ran away from her Season like the cur she is. She would make you a wretched wife."

"Your consideration for my happiness overwhelms

me," Malcolm replied. Inspiration struck. "And since you are so solicitous, I must admit to a peevish digestion. Makes me quite dyspeptic. Violent even. Poor bloodlines, I suspect. So, instead of inflicting myself on you further, I will take my leave." He rose and bowed to Elspeth, pitying her from the core of his being. "Your servant, Lady Elspeth. If you have need of my services, please let me know."

The girl glanced up with gratitude in her smile. "Thank you, Lord Breckonridge. I will remember that."

He had escaped before her mother could wonder at his meaning.

The following day a very humble Micky sent him word that Miss Compton had apparently left the Season all those years ago to go home and care for her ailing cousin. The story didn't match that of Lady Renderly, but he preferred to believe Micky anyway. Having therefore no unsatisfactory reports of the lady, he knew he had to make an appearance. Surely he owed her as much. Leaving Parliament early, and raising no few brows in the process, he presented himself on her doorstep at three in the afternoon.

He was not a little surprised to find several gentlemen there before him, though they most likely were there to court Miss Persephone. One strapping blond fellow obscured the crimson velvet drapes on the window of the little sitting room into which the elderly butler had shown Malcolm. A scrawny, dark-haired lad attempted to lounge on the crimson and gold lion-footed sofa in front of the black marble fireplace. The bright-coated Barrington, today in a wool superfine coat of an impossible shade of lime, clashed with the crimson-hung wall against which he leaned. But Malcolm could not help noticing that while the gentlemen exhibited various stages of ennui and frustration, the room itself was spotless. Miss Compton knew how to manage a household.

Neither Sarah nor her cousin were in evidence, however, although the butler brought the callers lemonade on a tray, his hands shaking so badly the liquid sloshed over the tops.

"Miss Sarah will be down shortly," the man murmured in a throaty voice to Malcolm.

"What about Miss Persephone?" the blond fellow demanded, snatching a glass off the tray.

"She'll be down when she pleases," the butler replied with far less charity. As he left the room, Malcolm noticed he walked with a limp. That she'd keep such a fellow spoke of the loyalty Appleby had mentioned. Small wonder her servants liked her.

Malcolm attempted to talk with the other gentlemen, but he had no sooner made their acquaintance than two left to be swiftly replaced by three others, including the Duke of Reddington. Reddington looked worse than Malcolm had ever seen him—green eyes hooded, tanned face lined. Even his usually impeccably tailored gray morning suit hung loosely on him. Malcolm nodded as the gentleman made his way to his side. The others engaged Barrington in conversation.

"Bit of a crush," Malcolm observed wryly.

"I've seen worse," the duke replied, eying the empty doorway with ill-disguised annoyance. "She's deucedly good at playing out her hand."

"I'm surprised you put up with it," Malcolm observed. "Is any woman worth such a price?"

The duke shook his head. "Have you ever seen her smile? It's like the sun at the end of winter. She is accomplished, intelligent, spontaneous. She can be charm itself. Her one failing appears to be that she knows it."

Suddenly Barrington stiffened, long nose up like a hound to the scent. His two conversation partners, one short and squat, the other tall and muscular, shoved each other in an attempt to reach the door. Before either succeeded, Miss Persephone Compton floated into the room. She favored each of her callers with a pleasant smile and they all started talking at once, clustering around her like bees to a bright, fragrant flower, elbowing each other to get closer. The duke shook his head, clucking.

"Lost, every last one of us. I wonder who'll win her favor today?"

Malcolm watched as Miss Compton allowed Barrington to monopolize the conversation. Barrington was obviously so overcome that he stuttered. The other two laughed. Miss Persephone smiled sweetly, laying a hand on his arm in encouragement. As Barrington turned a shade of red to match the walls, the other two glared.

Behind them, Sarah entered the room. While the younger Miss Compton was dressed in a frilled gown of pink satin, with bows along the draped hem, Sarah wore a simple gown of gray poplin. He'd have wagered it only deepened the color in her expressive eyes. It certainly did nothing to hide her womanly curves. She calmly joined the group, offering a smile here, a comment there. The short fellow lost his scowl. The tall fellow's arms relaxed from where they were crossed over his broad chest. Even Barrington managed to utter a full sentence to her. As Persephone giggled over something the tall fellow bent to whisper in her shell-like ear, Sarah saw the other two seated nearby. Looking up, she caught Malcolm's gaze on her and rewarded him with a blush. Malcolm found himself heartily glad he had come to see the elder Miss Compton.

Beside him, the duke straightened. Persephone was making her way in their direction, her rosebud lips warm in greeting, her violet eyes alight. The duke's wide mouth settled in a satisfied smile. That quickly changed as the girl spoke.

"My Lord Breckonridge, how good to see you."

Malcolm sketched a short bow. "Miss Persephone, always a pleasure. Excuse me while I pay my respects to your cousin." He moved past, but not before he saw her frown as well. In a moment, he was at Sarah's side.

"My lord," she murmured in her husky voice, curtsying.

He swept her an elegant bow. "Miss Compton. Good of you to receive me."

She took a seat in one of the two chairs placed near the door. He took the other, noting that the position afforded an excellent view of the rest of the room. Sarah was eying her cousin, who had engaged the duke in conversation. Neither seemed pleased by the event. The rest of her suitors looked positively green. Barrington's hue matched his coat.

"Your cousin is quite the success," he commented.

Sarah nodded. "Quite. Yet you appear to be immune, my lord. Or are you merely trying to awaken her interest by appearing disinterested?"

"Not in the slightest," Malcolm assured her. "I prefer my women mature and sensible, like present company."

She did not blush but regarded him steadily, eyes

slightly narrowed so that her long brown lashes hid their color. "And do you think the characteristics like maturity and sensibility compliments, my lord? They strike me as something one might say if one did not want to speak one's true opinion."

He quirked a smile. "If I were speaking about an act, I might agree with you. However, I assure you, I meant them as compliments of the highest order." He reached out and squeezed her hands where they lay folded on her lap, marveling again that they felt so small within his own. "Have no doubts who I have come to see, Miss Compton."

As he pulled back his touch, a blush crept over her round cheeks. "My lord, you flatter me," she murmured. "But thank you. And do not think I am unaware of what a sacrifice this visit is. Isn't Parliament in session this afternoon?"

"It is," he said, pleased she would think of that. Her awareness of his needs would only help their union. With the thought came the realization that he fully intended to offer for her, and the sooner, the better. It appeared he had made his choice without knowing it. He smiled to himself, and she cocked her head.

"What is it, my lord?"

"Merely that I realize you and I have a lot in common," he replied.

She raised an eyebrow. "Indeed? I would not have guessed. What do you find that we share?"

"An appreciation of how much work it takes for others to live a life of ease," he extemporized. "The desire to make a difference in the world. The tenacity to make things happen."

"You see all that in me?" She appeared surprised.

"Like knows like, my dear," he replied, certain of

himself. "I'd also wager you're tired of your cousin's circus. Tell me you have wanted a place of your own."

"What lady has not dreamed of her own establishment?" she replied. "I will remedy that when my cousin is safely wed."

He was surprised to feel a finger of fear crawl up his spine. "You are spoken for, then?"

She smiled. "In a way. I hope to teach. Lady Wenworth has offered me a place in the Dame School on her estate."

He remembered Appleby saying she was friends with the Darbys. Surely this position was only a way to rescue her from a drab future. His proposal would be even better.

"Do you like children, then?" he asked.

Her smile deepened, revealing her enchanting dimples. "Yes, I do, which believe me is a surprise after raising Persephone." She seemed to recall herself and bit her lip before continuing. "That is to say, I believe I will enjoy teaching."

She looked so delectable that Malcolm could suddenly imagine any number of things he'd enjoy teaching her as well. His thoughts must have shown in his eyes, for she blinked rapidly, color fading. Before she could respond, however, Persephone appeared at her side.

"My but how serious you look," the girl proclaimed. She smiled charmingly. Behind her, the duke and her other admirers looked far less amused. The short fellow crowded territorially behind her, his taller peer at his heels. Barrington craned his neck to see around them both. Only the duke kept his distance, mouth in a thin line of distaste.

Sarah's blush returned. "Lord Breckonridge and I

were just discussing teaching," she offered her cousin as if she had somehow been caught at some prank.

The girl affected a serious look, but Malcolm could see she put it on as she might a new gown. "Oh, yes, teaching. Sarah is frightfully good at it. Look at all she's taught me."

"You need no teacher, Miss Compton," the taller of her beaux protested. "I vow you are perfect as you are."

Malcolm refused to add to the exaggerated praise. Sarah kept her eyes on her hands. Persephone did not so much as look at the fellow.

"But are you not a teacher yourself, Lord Breckonridge?" she continued. "You teach the other lords how to vote. Your prowess on the floor of Parliament is legendary."

"You are too kind," Malcolm said, fully meaning it. Sarah looked acutely uncomfortable, and the duke, who had rarely spoken a word in defense of an act himself, looked ready to eat Malcolm with a bit of vinegar.

"Not at all," Persephone breathed, eyes for him alone. "What you do is amazing. I vow I could never declaim before an audience."

"You give yourself too little credit," Malcolm quipped, watching her audience watch her.

"Here, here," the short fellow piped up. Immediately the tall fellow chimed in. Even Barrington managed a word in her defense, though it took him several tries to do so. The duke alone raised an eyebrow for Malcolm's benefit. Sarah made a study of her hands, mouth tight as if she would otherwise burst into laughter.

"Perhaps," Persephone continued, seemingly oblivious to the currents eddying around her. "But only men get to make pretty speeches in Parliament." She pouted. "We women must be content to influence from the home."

Malcolm cocked his head. "I think you would have no difficulty in that arena either, Miss Persephone," he told her.

She smiled, but to Malcolm, the look held little charm and a great deal of calculation. "I'm glad we are agreed on that score, my lord."

"And you, Miss Compton," he said, returning his attention to Sarah to find her watching him with narrowed eyes. "Would you be content to influence from the home as well?"

Persephone gave her gossamer giggle. "Oh, my lord, Sarah has never been known to have strong opinions."

"I have strong opinions, Cousin," Sarah corrected her with quiet firmness. She put up her chin, which, Malcolm noticed for the first time, had a decided point to it. "I simply keep my opinions to myself. In answer to your question, my lord, I do not believe a wife should be seen and not heard. If I had an opinion on a matter, I would state it. I would not change my opinion simply to suit my husband's whim. However, if he could convince me that he had the right of it, I would not be shy in supporting him."

"She is quite loyal," Persephone seemed to feel compelled to assure him. "That I cannot argue with. But I fear, Cousin Sarah, that you are too shy to be so bold in stating your opinion. Isn't that why you left the Season so many years ago? Why, you cannot even stand to stay a Season in London now. You are forever nattering on about returning to the country."

Had Lady Renderly hit the nail on the head after all? If so, he could see no sign of the shy girl she must have been. Indeed, she took her cousin's teasing sitting as still as a queen faced with a recalcitrant peasant. And the supposedly charming Miss Persephone Compton came off the decided loser. She treated Sarah like an elderly aunt, or the poor relation, Malcolm realized with a pang. The woman deserved better. Small wonder Lady Wenworth wanted to rescue her. He felt an overwhelming urge to do the same.

"But surely you would not leave us, Miss Persephone," the tall fellow begged. Barrington and the short fellow both spoke at the same time, drowning each other out. Persephone turned to reassure them that she adored London. Malcolm easily ignored them, turning to Sarah to find she had once more paled.

"I hope you are enjoying the metropolis more this Season, Miss Compton," he told her.

Sarah's smile to him was strained. "In truth, I have not had an opportunity to see much of it, my lord. I find my time devoted to chaperoning my cousin. However, I will admit that I enjoy the country."

"Fah on the country," Persephone declared, showing that she had been listening to their conversation for all her admirers were still talking to her. "I could not live the sedate life Sarah craves."

"To each his own," Sarah said with evident stubbornness. "Now surely we have better things to discuss than my simple preferences."

"Quite right," muttered the short fellow. Malcolm shook his head, offering his shoulder to the rudesby.

"On the contrary, Miss Compton," he assured her. "I for one would like to hear all about your preferences."

Persephone sucked in a breath. The duke quirked a smile. Sarah's eyes widened.

"You are too kind, my lord," she managed. "I would not presume to bore you."

"I'm sure nothing you can say would bore me," Malcolm replied. Conscious of Persephone and her suitors watching with varying degrees of interest, he rose. "However, it strikes me that what I have to say should be said in private. Would you grant me the honor of an audience, my dear?"

Persephone darted forward to touch his sleeve. "My lord? Are you certain you will not stay?"

Malcolm lifted her hand away. "Quite certain, Miss Persephone. Your servant, as are all others in this room. Excuse us, please, gentlemen."

The beaux bowed, and the duke inclined his head, even as Sarah rose.

"This way, my lord," she said, and he liked the thought that she sounded just the least bit breathless. She glided from the room with Malcolm following. The last glimpse he had of Persephone Compton was her perfect mouth in the shape of a perfect circle of amazement.

EIGHT

Sarah felt as if her stays had suddenly tightened. She could barely breathe, and her heart was hammering so hard she was amazed it didn't burst from her chest. She was equally amazed she could put one foot before the other, yet she managed to walk across the hall to the library and motion Malcolm Breckonridge into one of the leather-backed chairs waiting there. The library was a proper room, all leather-bound books and gleaming wood surfaces. The library was a place to conduct business, a place to educate oneself. Unfortunately, sitting across from him, watching the late afternoon sun from the tall windows make silver highlights in his dark hair, she found herself unable to speak. This would never do. She cleared her throat and met his gaze. There was nothing guarded in his movements or demeanor. He obviously knew what he wanted and was secure in the outcome. She didn't know whether she had the strength to hear him out.

She forced herself to sit politely, hands clasped tightly in her lap. She was glad she wore gloves, for surely her knuckles were turning white.

"I don't intend to eat you," he said gently.

She managed a smile. "I did not think that you did, my lord. I must admit, however, that I am at a loss as to why you might wish to speak with me in private."

Unless, of course, he wanted to ask about Persephone. She found she did not have sufficient Christian charity to wish that to be the case.

"I understand my request might seem rather hasty," he agreed easily. "However, I hope you will hear me out. I have a proposal for you, one I believe will benefit us both." He paused to eye her, and she could not even draw a breath. He could not mean the kind of proposal she thought he meant. Yet her heart leaped at the thought. The mighty Malcolm Breckonridge, swept away as easily as the least of Persephone's beaux, by a sweet-faced lady from Suffolk.

As quickly as she conjured the image it evaporated like a soap bubble in the sun. Surely Lord Breckonridge had more sense than that. They had only just met. While he looked quite intent, she could not see any great passion smoldering in his eyes. Surely he wanted something else from her. She composed her mouth into a smile.

"A proposal, my lord? What would that be?"

He leaned forward. "How would you like children of your own to teach?"

Sarah blinked. Did he think to offer her a teaching position? Had he a Dame School on one of his estates? But surely he would not bring her to this private place with such a request. She must have mistaken him. "Do you mean children I would bear or children for whom I would be responsible?" she probed.

"Your own children, to be sure," he replied. "I'm speaking of your own home as well. A town house, or an estate, where you are in charge."

That did sound suspiciously like a marriage proposal. But shouldn't he be down on one knee? The least of Persephone's suitors would be more impassioned than this, and they had far less experience in public speaking than Malcolm did. He was also an accomplished debater, she reminded herself. He was trying to convince her of something, but what eluded her. Much as she would like the topic to be marriage, she simply could not convince herself of the fact.

"Sir, do not tease me," she said. "If you have something to say to me, please do so."

He raised an eyebrow and leaned closer. His craggy face dominated her field of vision, and she could not look away from those midnight eyes. "I know you value plain speaking, but I feel I must make sure you understand the benefits of what I am proposing. As I said, I would like to make sure we each get what we want. But I find myself uncertain as to exactly what you might want, Miss Compton."

Her gaze settled on his lips. She was sure it did so only to relieve the pressure of his dark gaze, but she found the sight fascinating. They were firm and tinted a soft rose, with the hint of a cleft below the lower one. She could imagine them touching her in the most interesting places. Stunned, she lowered her gaze and took a deep breath to purge these strange thoughts. "I'm afraid what I want, my lord," she heard herself say, "is not yours to give."

"I sincerely hope that is not the case," he declared. He rose to pace, and Sarah slumped in relief. Widening the distance between them was surely a good thing. Yet, glancing up, she saw with dismay that having a full sight of him only made her stays seem tighter. His long legs were shown to advantage in the tight-fitting gray trousers as he strode about the little room. The dark coat emphasized powerful shoulders. She was reminded of the lion at the Tower Zoo, magnificence caged. She dropped her gaze to her hands once again, interlocking her fingers until she could barely unclench them.

"I would contend, madam," he said in what was surely his most persuasive orator's voice, "that I could offer you your dreams if you would but give me the opportunity."

Was he offering her some sort of bribe, then? Did he mean to offer her her own establishment if she would plead his case with Persephone? She did not want that to be the case; she could feel the bite of disappointment, strong and sharp. But he had said she would have her own children. What did that have to do with him marrying Persephone? Did he think to provide her with a husband just as Norrie planned to trot out her farmers? The conversation only grew more confusing by the second. She kept her eyes on her fingers, afraid of what she would reveal if she raised her head.

"If this is about Persephone, say no more, my lord," she told him. "I have heard this speech several times. I cannot pretend to have any influence over my cousin's choice of husband."

She heard him stop and could feel the frown in his response. "What has this to do with your cousin?"

Involuntarily, her head came up. "You are not speaking about Persephone?"

"Decidedly not," he assured her. He returned swiftly to the chair opposite hers and took up her hands in a firm grip. She did not dare look away.

"I will not deny that your cousin is a lovely young lady," he said. "But she is absolutely unsuited to my needs. You see, I have a dream as well, a dream for a strong England, as safe and prosperous within as she is protected from without. Some have named governance a noble calling, and I am honored that it is mine. But to live up to that calling, I must have help."

Sarah frowned. For a moment she had been sure he meant to propose marriage to her again. Disappointment shot through her, tainted with disgust at her easily duped heart. How could she keep entertaining that notion? She had never been gullible before. "I shall do whatever I can to be of assistance to Parliament, my lord," she assured him. "Although I fail to see how I might be useful."

"You do yourself an injustice, madam," he assured her. "I have been considering this matter for some time, have looked quite extensively. I can safely say that you alone appear to have the qualifications to undertake this task."

Her frown deepened. Was he going to ask her to be a spy of some sort? She could not imagine a worse agent. Surely he'd seen how easily her face betrayed her inward thoughts. It must be something else. "Perhaps if you were to give me a few details, my lord," she ventured.

He let go of her hands and sat back, once more looking sure of himself. "I would be happy to elaborate. A gentleman in a single state can only progress so far in Parliament before questions are asked. In addition, it is my duty to continue the Breckonridge line. I have considered the matter fully, and believe I need someone who can not only manage a household, but polish my speeches, and assist me in entertaining. In short, Miss Compton, I need a wife."

Sarah wasn't sure whether to laugh or cry. How ironic, and how like the course of her life, that she had received her first and only proposal in the tone reserved for hiring a servant. She scanned his face again and saw only determination. The fire, the love that poetry, literature, and music celebrated, and she had been taught she had a right to expect with such a declaration, was missing.

"What you need, my lord," she corrected him, "is a good steward."

He leaned forward again, and she saw he was set on presenting his case. She could feel irritation building. Was she no better than a recalcitrant member of the opposing party? Did he truly think logic was the only thing at play here? It appeared so, for he launched into a speech. "I disagree. You see, I need one thing that no steward can provide. I need an heir. That requires a wife."

"It generally requires some amount of affection as well," Sarah felt compelled to tell him.

"Is it an impassioned plea you want, Miss Compton?" His eyes glittered dangerously. "I had not thought you shared your cousin's fondness for playing on the gentleman's desires."

"I certainly do not share it," Sarah replied. "But I'd like to point out, sir, that you apparently have no desires on which to play. Marriage, my lord, is not a business transaction."

"Oh, but my dear, it most certainly is." He rose again, obviously warming to his subject. She could imagine him pacing the floors of Parliament, meeting a gaze there, watching as heads nodded here. "Marriage is more than the union of two individuals. It is the melding of two families, the blending of two estates. It is the commitment of two minds to work as one toward a common goal. It is both our Christian duty and our God-given right."

Sarah put her hands together and clapped slowly. "Oh, very pretty, my lord. But you have missed the point entirely. Marriage is about far more than lands and minds merging."

He returned to sit beside her. "Do you look for passion as well? I have no fear that we would deal famously."

"Are you always this arrogant?" she asked, frowning.

He grinned. "Nearly always so, particularly when I am attempting to persuade someone to see my side. And have no doubts that I intend to persuade you, my dear Miss Compton. I have never met a woman more perfect to suit my needs."

Sarah shook her head. Why had she ever found this man the least agreeable? "And my needs have nothing to say in the matter?"

"Certainly," he agreed magnanimously. "Did we not agree that one of your needs is for a household of your own? I have estates in seven counties, as well as a town house here in London. You would have free rein to decorate them and entertain in them as you liked. My income is sufficient that you would never need be concerned about spending money, and I would offer you a considerable dower settlement."

"You resort to logic again, my lord," she replied. "I'm afraid that isn't going to work."

At last he frowned. "I don't understand."

She shook her head. "No, I truly believe you don't. I'm sure you see this as a great honor. You may even see this as a rescue of sorts, the poor, helpless spinster offered a wondrous new life by the wealthy titled gentleman. It is something out of a fairy tale. But I must refuse, my lord."

His frown deepened. "Is it that you fear the intimacy, that I will be as logical in my private life as I am here today?"

"I would not presume to wonder," she said, feeling her cheeks reddening.

His frown evaporated, to be replaced by a lazy smile. He reached out a hand to stroke her cheek. Heat spread from his touch, astonishing her in its intensity. Yet, knowing he was watching her reaction, she forced herself to sit ramrod straight and not lean into the touch as her body demanded. He ran a finger along her lips, and she raised her head, putting them out of reach, even as they tingled with his touch. He shook his head.

"It isn't that easy to evade me, Miss Compton," he murmured. "I believe you know that we would make a marvelous team. Let go of your pride and say you'll marry me."

The desire to agree was as strong as the demand of her body. She clamped her teeth together to keep the words from coming out. Was she such a spineless creature after all to be swayed by a simple touch? The very thought filled her with fury. She rose to her feet, forcing him to do likewise.

"I must refuse, my lord," she told him. "I believe it is customary to thank you for your offer. Therefore, I thank you. Now, excuse me. I should see to Persephone." She attempted to sweep past him, wanting only to escape. Her head was high, her pride higher. She refused to bear another burden of gratitude for something less than love.

She found his arm blocking her way.

"You owe me no more explanation than that?" he demanded. "I lay my heart at your feet and you spurn me so easily?"

She spared him a glance, finding his frown more astonished than angry. She felt a momentary pity for him; it was probably one of the only times anyone had refused him anything.

He would have to get used to it.

"You did not lay your heart at my feet," she replied. The firmness of her statement had some effect, for he withdrew his hand. "You did not even lay your prestige at my feet. What you laid at my feet was the position of a brood mare who will also pull your carriage. I've been pulling someone else's carriage most of my life, my lord. I intend to pull my own carriage in the future. I jolly well don't need to do it for a near stranger, no matter how rich or powerful or handsome or arrogant. The answer to your question is no, my lord. No, no, and again no. I do not need to marry for wealth or work. Most likely, I will never marry. But if I do, it will have to be like something out of a fairy story. The gentleman will need to be so madly in love with me that he can see no other course of action. And I assure you, I will feel the same way about him. Now, this interview is at an end. Good-bye, Lord Breckonridge."

NINE

As Malcolm stormed into Lady Prestwick's sitting room that afternoon, she deigned to look up. She was her usual composed self, perched on her camelback sofa with a partially finished piece of embroidery in her lap, needle poised in midair. She didn't even blink as he stalked up to her.

"She turned me down," he declared without roundaboutation.

She simply eyed him. "Miss Compton? Why would she do that?"

"Why indeed?" Malcolm snarled. He wanted nothing so much as to rail at the injustice, but he spotted Rames, the Prestwick butler, hovering in the background, jowls quivering. Prestwick had mentioned the fellow was a gossip. Malcolm affixed him with a black glare. "I won't eat your mistress, man. Give us a moment in private."

He swallowed, Adam's apple bobbing visibly, and turned his gaze to his mistress. "My lady?"

"It's quite all right, Rames," Anne told him. "If Lord Prestwick comes home while Lord Breckonridge is here, please show him in. Otherwise, you may leave me with his lordship safely."

It was a statement of the irregularities the fellow had no doubt seen when he had worked for the bachelor Prestwick that Rames did not so much as blink as he bowed and exited, shutting the double doors behind him.

Anne neatly took a stitch in her fabric. "So, Miss Compton did not wish to be your wife. That seems a bit odd."

"It's ridiculous," he spat, still too angry to sit. He paced the room instead, although even the long strides the green-hung room allowed did not diminish the emotions surging through him. "I obviously chose the wrong woman."

She raised an eyebrow and took another stitch. "Do you truly think so? She seemed perfect for you."

"Obviously, we were both duped," he told her firmly.

"I see," she replied. "A shame. Let me see, didn't you say you needed someone who is a good household manager? Is her town house ill-run then?"

"It is spotless," he admitted. "The servants are efficient, and the decorations are tasteful."

"Then I take it she overspends her budget."

"Not that I can tell," Malcolm replied, slowing his steps in thought. "Her wardrobe is behind the times; she does not appear to put a great deal of money into her looks."

"Is that not good? I believe you told Chas you didn't want someone who was fussy in fashion."

He thought of the way her simple gowns flowed down her well-curved frame. "She is not the least bit fussy, I assure you."

"Then she is not intelligent. She would not be able to find flaws in your logic."

Prestwick had obviously shared their entire conversation with his wife. Malcolm paused to regard her bowed head, looking for some sign of superiority, but she continued to stitch as if it were the most important thing she could do.

"I cannot say she is not intelligent," he replied. "In fact, she thinks she found a decided flaw in my logic."

"Oh?" The question was bland as if she were doing no more than asking his opinion on the weather. Malcolm shook his head.

"Do you want the whole of it then?"

She raised her head and smiled at him. "You did seem intent on telling me when you blustered in. Sit down, Lord Breckonridge. Perhaps we can discover what you have done to make the sensible Miss Compton take you in dislike."

"I did nothing," he protested, although he slumped into a chair across from her. The hardwood sides were not conducive to self-pity, however, and he was forced to straighten immediately.

"If you did nothing wrong, and she refused you, she is not the woman I thought she was," Anne said quietly. "Perhaps if you told me what transpired."

"The conversation is of little import," he replied with a wave of his hand. "I presented my case logically. She refused to deal in logic."

Now she frowned. "That seems most unlike Miss Compton. I would have said she was a very logical woman."

"If any woman can be so described," he muttered.

Anne flashed him a look that reminded him somehow of a master he had once had at Eton. "Most women can be so described, my lord. It is not *our* perceptions that cause most problems."

Malcolm sat a little straighter. "I beg your pardon, Lady Prestwick."

"You are forgiven," she replied, for all the world like the Prince Regent granting him a favor. "Now, please continue."

He shook his head. "Single-minded as well as determined. Very well, my dear, if you want the whole dreary story. I presented my case and Miss Compton told me she would not have me unless she loved me."

Anne took another stitch. "Very sensible, as I said."

"Sensible?" he sputtered. "You find that sensible? To appeal to as fickle an organ as the heart for something so important?"

She affixed him with that look again. "Quite sensible. If you expected otherwise, my lord, it is you who are the illogical one. Marriage is just as much about the heart as it is about the head. Perhaps more so."

"I'm getting quite tired of hearing this refrain," he informed her. "I have observed many excellent marriages in which neither party's heart was involved."

"And I've seen any number of wretched marriages in which neither party's heart was involved," Anne countered.

"You make my point for me. The heart is not a determinant in the success of a marriage."

"I disagree with you," she replied calmly, taking another stitch. He couldn't help noticing, however, that the fabric was nearly ripped by the force of her needle. "If you considered the logic of *my* marriage, my lord, Lord Prestwick would never have asked me."

Malcolm purposely did not look in her direction. Gossip abounded as to why Chas Prestwick had married the quiet Anne Fairchild. Most of the stories pointedly guessed that the gentleman had been caught being less than a gentleman, and Anne's widowed aunts would not let him escape. Still, even if that were the case, he could not imagine a more besotted or adoring husband than Prestwick. Nor a more devoted wife than the lady before him. "I would not dare compare my attempts at marriage with yours, Lady Prestwick," he said.

"That at least is sensible of you," she quipped. "We must all of us stand on our own in that field, my lord. So, Miss Compton could not give you her heart. Did you expect her to do otherwise when you had only just met?"

"I didn't expect her to do so even if we'd been friends for generations," he informed her. "As I said, her heart's feelings were immaterial to me. Logically, this is an excellent match. I expected her to see that, particularly as I took some pains to point out the benefits."

"Yes, somehow I would think you'd be good at that," she replied, taking another stitch. "I think perhaps I can see where you went wrong, my lord. However, before I offer any advice, I must know. How do you feel about Miss Compton?"

"I find her intelligent, trustworthy, and competent."

"Such high praise," Anne murmured. He frowned, feeling as if she were criticizing him, for all the sentiment was uttered with her usual quiet.

"I rather thought so," he replied, although the words sounded too much like an excuse to his ears.

"Then it is safe to say that your heart is not involved."

"No more so than in any other venture."

"I see." She set her needlework aside and patted down the skirts of her blue poplin gown. "That, of course, is the root of the problem, my lord. Marriage is not like any other venture. I daresay you would have put more thought and effort into campaigning for one of your laws than what you did to encourage Miss Compton to see your suit favorably."

He started to protest, but she met his gaze full on and the protest died in his throat.

"Consider my words before reacting, if you please," she told him. "That act last year, the one that so upset Lady Thomas DeGuis—how much effort did you put into seeing it go down in defeat?"

"Considerable," he admitted grudgingly.

"Define considerable," she insisted.

He sighed. "We both know it consumed most of my waking moments for several months. Very well, you've made your point. But surely a woman cannot expect me to devote my life to convincing her that marriage is a sensible course of action."

"There are some women who would expect as much. Somehow, I don't think Miss Compton is among their number. But if you are determined to have her as your wife, my lord, I am very much afraid you will have to court her."

He stared at her. "Court her?"

She quirked a smile. "You make it sound like torture. It is far less onerous, I assure you."

"Not from what I've observed," he replied, rising to pace once more. "Courting involves an extensive amount of time and effort. I must take her driving, I must meet her at the theater and the opera, I must languish in her sitting room on a daily basis." He stopped in shock. "Good God, I'll have to attend one of those ghastly subscription balls at Almack's."

"I doubt you will have to compromise your sensibilities to that extent," Anne told him, and he could hear the chuckle in her voice. The chit was enjoying this. He rounded on her.

"Easy for you to say, my dear. I have the Widows and Orphans Act I'm trying to convince Liverpool to father through the system, and another three due to hit the floor before recess. There's talk of developing even stiffer gagging acts to stop the people from reforming Parliament. The stiffer the acts, the more likely we are to have a fight on our hands. England cannot stand a revolution of the magnitude we saw in the American Colonies and France. I appear to be the only voice of reason. To top it all off, His Royal Highness is demanding that we raise his allowance again, so that he can buy more fripperies for his blasted pavilion in Brighton, and I will not watch him buy Chinese lanterns while the troops who returned from Waterloo starve. I have no time for romance, madam. I have work to do."

She shook her head. "If you have no time to look for a lady, you have no time to be married to that lady, my lord. Do you expect your wife to sit quietly home while you slave away in running the country? I think not. Have you not said she is to work beside you as a helpmate? If you were training a man to help you, would you not spend time teaching him what you expected?"

"That is an entirely different matter," he pointed out heatedly. "He would already have made the commitment. If I was married to the woman, I would certainly spend time with her."

"A woman expects commitment sooner than a man, I fear," Anne replied. "She wants to see that you are sufficiently committed to her before agreeing to spend the rest of her life with you. I'm afraid there is no getting around it, my lord. Any woman who would be good enough to be the partner you seek will want you to court her before marrying her."

He let out a deep sigh. "I am well and truly trapped then."

"If that's how you see it, I'm afraid you are. I must admit, however, that there are women who would jump at an offer of marriage from you, with no more effort than you gave Miss Compton. I'd pity you for marrying them, but they would be less effort, in the beginning."

"No," he agreed with reluctant admiration. "You are right. I have not found anyone to rival Miss Compton in meeting my requirements. Very well, I must court her. Surely you can suggest some appropriate way to do that that will not jeopardize the career I'm trying to support."

Anne nodded. "I could make a number of suggestions, if you'd like. Sit here beside me, and let's see what we can contrive."

Malcolm moved to do as she requested. He had a deep feeling that he was giving away something very important, and was about to give up even more. But he was determined to marry. If courtship was what it took, he might as well get it over with.

TEN

Sarah wanted nothing more than to retire to her room and cry. She had never been so hurt in her life. Oh, it had been awful when her parents had been killed and Aunt Belle and Uncle Harold had preferred to shuttle her off to strangers rather than see to her needs themselves. And Persephone's gibes the last few months had cut her to the quick. But even those things had not been as cruel as her interview with Malcolm. To think she had felt the least attraction to the man! He was an unfeeling beast, a monster. She was heartily glad that she had warned him off Persephone before her cousin had had to see him for what he was.

Unfortunately, she could not indulge in tears. She had been away from the girl quite long enough. She forced herself to return to the sitting room, only to find with surprise that the room was empty of everyone but Persephone. Her cousin was standing by the window, staring resolutely out onto the street.

"Is something wrong?" Sarah couldn't help asking.

Persephone turned to her, mouth tight. "Lord Breckonridge stormed down to his carriage. What did you say to him?"

Sarah stiffened. "It is of no import. Suffice it to say that Lord Breckonridge will not be calling again."

"Why?" Persephone demanded, stalking away from

the window like a lioness who had sighted her prey. Her violet eyes narrowed dangerously, and she put her hands on her slender hips. Normally, Sarah would have tried to talk her out of the tantrum she could see coming, but at the moment, she longed for a good fight.

"None of your business," she spat. "I have to share enough of my life, thank you very much. This portion is private."

"Your life?" Persephone frowned. "What has this to do with *your* life? I demand to know why you are chasing Lord Breckonridge away from me."

"Away from you?" Sarah stared at her. "Persy, he came looking for me."

Persy waved a hand. "Don't be ridiculous. No one comes looking for you. *I'm* the Incomparable Miss Compton."

"You're the incoherent Miss Compton at the moment," Sarah informed her icily. "Lord Breckonridge no doubt thought he would try a more desperate woman with his unwelcome advances. I assure you, he came to see me."

"Desperate?" Persephone swallowed. "Did he offer you a carte blanche?"

Much as she would have liked to blacken his eyes, she could not blacken his name. "Nothing dishonorable, merely distasteful. I would rather not discuss it, Persy. Let it be."

Persy tightened her lips, but the words burst out anyway. "But we must discuss it. I thought he came for me, Sarah, truly I did. I had such hopes." Her lower lip began to tremble.

If she cries about the fact that the man who couldn't

love me doesn't love her, Sarah thought, *I shall be forced to slap her.*

"Hope is for nitwits and innocents," she said aloud. "Be glad you are the latter and stop acting like the former. You have any number of presentable suitors, all of whom would commit senseless acts of valor for the merest smile from you. Be happy. Now, go change. I believe you are forgoing the pleasure of Almack's tonight to allow the duke to escort us to Drury Lane to see Keene before he ends his run."

Persephone lowered her gaze and fiddled with her skirt. "I was. But I dismissed His Grace."

Sarah closed her eyes and took a deep breath. "May I ask why in the name of heaven you would do that?"

"I thought Lord Breckonridge was offering for me!" she cried. "I thought I no longer needed Reddington's stuffy attentions. I thought I was all but married."

"You didn't think at all that I can tell," Sarah informed her. "Persy, have you no refinement of spirit? Are all your suitors toys to you? Do none of them move your heart in the slightest?"

To her surprise, the girl colored. "My heart has been moved, but not where it should be. And do not ask me to explain that statement, for I will not."

Sarah raised an eyebrow. "You should know better than to make a statement you will not explain. Your mother would not allow it."

"But you will," Persephone said hopefully. She met Sarah's stern gaze with an importuning look of her own. "You know you will, Sarah. You know how it feels to love the wrong man."

"I know what it feels like not to be loved," Sarah

corrected her. "That is entirely different. Now, if you've lost your heart at last, you must tell me."

Persephone hung her head. "I would not say that I've lost my heart, precisely. I am merely intrigued. He is very handsome, and quite unattainable."

Sarah could imagine her cousin being infatuated with a man who appeared unattainable. That would have been quite different from her many suitors who were only too happy to lay their hearts at her feet. She sat on the sofa and motioned her cousin to do likewise. Truth be told, she wasn't sure she was ready to hear of her cousin's success in love when her own life was proving so very unsuccessful, but she had a duty as chaperon. And she needed to focus on something other than her own pain.

"Tell me more," she insisted as her cousin joined her.

"I met him at Lady Prestwick's ball," she confessed, violet eyes misty. "Lord Yarmouth introduced us. I had only one dance with him, but he watched us the entire time we ate with Lord Breckonridge, and he joined my group for conversation after Lord Breckonridge left."

"The fellow who looked suspiciously like Lord Byron?" Sarah asked, remembering. She would not have felt comfortable around the brooding fellow, but she supposed Persephone might find him as poetic as the other women had once found Byron.

Persy nodded. "The very one. He barely spoke two sentences to me, but I could tell he was interested in furthering the acquaintance."

"Indeed," Sarah replied, hiding a smile. "If he only spoke two sentences I wonder that you were sure he was alive, let alone interested in pursuing you."

"A lady can always tell when a gentleman is interested," Persy informed her, nose in the air.

"Really?" Sarah knew her cousin could not be so wise as she had just dismissed a room full of suitors for a man who was plainly disinterested. Yet Sarah had to own she was not so sure of the signs herself. She had begun to believe Malcolm might be interested, with his warm looks and pointed attentions. Obviously, she had been mistaken. Or rather, she had mistaken the type of interest. She had foolishly hoped for love and found only an offer of employment.

"How exactly does a lady know?" she mused aloud.

Persephone leaned forward, obviously willing to share her limited knowledge. "Well, for one thing, he looks at you in the same manner as you might look upon a luscious raspberry trifle."

Sarah tried to imagine Malcolm looking at her in so hungry a manner and blushed.

"For another thing," Persy continued, "he will ask you personal questions. Lord Wells asked me where I was staying and how long we'd be in London. He wouldn't have asked if he hadn't wanted to call on me, would he?"

"I would think not," Sarah had to agree. Malcolm had asked any number of questions about her, all of which an employer might ask. She could not see that as a sign of devotion as her cousin did.

"Finally," Persy said dramatically, "he will allow nothing to keep him from your side."

Sarah snorted. "That sounds decidedly inconvenient."

Persephone smiled. "Not in the slightest. It is delightful beyond words." She sobered. "Only Lord

Wells has yet to call, so I suppose he was not interested after all."

"It has only been a few days," Sarah reminded her, although she had felt the same way earlier about Malcolm.

"True," Persephone allowed with a sigh. "I shall not let his absence drive me into a decline. I still have any number of suitors, and more every day. Still, I would have much preferred to have caught Lord Breckonridge instead. Now, there was an eligible gentleman. He has a much greater fortune than Lord Wells, and he is much more powerful. I would have been the envy of every lady in London."

Sarah felt a chill at the words. Persy pushed aside the man who intrigued her for another who would make others envy her. Sarah could not imagine a less healthy attitude. But then, she reflected, she had never had a reason to feel that others envied her.

"It is a pity," Persephone said with another sigh, "that Lord Breckonridge was not brought to heel."

"You are better off without him," Sarah tried to assure her, even though a small part of her protested. "He thinks of nothing but himself."

Persy giggled. "Perhaps that is because he hasn't found anyone else better. If he approaches me in the future, I will not be shy about letting him see how wrong he is."

Sarah looked at her with alarm. "I would prefer that you keep away from him. You would do better attempting to mend this rift with the duke."

"Tish tosh to the duke," Persy said with a wave of her hand. "He had no more appreciation of me than your Lord Breckonridge. We will both find better gentlemen."

"You will find someone, I have no doubt," Sarah replied, unable to frown at her airy tone. "In fact, I would not be surprised if you hadn't found someone by this time tomorrow. I will simply be glad when this Season ends."

"Very well, if you insist," Persy replied. "But I intend to enjoy every moment of my visit to London. What do you say, Sarah, shall we go to the theater ourselves tonight? I wager if we send Timmons around, he could procure us tickets."

Sarah made a face. "In truth, I'd rather not go out tonight. I may ask Norrie to come visit. Would you mind staying in?"

It was quite apparent that Persy would mind a great deal, but she gave a tight-lipped smile. "No, certainly, if that is what you wish. Tomorrow will be a better day, Sarah, you wait and see."

Sarah wanted to believe her. She had certainly expected a brighter future before she met Lord Breckonridge. But his proposal, insulting as it had been, seemed to have changed her view. Just as the luster of Lady Prestwick's ball had dimmed when he had left it, so her life seemed to have dimmed without the prospect of him in it.

"I don't understand it," she complained to Norrie when her friend visited that evening. "I never expected to marry and I certainly don't want to marry without love, so why am I so blue-deviled?"

Norrie smiled consolingly. "Do you perhaps love him?"

Sarah frowned. "I didn't think so. Certainly I find him handsome. And I will admit I admired him before he made his proposal. I do not think I know him well enough to love him."

"Perhaps you are merely disappointed he is not the gentleman you thought him," Norrie offered. "However, it is nice that he chose you, you must admit."

"I suppose," Sarah allowed. "Am I overreacting? Should I have given his suit more consideration?"

"Not in the slightest," her friend declared. "You have the right to be loved, Sarah. And you said yourself you cannot abide a gift given out of anything less than love. You may be miserable now, but think how miserable you would have been if you had accepted him."

Sarah did think about it. Indeed, it seemed as if she could think of little else. She thought of it as she wrote her letter to her aunt and uncle because she could not admit that not only had Persy cast off the duke but Sarah had rejected what they would consider an excellent match. She thought about it that night as she brushed out her hair and her hand grazed the spot he had touched on her cheek. The memory was as warm as her skin. She could not help thinking about it as she was forced to sit the next day and watch Persy flirt with her endless stream of callers. Neither Lord Wells nor the Duke of Reddington appeared. There was also no sign of Malcolm Breckonridge. Sarah was just as glad. She wasn't sure what to say to him anyway.

It was late in the afternoon when Mr. Timmons drew Sarah aside. "We have a difficulty in the entry hall, Miss Sarah," he said in his wheezy voice.

Sarah frowned. "Difficulty? What's the matter?"

"Perhaps you should see for yourself, miss," he replied.

Catching Persy's eye to let her know she would be out of the room for a moment, Sarah excused herself and hurried to comply. Once out the door and down the stairs, she immediately saw the problem.

The entry hall was overflowing with flowers. Vase upon vase of roses sat upon the hall table, squatted on the marble-tiled floor, rested against the wood-paneled walls. Red roses brushed the mirror above the hall table; white roses cluttered the entry to the library; and pink roses gathered behind the etched front door. She looked at Timmons in exasperation.

"This is the last straw. We must ask Persy's admirers to restrain themselves. There cannot be a single rose left in London!"

Persy chose that moment to peer down the stairs. Seeing the flowers, her eyes widened and she hurried down to caper into what little space was left.

"Oh, roses!" she exclaimed, going first to one bouquet and then another. She touched a petal here, bent to sniff a flower there. Sarah watched her with a shake of her head.

"Really, Persy, this is too much. See who sent these and ask him to stop at once."

Persy giggled. "They are ostentatious, aren't they? Oh, what a dear. Let me find the card."

"Here, miss," Timmons offered with a deep sigh, handing her a small card. Persy took it eagerly and read the inscription. Sarah turned to the butler.

"Perhaps if we salted them about the rooms, the smell would not be so overpowering," she suggested.

"Perhaps we should move them all to Sarah's room," Persy said, voice decidedly piqued. Sarah turned to her with a frown, but it was nothing to match the frown on her cousin's face. Persy thrust the card at her and stalked back to the sitting room. Frown deepening, Sarah looked down at the card.

"Forgive me," it read. It was signed only, "Breckonridge."

The card dropped from her lifeless fingers, and she stared around at the dozens of roses. For her? He had sent all these to apologize to her? Did he care about her feelings after all?

The thought was wondrous. She had dreamed years ago that someone might truly love her and care about how she felt. She'd conjured fairy tales with Norrie about the gentlemen they'd meet and the love they'd find. The dreams had sustained her until her Season had proven them a lie. Since then she had been careful to whom she gave her heart.

No doubt that was why the thought that he might care frightened her as well. She had accused him of not loving her, but she had admitted to Norrie that she did not think she was in love with him. Now that she was faced with the possibility that he could love her after all, she wasn't sure what to do. Perhaps that was why she hadn't truly believed he would propose in the library that day. Love had seemed a faraway ideal, something remembered before the deaths of her parents, something echoed in her friendship with Norrie. She wasn't entirely sure why no one except Norrie had ever shown her what she believed was love, but she had wondered whether she might somehow have held them off. Now here was Malcolm, refusing to be held off, refusing to go away. She had no idea how to respond.

But one thing she did know.

It would take a great deal more than a surfeit of roses for Malcolm Breckonridge to wedge his way into her heart.

ELEVEN

"And then," Appleby stated with great relish, "Mr. Timmons reports that she took the roses and threw them in the trash."

Malcolm paused in the act of removing his shoes. It had not been a good day. In the first place, recent events had made the Marquis DeGuis more than cautious in openly endorsing any mention of reform. Respected as he was among the Tories, his support was key to Malcolm's plans to halt the spread of censure. Only an extended conversation with the fellow, and his astute wife, had brought him into reluctant agreement. In the second place, Viscount Darton was having trouble framing the Widows and Orphans Act in such a way as to please the conservative Tories, and Malcolm had had to spend several hours wrangling over the merits of "child" over "dependent." Despite his promises to Anne, he had not had a moment to spend in courting and had hoped the roses might carry on in his stead. Obviously, that was not the case.

"You're certain she saw the card?" he asked his valet.

"Most certain," Appleby reported giddily. "She ripped it in half and half again."

"If you tell me she danced among the pieces," Malcolm growled, "I shall hurl this shoe at you."

Appleby sobered immediately. "My apologies, my lord," he murmured with a hurried bow. "I had no idea the subject was so injurious to your sensibilities. You can, of course, count on me to temper my comments in the future."

Malcolm closed his eyes and took a deep breath. Patience, he had to have patience. "I am not a child, Appleby," he said at last, "and my sensibilities, as you put it, are not so easily injured by anything Miss Compton might do. Now, is there anything more you care to relate?"

Appleby thought hard for a few moments. Indeed, the fellow's face screwed up so mightily that Malcolm wondered whether he was having an apoplectic fit. Just when Malcolm was ready to leap to his rescue, the fellow's brow cleared. "No, my lord," he replied.

Malcolm almost left him alone, but there was one more piece of information he needed for the next step in his campaign, however badly it seemed to be going. "Did you have any luck discovering Miss Compton's favorite candy?" he probed. That question did not seem to overtax Appleby's abilities at least, for the fellow answered quickly enough.

"Chocolate almonds," he proclaimed, trotting to the wardrobe to retrieve Malcolm's blue-velvet dressing gown. Malcolm bent and finished removing his shoes at last, straightening and rising in time for Appleby to drape the robe over his shoulders.

"Chocolate almonds," Malcolm mused aloud.

"Yes, my lord," Appleby replied, tugging the robe down at the back. "Although she has been known to pass them up for rum centers."

"Get a box of each from Gunter's," Malcolm ordered. "I'll write a note to go with them."

"Very good, my lord," Appleby intoned. He returned to his business of preparing the room for Malcolm to retire.

Malcolm settled himself into the easy chair by the fire and reached for his Bible. The chair had been with him since his college days, the Bible even longer. Both were well worn and comfortable. The back and sides of the chair had long since been bent and crushed to fit the contours of his body. The tooled leather of the Bible, rubbed deep in places, fit his hands.

He thumbed through to one of his favorite passages, in the book of Exodus, and read again where Moses prayed to God to return His presence to the Israelites after they had built the golden calf. God had called the Israelites a stiff-necked people. Malcolm understood that phrase all too well. How many young lordlings had he had to shepherd through their first weeks in Parliament as they attempted to put their petty concerns into inappropriate laws? How many more seasoned nobs had he had to reason with when titled consequences were threatened by the public's welfare? There were moments when, like Moses, he could only pray for patience. There were times when, like God, he almost refused to favor them with his presence. But Moses had at least had a helper in Joshua. Malcolm had never found anyone whose judgment and temperament he trusted enough to work directly beside him. At least, not since Winston Wells.

He tried not to think about that time in his life. His older cousin, knowing his interest in politics, had arranged for him to get a seat in the House of Commons. He had had to work directly with a number of members in the House of Lords, one of them being Baron Winston Wells. Wells had been a fastidious man, as careful in his words as he was in his dress. While he leaned heavily toward the more popular Tories, he would listen while Malcolm expounded his increasingly Whig theories. Unfortunately, Malcolm had not been the only one to whom he had listened. It was in Malcolm's third year at Commons that he found Lord Wells had been selling secrets to the French.

He had been sick about the matter for days. He had come to care for the man as a father. How could he possibly turn the fellow over to the authorities? Finally, in desperation, he had appealed to the man himself. The next day, Wells had been found dead, with a self-inflicted bullet through his temple. Malcolm closed his eyes in memory, but the vision of Lady Wells's distraught face would not leave him.

Young Wells had been away at school then, but Malcolm had vowed to do what he could for the boy he had made fatherless. But even helping to pay for Rupert's schooling and giving the boy *entre* to Parliament when he had taken his father's seat a few years ago failed to fill the void in his heart left by Winston Wells's passing. Sarah Compton acted as if it would be easy to let someone fill his heart, a woman, a wife. She had no idea what she asked of him.

At length he realized that Appleby had finished and taken himself off for the evening. Malcolm had one last task to accomplish before retiring. He pulled out the portable writing desk from the table beside him and nestled it in his lap. He obviously needed to find a better way to apologize to Sarah. Surely that would not be too difficult a task. If he could find the words to assuage Lord DeGuis's concerns, certainly he should be able to write a meaningful apology to a woman.

But the words refused to come, at least to his liking. The first draft he threw away as too effacing. The second he ripped up as she had ripped up his card as too arrogant. The third was too wordy, the fourth too terse. At last he paused and stared into the fire. Anne Prestwick had told him he would need to put effort into this courtship, but somehow he didn't think this was what she had in mind.

Perhaps he should look further, find a woman who was less demanding. Surely some other woman would be happy to take his money and position and serve at his side without any messy entanglements of the heart. Yet, something inside him quailed at the thought of leaving Sarah behind. What was it about the intractable Miss Compton that drew him in? Her witch's eyes came immediately to mind, followed swiftly by the womanly curves that filled her gowns. Was it merely a physical attraction that held him, then? That made little sense as her cousin was even more beautiful and she attracted him not at all.

It was something more, then, something deeper. He refused to believe it had anything to do with his heart. He did not believe in love at first sight. No, a better explanation might be that Miss Compton had many of the traits he found praiseworthy, more, in fact, than any of the women he had met over the years. And he had been sporadically hunting for several Seasons before Anne Prestwick had been coerced into helping him. No, Sarah was a rarity. It might take him years to find someone with her qualifications, and time was running out. Therefore, it was imperative that he attempt to salvage their budding relationship.

He took out a piece of paper and twirled the quill between his fingers for a moment while he thought.

Then he dipped the tip in the ink and sent the quill flying across the page. He was not known for having a golden tongue to no effect. It was time he did what he did best.

It would take a great deal more than an excess of roses to win Persephone Compton's heart. Of this, Rupert Wells was certain. In fact, he was amazed Breckonridge had tried something so very common. Wells had had agents watching the Compton house for three days, ever since the Prestwick ball. He knew the vast number of gentlemen who had come calling. He'd read detailed accounts of their dress, their equipage, and their bouquets, all of which were designed to impress. The girl was an Incomparable after all. The eligibles flocked to her like pigeons to grain. He knew better than to join them. He must stand out from the crowd.

He had started the game at the ball by appearing to be cool to her. His demeanor had intrigued her, he was certain, for she had doubled her efforts to attract his regard. But he could not let too many days go by or she would likely turn her attentions elsewhere, perhaps even to Breckonridge. While he wanted to keep Breckonridge interested, he wanted to keep Miss Compton disinterested. The key was either ruining or hurting Breckonridge. If that meant ruining or hurting Miss Compton in the process, it was simply too bad.

But just as he could not denounce Breckonridge as evil without proof, neither could he show an open interest in Miss Compton without tipping his hand. He had hoped to further their acquaintance at Almack's Wednesday night. The ballroom boasted any number of places where a gentleman might snatch a private moment with a lady, if he were clever. Rupert knew he was clever, but Persephone Compton had not arrived for the dance. Now he had no choice but to make a more obvious approach.

His chance came Friday morning when one of his spies sent him word that Miss Compton had been spotted on Bond Street, shopping with only a maid and footman for company. He had excused himself from the private debate over the wording of the Widows and Orphans Act with a curt word to Breckonridge. He took private delight in the man's frown. It was not often he found an opportunity to insult the fellow twice in one day and get away with it. He was positively giddy by the time he reached the shopping district.

His man directed him to the milliners, where Miss Compton was trying on hats. He could see her through the window, her willowy frame wrapped in a ribboned pelisse of serpentine satin. Her curls glowed golden against the color. He walked past the shop for a block and waited, then was forced to retrace his steps twice more before she actually appeared. By then, he was more than a little put out with her.

Still, he tipped his high-crowned beaver and nodded to her as they passed. He would have had to have been blind not to see the eager light spring to her violet eyes. He certainly heard the eagerness in her voice as he made to continue and she hailed him.

"Lord Wells! How lovely to see you!"

He turned to find she had stopped and was smiling at him charmingly. Only the hint of pink in her creamy complexion told him she knew she was being forward.

He bowed. "Miss Compton. A pleasure. I trust you are having luck with your shopping?"

"Tolerable," she pronounced, waving a dainty hand

back to where a strapping young footman balanced a stack of parcels reaching nearly to his solid chin. "But I have such trouble making decisions on matters of dress. It is so difficult to judge what would look well on one."

"I would imagine anything would look good on you," he told her pointedly and had the pleasure of watching her blush deepen.

"You are too kind," she murmured. "Still, I value the opinion of a more seasoned person. Unfortunately, my dear cousin Sarah could not join me this morning."

Though he knew the spinster had been left at home, he was careful to evince surprise. "You are unescorted?" he asked, ignoring the little dark-haired maid beside her and the footman at her back. "That will never do. I'm certain your friend Lord Breckonridge would never approve of it."

At Breckonridge's name, she stiffened, putting up her little chin. "I do not care whether he approves or not. I am much put out with Lord Breckonridge, and you may tell him so."

Rupert hid a smile. So, she had already taken Breckonridge's measure. He might be able to use that to his advantage. He forced his face to remain unmoved. "How tragic," he drawled. "You must tell me how he came to earn your wrath. Would you allow me to walk with you a while?"

She batted her lashes before lowering her gaze. "Certainly, Lord Wells. But I hope we can find better topics of conversation than Lord Breckonridge."

So do I, thought Wells as he put her hand on his arm. *So do I.*

* * *

While Persephone poured her heart out to Rupert Wells, Sarah turned her attention to the correspondence. Having dispensed her cousin shopping, with the girl's maid Lucy (who Mr. Timmons said had been properly schooled in her role) and Jerym the underfootman, Sarah sat at the Sheridan writing desk in the corner of the library. She first sorted and paid the bills, noting with disapproval that the price of coal had risen again. Good thing Uncle Harold was well off. Another few guineas would never be missed. How did the poor fare? Perhaps this problem would be solved by one of the acts Malcolm was supporting.

She snatched up the next batch of correspondence and focused her wayward thoughts. She had put off writing to her aunt and uncle again last night. Today she noted the fact that Persy had several new suitors, carefully avoiding any mention of the Duke of Reddington. She still held out hope that her cousin would be persuaded to reconcile with the fellow, especially now that she knew Lord Breckonridge wasn't interested in her. Malcolm, Lord Breckonridge, was clearly not interested in anyone but himself. It was a decided shame, really, for with his sharp wit and handsome countenance he had much to offer a lady. She could easily imagine herself on his arm, strolling through an august set of personages, exchanging pleasantries, offering smiles of encouragement. She realized her pen had stopped moving and hastily dipped it in the ink again, scolding herself.

"These just came, Miss Sarah," Timmons said from the doorway, bringing her a pile of parcels and cards. Persy's admirers had been busier than usual. Sarah was getting quite familiar with the white boxes from the famous London confectioners of Gunter's. There were

three of them today, along with several dozen assorted calling cards and envelopes. She sorted through them, passing those for Persephone alone into one pile and those that included her into another. Her pile, as always, was decidedly smaller. That is, until she reached the boxes.

She was surprised to find that the two largest boxes were addressed to her. Her surprise melted into anger as she recognized the bold hand on the envelope affixed to the largest box. Did he think he could buy what she refused to give? Worse, did he think her price was so low that roses and boxes of candy would serve to do the trick? She should throw them out unopened.

But curiosity got the better of her. He could not know how savagely she had dealt with his earlier gifts. Why send more? Could it be that he really did mean to apologize for his insulting offer? With hands that trembled, and thoroughly disgusted with herself, she broke open the envelope.

"My dear Miss Compton," he had written. "I realized belatedly that roses might not have been an appropriate way to apologize. I'm not certain these sweets are any better. I believe I am coming to understand your position. Surely we both need to know each other better before making any decisions on a future. I was simply so gratified to find a woman of such rare intelligence, sense, good nature, and beauty that I rushed forward to seize her before some other fellow recognized her as a treasure. I promise to be more sensitive in the future, only say that you are willing to forgive me and give me another chance. Your servant always, Malcolm, Lord Breckonridge."

Sarah stared at the paper. What gammon. Intelligence, sense, good nature, and beauty, indeed. She liked to think she had the first two in good measure, but the third had been sadly lacking of late, and only a fool would consider her beautiful next to Persephone. *A fool, or a man in love,* a voice inside her said. She shivered. There it was again—that chance to risk her heart. He wanted another chance. Another chance to trample her tender feelings? Another chance to make a mockery of her dreams?

Another chance to fall in love?

For what if that was what happened? What if they both fell in love? What if she had a chance for a husband, a family, a home of her own? Shouldn't she take it? Shouldn't she try as she had never tried before? Was it such a very great risk?

"Oh, Sarah, you are mad to consider it," she told herself aloud. She dropped the note to knuckle her eyes. "What if nothing comes of it? What if he never gives you his heart? What if he cannot love anything beyond Parliament?"

What if you never find out? her heart protested. *What if you never see him again?*

She dropped her head to her arms and sighed. So many ifs. She wasn't sure how to deal with them. It had been so very long since she'd taken a chance. Perhaps that was all the more reason to take one now. Would it hurt so much if she failed to bring him up to scratch?

The answer, of course, was yes. He had the power to love her and the power to hurt her. If she opened herself to one, she opened herself to the other as well. She didn't know whether she had it in her.

As she lay on the desk, thinking, a warm sugary smell filled her nose. She straightened, inhaling. Chocolate. She'd shared boxes of chocolate almonds with her cousin years ago. When Persephone was twelve, they had made her nauseous and Sarah had had to eat the three boxes her cousin had received for her birthday. She hadn't had more than a handful since at late-night suppers when she was chaperoning. Aunt Belle had reasoned that if her dear Persephone couldn't have them, no one in the household could. Feeling wicked and wondrous at the same time, Sarah pulled off the lid from the first box. Her eyes widened at the dainty nuts nestled in the tissue paper. Selecting a large, luscious one, she dared to take a bite, letting the heady flavor glide across her tongue. Sarah groaned in ecstasy.

She must be a very shallow creature, indeed, she reflected as she tried the candy from the second box. It had a rum center, the taste tangy with the fine liquor. She licked the remainder from her fingers and lips, closing her eyes in delight. Then she shook her head. It seemed she was so easily bought after all.

Malcolm, Lord Breckonridge, was forgiven.

God help her.

TWELVE

Malcolm returned home that night with a spring in his step. Castlereagh, the Foreign Secretary, and Sidmouth, the Home Secretary, had been quarreling for days, but thanks to him, they were once more on speaking terms. Liverpool had pronounced the new version of the Widows and Orphans Act to be nothing short of brilliant. Wells had loosened up enough to gripe at him as he left the debate, which boded well for getting the young baron to show his passions. Life had returned to as normal a condition as possible for a leader in Parliament. He was actually whistling as he opened the door to his bedchamber. He stopped when he met Appleby's eager smile.

"What now?" he growled.

"I am saddened to report," his valet replied, the light in his bleary blue eyes belying his words, "that the boxes of chocolate met with the same fate as the roses."

Malcolm sighed. So much for an easy peace. "I suppose it's too much to hope she actually spoke to anyone on the matter. Did no one hear her complain of my treatment? Did she not berate the staff for her abuse?"

Appleby's face fell. "I did not think to ask, my lord."

"Never mind," Malcolm replied, moving into the room. "You said earlier her servants adore her. Somehow I doubt she's the type to take her feelings out on them."

"How refreshing," Appleby muttered.

Malcolm ignored him, sitting on the bed to tug off his boots. He had a sudden thought and paused. "Did anyone notice whether the boxes were empty or full?"

"I regret to say I didn't ask that question either, my lord," his valet replied.

His tone was so downcast that Malcolm could not help grinning at him. "Don't be hard on yourself, Appleby. You've been rather good at coming up with information, even with the restrictions I've put on you to avoid encouraging betrayal. Simply try in the future to remember that it is Miss Compton's feelings that interest me. What she throws in her trash is merely an indicator. Now, have you anything else to report?"

"Not regarding Miss Compton," Appleby admitted with a sigh. "Although I could regale you with tales of Miss Persephone."

Malcolm started to wave him off, then paused again. He had no interest in which suitors thronged the young beauty's sitting room or which dress she had deigned to wear that day. However, if his valet had information that would affect Sarah in any way, Malcolm should hear it. He needed all the help he could get in finding ways to present himself in a positive light to the lady.

"What have you heard?" he asked carefully.

Appleby stepped forward eagerly. "She has cut off His Grace, the Duke of Reddington, without so much as a backward glance."

"Pity." Malcolm shook his head. "Reddington was

hooked, if you ask me. The girl should have reeled him in."

"No doubt she thought him too small," Appleby said darkly.

Malcolm raised an eyebrow. "Oh? Will you tell me she's caught the attention of someone bigger? Not many can boast of fortune or family greater than Redington."

"It is rumored," Appleby said, pausing to lick his lips, "that she has set her sights on someone more powerful. Carlton, the duke's man, gave me very good odds."

"Indeed." Malcolm eyed him. "Most of the gentlemen in power are married, I know to my sorrow. Don't tell me she has eyes for Wells, that misanthrope. He'd eat her for breakfast and spit out the crumbs."

"No, my lord, not Lord Wells, although I believe she has been seen walking with him," Appleby assured him. "I regret to say, my lord, that she appears to favor you."

Malcolm started. "I hope you had the good sense to bet against that notion."

Appleby fidgeted. "Well, my lord, the young lady is quite lovely, and as I said, the odds were very good."

"You've wasted your blunt," Malcolm informed him. "I've already told you I prefer her older cousin. I hope this Carlton fellow didn't take it as proof against me that you accepted the wager."

Appleby licked his lips again, avoiding Malcolm's gaze. "I . . . I could not say, my lord. Would you like some assistance with your boots?"

"Yes," Malcolm replied, holding out a foot. His valet obligingly straddled his leg to yank off first one and then the other Hessian. As soon as he was done, however, Malcolm dismissed him. He had had quite enough gossip for one night.

As his valet slunk out, Malcolm shook his head. Could nothing go right with this courtship? He hardly needed half of London speculating about his matrimonial pursuits. Of course, it was possible that Sarah had the good sense to hire servants who did not gossip, and so she would not hear the rumors. On the other hand, someone in that house gossiped all too well, or Appleby would not be able to relate his stories. Hadn't he mentioned this Timmons fellow? Malcolm seemed to remember that was the butler's name. All he could hope for was that the fellow and the rest of her servants would realize that someone like Malcolm could not possibly be interested in Persephone Compton.

He shuddered at the very thought of aligning himself with the mercenary little charmer. Of course, he could hardly go around telling people that. Nor could he tell Sarah how unattractive he found her cousin. He would have to hope she recognized how attractive he found her and that that would suffice.

To ensure Sarah had no doubts, he made time the following day to call. As usual, a half-dozen fellows kept a rotating vigil at Persephone's shrine. The girl was gowned in a demure sprigged muslin with simple lines and only a single ribbon under the high waist, but the coquettish glances she bestowed from under lowered lashes belied her innocence. Sarah, on the other hand, wore a long-sleeved gray poplin gown that was understated and elegant and drew attention to her changeable eyes. He turned to her immediately, raising her hand to his lips.

"Miss Compton, your eternal servant," he greeted her. When Persephone paused in her conversation, clearly expecting a similar salute, he merely nodded. The girl's sunny countenance immediately darkened. Was it true, then? Had the girl set her cap for him? He purposely turned his back to her to lead Sarah to a more private seat. He could feel the girl's eyes drilling into him. He ignored her.

Sitting beside Sarah on the sofa, he saw she was regarding him with a raised brow.

"And what has Persephone done to so earn your enmity, my lord?" she asked, smile teasing.

"I have no idea," he replied. "Nor do I care. Be assured I came here only to see you."

"I am flattered," she murmured, lowering her gaze.

He chuckled at the maidenly posture. "You've been taking lessons from your cousin, I see. I warn you, I am immune to the fluttering of eyelashes."

"For which we should all be grateful," she quipped, looking up again. "Imagine what laws we would have if you succumbed so easily."

"I shudder to think," he replied, pleased that he could see her eyes again. Green as light, as fine jade shone among the blue. "I have more than once been encouraged to proclaim a national holiday on Brummell's birthday, even after he insulted the prince by calling him fat."

"Well, His Highness has grown large," she remarked with a grin that showed her dimples to advantage. "Of course, I am not the best judge, not being a noted leader of fashion like Mr. Brummell."

"No, I rather think you set your own fashion," he replied approvingly. "In fact, did not your cousin tell me that you collect rocks?"

She sighed. "Oh, I hoped you'd forget that."

He raised a brow, intrigued. "Why? Is there is some scandalous story behind the pastime?"

"Nothing scandalous. Merely silly."

"I find it hard to believe you would do anything foolish, Miss Compton."

He watched as the color grew in her cheeks. She did not like talking about herself, particularly anything close to her heart. While he admired her humility, he felt a driving desire to know everything about her. The desire surprised him, but he told himself the interest was surely expected since he intended to make her his wife.

"Then perhaps I should tell you the tale merely to prove you wrong," she threatened. "I suspect it might be a novel experience for the great Viscount Breckonridge."

"Not as novel as I'd like," he admitted. "But pray do not let that stop you."

"Very well," she conceded grudgingly. "It started when I was in school. I studied at a private school near Wells, the Barnsley School for Young Ladies. I was from one of the less exalted families, and by far one of the oldest to start. Many of the girls had been there since they were six. They were a rather close-knit group, slow to accept newcomers. I found it expedient to keep my eyes on the ground and my mouth closed."

He could imagine how difficult it must have been for her. The same bewilderment he heard in her voice he'd seen in the eyes of some of those newly elected to Parliament. "Did no one offer you help?" he asked.

She nodded. "Several, most of whom are my friends to this day, though we keep in touch only through correspondence. But before they stepped forward, one of the other girls demanded to know why I kept my head bowed. I think she thought to shame me into confessing myself less than she was. I told her the first thing that came to my mind. 'I collect rocks and I am never certain when I'm going to find an unusual specimen.' "

"Very original," he commended.

"Very ridiculous," she countered, wrinkling her nose. "I kept my head down even while we were inside, and I certainly couldn't have expected to find many rocks on Miss Martingale's clean floors. But I must have told the story with sufficient conviction, for she believed me. After that, they all took great pains to point out likely specimens on our daily constitutionals about the grounds."

"You found a way to appear interesting in their eyes," he surmised. "They were only looking for an excuse to like you."

"Perhaps," she allowed. "But I didn't see that as a child. I became rather cavalier about the whole thing, refusing this rock as too common, that rock as too dull, another as too shiny. I'm ashamed to say they only doubled their efforts. It became something of a prize to find a rock I would accept. After I left the school, I'd still receive rocks in the mail from classmates. My aunt and uncle never knew what would arrive in the post. Even Persephone thinks I collect the things, as you know. I suspect it was merely a way to get attention."

"So, you do share a few traits with your cousin," he joked.

She smiled ruefully. "I suppose so. Thankfully, I grew out of it. Besides, Persephone appears to collect gentlemen. I only collected rocks, with no feelings at risk."

He glanced to where a half-dozen gentlemen were vying for the girl's attention. Persephone caught his gaze on her in mid-yawn and turned the movement into a simpering smile. He shook his head, returning his attention to Sarah. "I cannot imagine how so many gentlemen find themselves so hopelessly enthralled with your cousin."

"Of course," she replied, and he noted that all merriment had faded from her smile. "The great Lord Breckonridge would never be so taken with any lady."

He had stepped into a trap of his own making. His comment had obviously reminded her of their earlier discussion, something he had hoped to make her forget. He knew he could spout any number of pretty phrases to assure her of his devotion, but he found he could not lie to her. His conscience forbade it, and she wouldn't have believed him anyway.

"I see I am not forgiven after all," he murmured instead.

She sighed. "I'm sorry, my lord. I have no right to withhold forgiveness, not when you've tried so hard to make amends. Besides, you are merely being yourself."

Somehow that still sounded like he was less than he should be. "And what would you have me be, if you could change me?"

She regarded him with narrowed eyes. "That is a very large if, my lord. I prefer to deal with reality."

"What, do you never dream of what could be?" he challenged.

"That is a foolish pastime for one in my position," she replied so primly that he knew he had touched on something. "Dreams are surely for people with position and power."

He frowned. "I could not agree less. Everyone has a dream. People of position and power often forget that and are content to let things stagnate. We need visionaries, Miss Compton, people who aren't afraid to reach for their dreams, to make a difference."

She met his gaze, and he could see swirls of silver in the blue of her eyes, like fairies dancing on a pond.

"One cannot make a difference," she said, "unless the rest of the world concedes the difference."

"To hell with the rest of the world," he growled in return. "Sometimes the only person who sees the difference is the person who made it. We can ask for no more than that, Miss Compton—to know in our hearts that the world is a better place because we passed through it."

"You make it sound so easy," she protested. "The world conspires against us. We are tiny people, insignificant in the scheme of things."

"That you will never make me believe, my dear," he replied. "The smallest ant can carry many times its weight. A single twig can stem a flood."

"A single word can change a life?" she ventured.

"Precisely." He beamed at her.

She gave him a reluctant smile in return. "You almost make me believe in miracles, my lord."

"Almost?" He scratched his chin. "I'm slipping. I could have sworn that speech would sway the vote in my favor."

Instead of laughing as he intended, her smile faded again. "Is it so imperative that you win?"

"Of course. That is how *I* make a difference, Miss Compton."

"And what of your opponent, the one who loses if you win?"

"Ah," he replied, "but you look on it as if it were black and white, a winner and a loser. True politics is shades of gray. The challenge is finding the single most perfect solution in which everyone perceives himself a winner."

She cocked her head. "Is such a thing possible?"

"Sometimes," he admitted. "I wish it were always. It is my dream to make it so."

"It is an honorable goal," she acknowledged. "I can see why it inspires you."

Suddenly he felt sheepish. He had come to court her and instead climbed into a pulpit to preach. He sighed. "I must beg your forgiveness again, Miss Compton. I can't seem to stop giving speeches even when I leave the halls of Parliament. You must find me insufferable."

At last her smile returned to its usual warmth. He felt himself basking in the glow of it. "Not insufferable, my lord. I find your passion inspiring. Indeed, you have given me a great deal to think about."

He wanted to ask her if their talk had changed her mind about his proposal, but his statesman's instinct warned him that it wasn't the right time. Instead, he smiled back at her. As he watched, the blue deepened in her eyes, drawing him in. Without realizing it, he leaned forward. She leaned toward him as well, faces closing the distance that hearts could not.

"Well, Cousin Sarah?" Persephone demanded suddenly from beside him, hands on hips. "Lord Weston has asked us to join him at the theater tonight. May we go?"

Sarah blinked, straightening, and Malcolm had a moment to collect himself. Good God, had he been about to kiss her? In full view of Persephone and her flock of devotees? What had he been thinking? In truth, he couldn't remember thinking at all, only feeling. It was a singular experience, and while it shook him, he could not say he was adverse to it.

Sarah seemed similarly shaken. "Tonight? I believe we have something planned. Something, I think. Something important?"

Persephone frowned, hands dropping. "Cousin Sarah? Are you all right?"

Malcolm seized the opportunity. "Perhaps what you forgot, my dear, is that you agreed to accompany me to the opera tonight. Isn't that right?"

Sarah's gaze focused on him with obvious difficulty. The blue had cooled significantly, he could see. Her eyes appeared as chill as the sky in midwinter. He waited for her to denounce him.

"Yes, of course," she murmured, looking back at Persephone. "We are going to the opera with Lord Breckonridge this evening. Perhaps Lord Weston could be persuaded to take you to the theater tomorrow. I understand from Lady Wenworth that Keene has extended his run, and I know you so wanted to see him."

Weston, a tall, gangly fellow newly ascended to his title, nodded eagerly. Persephone smiled sweetly. "What a lovely suggestion, Sarah. I'd be delighted, Lord Breckonridge, Lord Weston."

Her admirers led her off.

"Well done, Miss Compton," Malcolm said. "You see, it is possible, a solution in which everyone wins."

Sarah eyed him, face thoughtful. "I understand the concept, my lord. I'm just not certain of one thing. What exactly have I won?"

THIRTEEN

What had she won, indeed? Sarah had to ask herself that many times over the next few weeks. To her amazement, Malcolm became a frequent caller at the house on Curzon Street. He appeared at least three times a week just to visit. In addition, he escorted her to the park, on walks about the neighborhood, on drives out to the country. He took her to the opera and plays. He even took her to see the menagerie at the Exeter 'Change. She was fascinated by the tigers, whose prowling grace reminded her not a little of the man beside her. But when the keepers brought in a hunk of raw meat for the animals, she had turned her head into Malcolm's coat to blot out the sight of the sharp white teeth. His arms came around her easily, his dark head bending so that he could whisper reassurances in her ear. This public display would have been scandalously delightful if she hadn't caught herself wondering whether he'd known she'd be so affected.

One fellow in the crowd obviously thought so. "Feed 'em some more, Phil," he called. "Maybe she'll cozy up to me."

"Why'd she do that when she's got the biggest bloke in the room," a woman had chided. "Here, deary, move over. I'm scared too. Perhaps I can get a hug out of it."

"I regret, madam," Malcolm had replied, "that I have found the only woman for me."

He had whisked her out of the building with her cheeks still blazing.

He had taken other liberties as well, though in truth she could not say he had ever been less than a gentleman. When the music trembled with emotion at the concert by the Philharmonic Society, she found her hands trembling under the gentle pressure of his. When she went to dismount from a ride in Hyde Park, she found her heart pounding louder than the sound of horses' hooves as he lifted her down against his strong body. And when the fireworks exploded over Vauxhall, the sparks were nothing to the fire inside her as he pressed his lips to hers.

But even as each of his touches left her shaken, her mind was not so easily moved. She could not fail to notice that he never seemed too affected by their proximity. Indeed, his goal with all these entertainments and embraces seemed merely to prove to her that they would make a marvelous pair. There were times when she knew by his smile that he thought he had made his point. She refused to give him the satisfaction.

As the days passed, she also refused to remain alone in his company for long. It was not that she didn't trust him. Rather, she did not trust the reaction of her traitor body. She insisted that either Norrie or Persephone accompany them on their outings, as her chaperon. She wasn't certain how her cousin would take to such a responsibility. Certainly Persy generally preferred to keep all attention to herself. Yet, she was a delightful companion, walking beside Lord Breckonridge and joining in their conversations, occasionally drawing off by herself so that they would have a few moments alone. Sarah wasn't sure what to make of it, but she decided it was better not to question her cousin.

She did do her best to ensure that Persephone was also spending time with her various suitors. When she could not go with the girl, she had Norrie accompany Persy instead. She had a duty to her aunt and uncle, after all. They had come to London to find Persy a suitable husband, even though the girl had yet to show a preference. She did not like to think what Aunt Belle and Uncle Harold would say if they knew half the time was being devoted to Sarah's needs. Not that they would begrudge her the chance. They simply wouldn't have thought it possible.

At times she wasn't entirely sure it was not some dream. Malcolm was unlike anyone she had ever met. His conversation was witty and well informed. His demeanor was generally polite and kind. He gave her all his attention. Even when they were in a crowd of people, his touch, his smile, would let her know she was foremost in his thoughts. It was just so easy to lose herself with him. One could not ask for a more devoted suitor.

And yet, she did ask. The more she was in his company, the more she caught herself wishing she had more of him. Even when he kissed her, she sensed a distance, though truth be told, she wasn't sure whether it came from him or her own heart. She could not say he was overly demonstrative. Indeed, he seemed to treat nearly everyone they met with the same friendliness. She supposed that was part of his position. A leader in Parliament must surely have to maintain an openness in communication with his fellow members.

Certainly everyone she met seemed to hold him in high esteem. The one person who did not was Lord Rupert Wells, and she had been in his company for so short a time she could not be certain she had really sensed the tension between them.

It had happened in Hyde Park. Malcolm had driven her and Persephone to the gathering place of the haute ton, where they disembarked to stroll among the grounds. Paths led through greenery and blooming flowers. Ladies in bright muslin held parasols to shade them from the heat of the summer sun. She walked on Malcolm's side, arm through his, while Persephone walked on the other side. Malcolm had been pointing out a boy launching a small boat onto the wide green waters of the Serpentine when her cousin had sucked in a breath. Sarah had leaned forward to regard her cousin, only to meet the gaze of Lord Wells, who was passing them.

Dark eyes glittering, Wells tipped his top hat, offering them a bow.

Persephone looked quickly away, coloring. Malcolm paused immediately.

"Good afternoon, Wells," he remarked. "Do you know my lovely companions?"

"I believe we have met," Wells intoned. "I will not detain you. Enjoy your walk."

Persephone's lower lip trembled, but she put up her head as if she didn't care that he had been short with them. Malcolm frowned, but continued walking. Glancing back, Sarah had seen that Wells had stopped to regard their passage. In his eyes was a look of simmering heat, quickly covered. She could not tell whether it was directed at Malcolm, or Persephone.

She did not feel comfortable asking Malcolm about

it, but she did ask her cousin later when they were once more alone at home.

Persephone raised her brows, the picture of innocence. "Lord Wells?" she asked. "I cannot think who you mean."

Now Sarah raised her brows. "Oh, come now, Persy. Do you have so many beaux that you no longer remember them all? Besides, wasn't Lord Wells the gentleman who so intrigued you at Lady Prestwick's ball?"

"Oh, I suppose," she replied begrudgingly. "It's just that when I'm with one gentleman, I try not to pay undue attention to others."

Sarah refrained from commenting. Persephone had gladly spurned any number of gentlemen when a more eligible candidate had appeared at her side. If her cousin had decided to mend her ways, Sarah did not want to say anything to discourage her.

Nor could she find it in her heart to discourage Malcolm. She could not deny the joy in having a suitor of her own, to have a friend with whom she could carry on a conversation. She enjoyed catching his eye when Persephone or one of her beaux made a cake of themselves. She liked sharing his smile when Norrie brought her a rock from Kensington Gardens. She felt just as contented in a spirited argument with him as in a deep philosophical debate. He seemed to enjoy her company just as much. Certainly he continually sought it. If only she could be certain these companionable feelings were growing into love. Then she might be willing to open her own heart.

As the Season neared its end in late July, she knew they were nearing a critical point in their courtship. Parliament would be in recess, and the eligibles would be leaving the city for their cooler country homes. Malcolm would surely press her for an answer. Worse, Persephone had yet to decide upon a winner in the contest for her hand, a contest that was also nearing a peak if the throngs of admirers in the sitting room were any indication. She had actually had to stop two arguments before they disintegrated into fisticuffs, and had heard through Mr. Timmons that there had been a duel fought in Persephone's honor. Thankfully, no one had been seriously hurt.

Even Persephone was showing the strain, however. More and more the girl begged for quiet times to herself, sitting alone in the garden behind the house or taking a constitutional about the neighborhood with only Lucy for company. Her creamy skin had become more pale, it seemed to Sarah, her eyes fatigued. Yet, when Sarah had tried to cheer her with the reminder that they would surely be returning home soon, her cousin had merely glowered at her.

"You may smile about it," Persephone complained. "You like rustication. I vow I will expire if I am forced into retirement so early in my career."

"Your career?" Sarah couldn't help but smile. "Pray tell, do you intend to make a life's work of this courting?"

Persephone tossed her head. "Certainly not! But I will continue in my quest until I have won the perfect man. That may take a few days or a few years, as fate decrees."

Sarah felt her smile fading. Years? Was that her future if she refused to marry Malcolm, to be forced to trudge in her cousin's wake through one Season after another? Even if Aunt Belle took over the task, would Sarah feel comfortable going to Wenworth with Norrie if her cousin was not well settled? The prospect of returning to the country looked more dismal every second.

Even Norrie was perplexed. "You must do as you see fit, of course," she had said when Sarah had told her of Persephone's intentions. "I admire your loyalty to the girl, especially when she does not appear very loyal to you."

"Persy is young," Sarah replied. "She doesn't understand how she hurts people."

"Will she learn if we keep shielding her?" Norrie asked with a frown. "Not that I would wish any ill on the girl, but sometimes I think a broken heart would do her good."

Sarah shook her head. "I cannot wish for that either. Let us hope instead that she meets her true love soon, if such a person exists."

"You sound like you doubt that," Norrie chided. "Is it for Persephone or Sarah that you fear?"

Sarah sighed. "Both, I suspect. Tell me again, Norrie. When you fell in love with your Justinian, how did it feel?"

"Amazing, frightening?" Norrie cocked her head, gazing off into the distance, deep blue eyes unfocused. "Wanting to love, wanting to be loved, wanting to be certain." She blinked and refocused on Sarah. "But don't pattern your hopes on mine, love. You know Justinian and I very nearly didn't make a match of it, and wouldn't have if not for the interference of a small black kitten and a determined dowager. What does your heart tell you?"

"I wish I knew," Sarah returned with another sigh. "I fear it has been too long since I listened to it. I don't know what it's saying anymore."

Norrie squeezed her hands where they were folded in the lap of her dress. "Keep trying, Sarah. I know you have the capacity for great love. You show it in your devotion to Persephone, in your loyalty to your aunt and uncle, in the very fact that you've answered my tedious letters all these years."

"Hardly tedious," Sarah protested with a smile.

"Not for the last three years anyway," Norrie agreed, answering her smile with one of her own. "Now, try to cheer up. The Season is nearly over. With any luck, you will be coming home with me."

The thought would once have been enough to cheer her. Now she could not look at the future without cringing. She was nearly as blue-deviled as Persephone when Lady Anne Prestwick came to call one afternoon near the first of August. Still, she roused herself to welcome the young countess.

"Persephone will be so sorry to have missed you," she told Anne as she sat beside her on the sofa in the sitting room.

"She's out with one of her suitors, I suppose," Lady Prestwick murmured with an indulgent smile. "Did she tell you we met the other day on New Bond Street?"

Sarah shook her head. "No. Was this Tuesday? She and her maid went shopping."

"Yes, that's right," Anne replied. "You might ask her about the occasion. I was under the impression she was rather upset."

Upset? What had Persephone been up to? Sarah couldn't remember noticing anything out of the ordinary when the girl had returned. Indeed, she had seemed inordinately pleased with her purchases. "Perhaps she was tired," Sarah ventured. "She does have a tendency to overdo it when shopping."

"A singular habit," the countess remarked as if she did not share it. Eyeing the fine silk of her lavender-striped walking dress, Sarah somehow thought she was more familiar with the shops on New Bond Street than she intimated. "But I suppose common among the young ladies on their Season. And she is so very popular. Every time I see her she is on the arm of another beau. Has anyone risen above the others?"

"Not that I can notice," Sarah admitted with a sigh.

Anne grimaced. "Ah, well, she is young. Time enough for her to find the right man for her. And you, Miss Compton? Have you made any decisions?"

Sarah regarded her, suddenly remembering the connection between this innocent-looking woman and Malcolm. Lady Prestwick had been the one to contrive the ball at which Sarah and Malcolm had met. Lady Prestwick was rumored to be his confidante. Did she know that Sarah had already refused him once?

"Nothing definite," Sarah hedged, picking at the folds of her spruce poplin gown. "But, as you say, there is time."

"Less than you might think," Lady Prestwick assured her. "I believe Lord Breckonridge is at that point in his life where he believes he must marry. You must know he is determined that you be that bride, Miss Compton."

"I am not ready to discuss my relationship with Lord Breckonridge," Sarah replied stiffly.

Anne sighed. "I'm sorry. I didn't mean to intrude. It is simply obvious to me that you would make him an excellent wife. I know he shares that belief. Yet, I sense you doubt it. Is it being a viscountess that disturbs you? I know I would have feared it, had I known Chas was an earl when I accepted him."

"How could you not know?" Sarah asked with a frown.

"I did not know his brother had died," Anne explained. "When I accepted him, I thought I would be marrying an impecunious second son. Imagine my chagrin to find myself a countess."

Sarah smiled. "Somehow I doubt you would have refused him had you known."

"Oh, no," she replied with a firm shake of her head and a smile of her own. "I adored Chas, from nearly the first moment we met. My only hesitation in marrying him was that I feared he did not love me."

Sarah could not have changed the topic if she had tried. "Why were you in doubt? Was he too cool?"

"Cool? Chas?" Lady Prestwick laughed. "My dear, I thought his exploits were legendary. My husband had a tendency to enact the most charming escapades. He is an avid racer. At one time he held the record for curricle and pair to every spot within a fifty-mile radius of London. He once recited a scandalous love poem to me in front of two hundred of London's finest. Oh, no, Chas is most assuredly not cool, Miss Compton. That wasn't what I feared. No, I was afraid he married me out of honor. You see, we caused a bit of scandal."

"Really?" Sarah breathed, trying to imagine this elegant little woman doing anything as wild as her husband.

"Really," she replied with a fond smile. "But he was able to convince me to my satisfaction that he loved me." She cocked her head to eye Sarah. "I take it Lord Breckonridge has not been so satisfactory?"

"Not nearly so," Sarah admitted. "In fact, he has

never claimed to love me, and he has only once stolen a kiss."

Anne shook her head. "The cad. I had no idea he was being so lukewarm. Perhaps you should kiss him first next time."

Sarah stared at her, feeling her color rise. "How can you suggest anything so forward?"

"So, you are just as unwilling to show your feelings," she surmised before calmly shaking her head. "What am I to do with the pair of you? I think I must invite you and your cousin to Prestwick Park for a fortnight."

Sarah put a hand to her head. "I'm sorry, Lady Prestwick, but I'm having a difficult time following your line of reasoning. You berate me for not being forward and then invite me to visit?"

She smiled. "Precisely. London moves too quickly, and Parliament is a persuasive mistress for men like Lord Breckonridge. A few weeks in the country will allow you both some time to reflect. Please say you'll come."

Was it that simple? She gazed at the little countess, who sat contentedly smiling at her. Could she just whisk Malcolm away from the bustle of London to get him to declare he loved her? Would her heart unbend away from the town where it had permanently stiffened? Wasn't it worth the chance to find out?

"I would have to ask my aunt and uncle," she realized out loud. As soon as she said it, she knew they would not approve. While Lady Prestwick was becoming a renowned hostess, it did not sound as if there would be any eligibles at the estate. It would be a waste of Persephone's time. Surely her aunt and uncle would forbid the visit.

"Let me write them," Lady Prestwick begged, rising. "They are in Suffolk, are they not? I'll send a note this afternoon. I'm sure I can persuade them to let you come."

Looking at her, Sarah somehow thought she could. She nodded her agreement, rising as well.

Anne Prestwick reached out to give her a quick hug. "Wonderful. This will all work out beautifully, you'll see. Now, I must go. I need to tell Chas we'll have company."

"He doesn't know?" Sarah asked in surprise as they separated.

She laughed. "Of course not. I only just thought of the idea. Don't look so worried. I told you, Chas thrives on excitement. He'll be delighted to have company, particularly when he hears who. We generally keep any entertaining to a minimum at Prestwick Park; it upsets the dowager countess. Luckily, Lady Prestwick is visiting my Aunt Millicent for the summer. So, we'll have the place all to ourselves. I promise you, everyone will be pleased with the arrangement."

Sarah wasn't so sure that would be the case. However, Persephone was delighted with the idea.

"It's like extending the Season," she declared. "How very clever of you to achieve it, Sarah!"

Sarah hardly felt clever, but Norrie was nearly as effusive in her praise of the idea as Persephone had been.

"How wonderful!" her friend had proclaimed. "You will have Lord Breckonridge all to yourself, and you can come visit me every day if you wish." She handily ignored the fact that Sarah could hardly do both at the same time. "I shall have to send a card round to Lady Prestwick thanking her for her kindness," Norrie added.

Even Sarah's uncle and aunt acquiesced. Aunt Belle went so far as to praise Lady Prestwick's condescension. Sarah wasn't sure what to make of it.

But, like it or not, she was on her way back to Somerset.

And maybe into Malcolm's heart.

FOURTEEN

Rupert could not imagine how Persephone Compton had inveigled her way into Breckonridge's heart. He crossed his arms over his chest as he waited for her in the shadow of the mews behind the house on Curzon Street. The spinster had wanted to go shopping, and Persephone had promised to plead a headache so that she might meet with him instead. Yet, the carriage and grooms had been gone for over a quarter hour and still he waited. Really, the chit was becoming tiresome.

He stiffened as he heard the kitchen door of the town house open. But the whisper of fine silk told him who approached. In a moment she was at his side, rosebud lips parted breathlessly. He swept her into his embrace, crushing her mouth beneath his own. He had found she preferred his caresses just the least bit impetuous. He suspected it made their little game seem more dangerous to her, showing the desperate nature of what she called their forbidden love. Even now she trembled in his arms. How much more would she tremble if she knew how very little she meant to him?

He raised his head at last, and she snuggled against his chest with a satisfied sigh.

"How I shall miss you while we're in Somerset," she murmured.

Rupert frowned. "Somerset? When are you going to Somerset?"

"At the end of the week," she replied. "Lady Prestwick invited Sarah, so of course I must go along."

They were removing her? Did they conspire against him? Had he given himself away so badly? No, he thought, his grip on the girl tightening involuntarily. More likely *she* had given him away.

She obviously mistook the pressure. "Do not fear, my darling baron," she murmured, tilting back her head to gaze up at him. "I will not forget you. I promise."

"Is that what they intend?" he demanded, jaw tightening. "Have we been discovered?"

"No, no," she protested. Her violet eyes were clear, her expression fervent, and he had no choice but to believe her. "I told no one, as I promised you. Only my maid knows of our trysts and I am convinced she would not betray us."

"You pay her well, then," he mused, relaxing.

She giggled. "I have no doubt my father pays her adequately. But Lucy serves me well for another reason. There is great prestige in serving a titled lady."

"And you think to be one soon?" he probed.

She had the good sense to drop her gaze to his waistcoat, toying with the top silver button. "Perhaps. But the gentleman has yet to ask me."

She could have meant Breckonridge, or she could have been angling for a proposal from him. He knew enough to take the bait without being hooked. Besides, marriage was not in his plans. She had caused him enough trouble that he had decided she must be ruined along with Breckonridge. At least that added a little spice to the deception. He could certainly follow her to Somerset and finish his seduction—it would be so much easier to get her alone in the country. But Breckonridge might never know of it. The man covered his interest in the girl behind this ridiculous courtship with her cousin. Why else invite the girl along at every opportunity? Yet, she could not bring him to heel in the country.

"One day out of my sight is too much," he vowed, and she rested her head against his chest again. "You cannot go. If you will not think of me, think of your other devoted followers—Barrington, Cotell, Breckonridge."

She gave another of her gossamer giggles. The sound grated on his nerves.

"I *will* leave a hole in Society, won't I?" she said, complacent in her overblown self-worth. "But I am convinced you will survive somehow until my return. Besides, I understand Lord Breckonridge is coming with us."

Despite himself he stiffened. "Breckonridge plans to rusticate? When?"

"He leaves when Parliament recesses," she replied smugly. "So, you see, I shall have him all to myself. Who knows what can happen in the country?"

Who knew, indeed? Rupert's thoughts tumbled over each other like a troop of gypsy acrobats. If Breckonridge meant to rusticate in Somerset, it could only mean one thing. He was indeed serious in his pursuit of the girl and intended to spirit her away somewhere quiet to tell her so. Rupert had to time his seduction perfectly—after the engagement but before the wedding. And the girl had to be willing; a rape would merely prove Rupert the scoundrel. Yet, Somerset was so very rural. There'd be no audience to Persephone's tearful betrayal: he knew she'd cry—he'd imagined it too many times. He narrowed his eyes.

"How many others go with you?" he asked.

She glanced up coyly. "Are you jealous? I'm sorry to have teased you. Only Sarah and Lord and Lady Prestwick will be in attendance, besides Lord Breckonridge."

Only the Prestwicks? Ah, but that would mean their butler would be along. Rames was a noted jabbermouth, he knew to his pleasure. Between the Prestwick butler and Breckonridge's fool Appleby, his own valet always had a story to relate. Appleby might protest aloud that Breckonridge was courting Sarah Compton, but the man's money was on Persephone. With such a set of gossipers in attendance, news would reach London soon enough.

"Surely Lady Prestwick can spare an invitation for a friend of Breckonridge's," he said aloud.

He could see her frown. "I'm sure I would not presume to ask," she said primly.

Wretch, he thought. It was clear she sought to punish him for not offering. She so much as flaunted Breckonridge in his face. It was a dangerous game. "And if I were to follow you?" he pressed. "Do you expect me to live off the crumbs of your affection?"

"Crumbs?" She raised her head and broke from his grip. "Crumbs? I risk my reputation, my honor to be with you and you call it a crumb? Perhaps you would like to visit via the front door like the rest of my suitors, my lord."

She was as slippery as an eel and twice as cunning. He made his face penitent.

"Have I not explained why we cannot be seen in public? Do you think I like the fact that the inheritance is not mine until October? Your father would never accept me as a suitor now. Would you have wanted me to be content to worship from afar? To see you go to another?"

"Never!" she cried, throwing herself back into his arms. "Oh, Rupert, it is all so very tragic and romantic. Will you really follow me to Somerset?"

"To the ends of the earth, if need be," he assured her. *Anywhere, just so long as justice is served, and Breckonridge is humbled.*

Malcolm had to admit that Anne Prestwick was a genius. First, she convinced Sarah to attend a house party where Malcolm could have her all to himself, and then she had the foresight to have her husband deliver the news to him.

"Is she mad?" Malcolm had raged at first. "I can't leave London. Parliament won't recess until the end of the week, and there are any number of laws that must be moved forward in that time or languish until next session."

"If you don't come," Chas had replied, leaning against the doorjamb of Malcolm's untidy library, "it will be you who languishes until next session, Malcolm. Anne is adamant. If you wish to marry Miss Compton, you must come."

He had groused for some time, but eventually realized that the Prestwicks were right. Sarah would no doubt be returning to the country soon, and Persephone might agree to wed any day. Even if Sarah did not accept Lady Wenworth's offer to teach, it was highly possible she would not be back in London next

Season. If he wanted her, he needed to convince her of that fact.

As he rode through the arched wrought-iron gates that announced the drive of Prestwick Park, he knew he had made the right decision. In the green of the country, he felt the last vestiges of his London stresses slough off his shoulders like snow from a roof in a spring thaw. He hadn't ridden in ages. There were any number of fine horses scattered among his various estates, but he seldom had time to ride during his rare visits. He found himself glad Prestwick had suggested riding from London rather than sitting in a stuffy carriage.

Of course, he would likely pay for the ride for a few days. After the first night, he had been stiff and sore, envying Sarah and Persephone, who came behind them in a coach. On this, the third and final day out, he wasn't sure his tailbone would ever be the same. Still, the day was warm and honey-scented, the sky a cloudless blue, and the rolling green hills of Somerset hugged him on all sides. Through the oaks that lined the drive he could see the red-brick great house, and beyond it, the rising gray mass that was the Mendip Hills.

He had not visited Somerset before. His mind immediately went to cataloging those members of Parliament who came from the area. The reclusive Earl of Wenworth had his seat just north and west of the village of Wenwood, which Prestwick had said was a few miles along the nearby River Wen. They'd need his vote on that Marriage Act next session. As Sarah was a particular friend of the countess, perhaps she could introduce him. Then there was the American chap, the Earl of Brentfield, whose lands ran along the eastern boundary with Prestwick Park. He'd been quite vocal in his opinions; indeed, the radical reformers were rather hoping they could persuade him to join them. Perhaps it was time for a heart-to-heart chat with the fellow. He had a charming wife, if Malcolm remembered—quite the accomplished artist. Perhaps Sarah would enjoy meeting her.

He shook his head at himself as he guided the horse up to the gleaming white-columned porch. Funny how he was beginning to see Sarah at his side in all his future dealings. It was a dangerous trait. He had less assurance that she would accept him now than when he had first proposed.

But certainly more hope. He would not be the only one more comfortable here. Sarah had said she enjoyed the country. Though he suspected her home was more rustic than this, perhaps Prestwick Park would do. He glanced around at the house in front of him, as grooms scurried forward to take his horse. Eight windows faced the drive, wings stretched backward toward the hills. Likely there was a garden behind the house. It was a graceful place, a comfortable place. Surely he and Sarah could come to a meeting of the minds here. All he could do was try.

Sarah was almost as certain when she and Persephone stepped down from the carriage some time later. Prestwick Park was larger than her aunt and uncle's estate by some degree. Even Persephone blinked in wonder as they entered the rotunda and gazed up at the domed roof two stories above them. A carpeted corridor stretched away to their right, and doors led off to their left. Immediately before them swept the great stair, curling around the room to the upper floor. Sarah would never have known where to go first if a helpful footman hadn't led them to Lady Prestwick, who welcomed them warmly. Her welcome was nothing, however, to the reception Malcolm gave Sarah after she had had a chance to change from her traveling clothes in the lovely bedchamber Anne had given her.

She found him loitering in the corridor just down from her room. His aimless perusal of a painting of a cavalry charge made her wonder whether he was actually waiting for her to appear. His smile as she greeted him was tender, and he took her hand and brought it to his lips.

"Thank you," he murmured, "for agreeing to come and agreeing to give me this chance."

She was not sure how to answer him. As if sensing her discomfort, he turned her hand in his so that he could see her palm. "Such a small hand," he mused, stroking it with his thumb. She would not have thought it possible, but each movement seemed to be centered in her belly. "Do you know you hold my fate in it?"

"Nonsense," she said, pulling back. Yet her own hand moved to touch the spot he had stroked. He smiled at her, head bending nearer.

"Good afternoon, Lord Breckonridge," Persephone caroled, joining them. Malcolm stepped back and greeted her cousin kindly, and Sarah had no choice but to fall in with the two of them as they proceeded back to the main floor.

She was not certain what to expect of their visit, but was pleased to find that their lives immediately settled into a comfortable routine. Anne Prestwick proved herself as able a hostess in her own home as she had at Almack's. The food was good, frequent, and plentiful; the companionship as close or removed as one could wish. Sarah rode with Persephone every morning after breakfast. Sometimes Malcolm joined them. Other times, she suspected, he cornered Lord Prestwick for a debate on matters from Parliament. When Lord Prestwick could stand no more, they played billiards or went hunting in the oak woods surrounding the house.

However he had spent the early morning, Malcolm usually welcomed Sarah and Persephone back from their ride and spent the rest of the day with them. Lord and Lady Prestwick took them to see the famous caves at Cheddar Gorge and the sweeping golden cathedral at Wells. They drove through the surrounding vineyards and saw the waterfall behind Wenwood Abbey. Sarah was pleased to find Anne Prestwick a companion who actually took the time to seek her out and ask her opinion and advice. She was certainly not used to receiving such attention.

She worried that Persephone would take it amiss, but her cousin was charm itself. She smiled and conversed with everyone, even when Sarah was certain the girl must be bored to tears with none of her usual suitors to pay her court. Yet, Persephone seemed happy, going so far as to tease Lord Breckonridge and play billiards with Lord Prestwick. She also spent considerable time alone, wandering in the gardens, taking Lady Prestwick's pony cart for short jaunts up the drive. Sarah wasn't sure what to make of it, but she thanked God that the girl appeared to be coming to her senses at last. Perhaps Lady Prestwick was right. What they had all needed was time away from London.

Now, if she could just determine what to do when Malcolm next proposed.

FIFTEEN

Rupert was also enjoying the country. It was indeed far easier to get Persephone Compton alone. They met at the end of the Prestwick Park drive when she drove the pony cart. They met in a clearing when she ventured into the woods beyond the house. They met whenever he could slip into the Prestwick garden unseen. She had yet to allow him sufficient time to compromise her, but her trust in him was growing along with his desire to bring this charade to an end. Accordingly, he encouraged her to meet him beneath the rose arbor in a secluded corner of the garden on the fourth day of their visit.

"So, you are yet unencumbered?" he asked after he'd stolen a kiss.

"Yes," she replied, and he could not tell whether or not she was pleased by the fact.

"But you will accept Breckonridge if he offers?" he pressed.

She sat on the bench under the arbor and bent her head to a rose that grew through the white latticework. The warm color of the flower was no deeper than her own lips. Somehow, he thought she knew that.

"I had once hoped to become Lady Breckonridge," she confessed. "But now . . ."

Now she was turning to him. Rupert smiled as his

gaze lingered over the rise and fall of her breasts. "You are steadfast in your love for me?" he asked.

"Of course," she murmured, more to the rose than to him. "But you cannot expect me to wait forever."

"No, certainly not." No more would he wait. He reached down to take her hand and pull her to her feet. She gazed up at him. The innocence in those violet eyes was for once the truth. But not for long.

"I am finding it just as difficult to wait," he murmured, running his hand up her arm to her shoulder and bare neck. She shivered in obvious delight. "But first, I must have proof of your devotion to me."

She blushed. "Of course. Would you like a handkerchief to wear next to your heart? Or perhaps a lock of hair?"

Rupert pulled her close. "I had in mind a more substantial demonstration." He covered her mouth with his. She did not resist him. In fact, she leaned into the kiss, opening her mouth to let him drink of her. Loosening his hold ever so slightly, he brought up one hand to cup her breast.

She recoiled immediately, rearing back to slap him. "My lord, you ask too much!"

Her voice had turned shrill even as her eyes flashed fire. He cared less about her wounded sensibilities, but he could not allow her to betray him. Even now he felt as if eyes watched him through the rosebushes surrounding them.

"I think perhaps you should come with me," he told her, recapturing her shoulder. She flinched away from him, and he tightened his grip. Eyes widening as if she understood her danger, she yanked away from him with strength he did not know she possessed. With a sharp rip, the lace collar of her gown tore under his fingers.

"Now see what you've done," she cried, eyes tearing. "You are a beast, Rupert Wells. I will never forgive you. I will go and marry Lord Breckonridge, and it will serve you right."

She turned on her heel, and even though he sprang after her, she ran through the garden like a doe pursued by hounds. Catching a movement out of the corner of his eye, he ducked behind a statue of a Greek maiden. His heart nearly burst in his chest.

But no one came after him, nor did he hear any movement in the garden around him. After some time, he convinced himself to move away from the house and off the estate.

He had damaged his chances with the conniving Persephone. The very idea of the time wasted sickened him. Of course, it was possible she might be brought to forgive him, but he didn't think he could stomach the groveling necessary to bring that about. Yet, he had to try.

He refused to leave Somerset empty-handed.

While Sarah had been delighted in her cousin's behavior up until that fourth day, Malcolm was not so sanguine about Persephone Compton's turnaround. While, he too was pleased to see Sarah given her share of attention for once, he could not help but feel that something was wrong with Persephone that she did not protest. His impression was proved correct when he happened to stumble upon the girl returning from a walk in the garden with her eyes red-rimmed.

"Is something the matter, Miss Persephone?" he asked.

She jumped, gaze rising swiftly to his face and just as swiftly dropping. "The matter? No, no, of course not, my lord. Why would you ask?"

"I'm not used to seeing you cry, my dear," he replied gently. As he looked closer, he could not help but notice that the lace trimming on the neck of her pretty gown was torn. "I can understand why you may not wish to confide in me," he continued, concern rising. "Shall I go get your cousin?"

"No, thank you," she said. "And I'm sorry if I appeared blunt. I did not expect to find you alone. You have been spending a great deal of time with my cousin."

"That is the way it is, when one is courting," he assured her, wanting to leave no other impression.

She frowned, though her gaze was still on his toes. "It is true, then? You intend to offer for her?"

"That, Miss Persephone," he informed her, "is a matter between me and Miss Compton."

She raised her head at last, violet eyes misty with tears, rosebud lips trembling. He was certain not one of her suitors would have been able to withstand such a look and thanked God yet again that he was not in their number.

"Is there nothing I can do," she breathed, pausing to run her tongue along her perfect lips, "to convince you that this match will only bring unhappiness to you both?"

Malcolm shook his head. He knew he had a tendency to overestimate his abilities, but it didn't take arrogance to tell him the girl was indeed set on attaching him for herself. "Somehow, I do not think it is your cousin's happiness that concerns you."

She misunderstood, but on purpose or not he could not tell. "You are right, my lord. It is and always has been your happiness that interests me. While I adore Sarah, it is clear to me that she will not make you the kind of wife you need."

"I disagree," he told her quietly. "Your cousin is intelligent, capable, and likable. She is imminently suited to meet my needs."

"She is retiring, self-effacing, and plain," Persephone countered. "She is also penniless. Besides, she would be completely unhappy being Lady Breckonridge. I tell you this for her sake as well as your own. I do not want to see her hurt."

"And you think a sudden transference of my affections won't hurt?" he demanded.

She had the good sense to color. "Certainly, in the short term. But in the long term, she will thank you for it."

Malcolm shook his head again, as much at her ploys as his refusal to believe them. "Miss Persephone, I understand your position. I'm sure you find it well grounded. However, I find it totally without basis. If your cousin will have me, I mean to make her my wife. I suggest your time would be better spent preparing for her wedding than trying to prevent it. Good day."

He moved past her as she cast her gaze demurely down again, but not before he saw her eyes narrow in anger and humiliation. The emotion, however, did nothing more than register. His concern was for Sarah.

The only other surprise the first week was the arrival of Lord Wells. It was not so much that Wells would follow him to Somerset that was surprising, particularly as they had more preparations to make to ensure the Widows and Orphans Act passed next session. That Lady Prestwick would refuse to allow him entrance to Prestwick Park, however, was a shock. And that Malcolm would not even have known of it if he hadn't been passing the library was beyond anything he could have expected.

They had returned from church services in Wenwood, partaken of a light luncheon, and disbanded to change to their more casual country attire. On returning downstairs, he had heard music coming from the forward salon, which faced the drive, and, hoping to find Sarah, had gone to investigate. He was just passing the library at the foot of the grand stair when he had been stopped by Wells's unmistakable drawl.

"I simply thought to relay a message to Lord Breckonridge," he was saying with his usual coolness. "I assure you, Lady Prestwick, it was not my intention to insinuate myself into your charming little house party."

"I'm very glad to hear that, Lord Wells," the lady of the house murmured. "Because you must understand that I would not have allowed you to do so. I will make myself clear, sir. I know what you are, and you are not welcome in my home."

Malcolm frowned. He would not have thought it possible that the level-headed Lady Prestwick would be swayed by gossip. Wells deserved better than to be judged by his father's actions. Malcolm squared his shoulders, prepared to ride to the rescue, and strode into the room.

"Lady Prestwick," he began, watching with satisfaction as both the occupants of the room stiffened. The Prestwick butler, Rames, in fact, was the only one to look pleased to see him, his jowled face relaxing in obvious relief. "I beg your pardon. I thought to ask you about your plans for the evening and didn't realize you were entertaining. Good to see you, Wells."

Wells bowed. "Your servant, my lord."

"Lord Wells has an urgent message for you," Anne said, rising. "I trust you to see him to the door when you're finished."

"See him to the door?" Malcolm replied, keeping his tone light. "Surely you can spare us some time, Wells. I'm certain Lady Prestwick wouldn't mind making room for a gentleman I consider a friend."

He knew he was putting Anne in a difficult position, but was confident her good sense would allow her to realize she may have misunderstood the fellow. Wells eyed her expectantly.

To Malcolm's surprise, she straightened, raising her chin so that their gazes might meet. He had never seen her look so implacable.

"I'm afraid that won't be possible, my lord," she replied. "I'm sure Lord Wells understands the wisdom of my position. Good day, sir."

She swept from the room, leaving Malcolm to gaze after her, perplexed.

"What the devil was that all about?" he demanded.

Wells shrugged, but the bitterness in his voice belied his casual air. "What do you expect? No doubt she dislikes cowards and traitors."

"As you are neither," Malcolm informed him, "I do not see how that signifies. I will speak to her if you like."

"No!" As Malcolm frowned at his vehemence, the young man colored. "That is, I have no need of your protection, my lord. I prefer to stand on my own merits."

Malcolm nodded. "I understand. Let us speak no more about it. You said you had a message for me?"

"Yes," he said, and Malcolm had the impression he was pleased to turn the conversation onto other topics. "Lord Liverpool asked me to relay a request. It seems he is unsure how Prestwick, Wenworth, and Brentfield plan to vote on several key issues next session. As you were in their vicinity, he wondered—"

"Whether I would sound them out," Malcolm concluded. "Certainly, though I make no promises not to attempt to sway any Tory tendencies I detect. I trust you have the measures in question outlined?"

"I have," Wells replied, pulling a piece of parchment from inside his coat. As his hand moved away, Malcolm caught sight of a brace of dainty pistols clamped to the young baron's waist. Apparently Wells was serious about his duty in delivering the note, to the point of fending off highwaymen on his ride from London. On the other hand, the fellow was dressed in the dove-gray morning coat and darker trousers as befitted a cultured gentleman on a London social call. He had hardly ridden from the capital that day, which made Malcolm wonder where he had spent the night.

"Will you return to London immediately, then?" Malcolm asked, raising his head from a perusal of the paper.

"Shortly," Wells hedged. "I had some business in the area. No doubt that's what prompted Lord Liverpool to trust me with the message."

"Liverpool trusts you," Malcolm assured him. "You've proven yourself able and shrewd."

"I certainly hope so," Wells replied, reaching for his top hat on the table near the chair. "If my business goes as planned, I may give them all cause to look at me differently. Is there anything else I can do for you, my lord?"

"Tell Liverpool I'll do my best to help the cause," Malcolm replied, walking him toward the door of the library. "And assure him I'll see him in January for next session's opening."

Wells bowed. "Your servant, my lord. I hope your stay in Somerset is enlightening."

"It already has been," Malcolm assured him, leading him out of the room and across the rotunda toward the front door, where two strapping footmen stood ready. "I believe I am close to achieving my objective."

"Miss Compton has agreed to accept you then?" he asked pointedly.

"Was there any doubt?" Malcolm joked. "You should know I don't turn aside from my chosen path easily, Wells."

"Indeed," Wells drawled. "I simply assumed that as she has refused so many, even you might have trouble bringing her to heel."

Malcolm stopped, frowning. "Refused so many? What have you heard?"

"It is common knowledge, my lord," Wells replied, stopping as well and lowering his voice to keep the footmen from hearing. "Miss Persephone Compton has sent a great number of gentlemen packing. Look at His Grace, the Duke of Reddington."

Malcolm grinned, relieved. He wasn't certain he could have stood to hear that Sarah was a heartless temptress. "Don't tell me you fell for the gossip as well? Yes, I know all about Miss Persephone's escapades. It does not signify. I am courting Miss Sarah Compton."

Wells blinked, paling. "Miss Sarah Compton? Are you sure?"

Malcolm chuckled at his shock. "Quite sure. Don't look so chagrined. Even my valet had the temerity to wager against it. I will not deny that Miss Persephone is a beauty, but she cannot hold a candle to her cousin. Next time you see the two of them together, study them. You'll see I picked the right lady for me."

"Of course, my lord," Wells murmured, although Malcolm thought he still looked shaken. "I quite see what you mean. Indeed, I cannot understand why I did not see it sooner."

"It doesn't matter," Malcolm assured him. "Just believe me when I say the issue will be resolved shortly. Safe journey, Wells."

Wells bowed again and left. Pausing, Malcolm no longer heard music from the forward salon. He turned to the stairs, shaking his head. He had thought at first that Persephone's beauty was blinding everyone to his motives. If even the young baron, who knew him fairly well, thought Persephone Compton was his bride of choice, perhaps it was his own behavior that was suspect.

It was obviously time to make it clear to one and all that his Incomparable Miss Compton was Sarah.

SIXTEEN

Rupert stalked out to his waiting horse and threw himself into the saddle. He ignored the groom who stood expecting a tip for his service and drove his heels into the beast's flanks. He barely felt the jolt as the sorrel gelding broke into a gallop. All he could think was that he had failed.

Failed. The word echoed to him in the horse's pounding hooves. He had let Persephone Compton's attraction blind him to the truth. All his strategems, all his work, for nothing. He was as weak as his father after all.

No, no, never that. He reined in the gelding before they reached the bottom of the drive and urged the animal into the oak woods. No, he should not see this as failure. It was a singular defeat, to be sure, one that had cost him precious time and effort. How could he have put all his trust in that simpering tart? He grimaced as he thought of what she had driven him to. Because of her refusal to meet with him, he had had to concoct that Banbury tale about Liverpool to enter the house and see for himself what was happening. In truth, Liverpool had mentioned it was a shame Breckonridge wouldn't be working while he was rusticating, so the risk was low that he would be displeased that the fellow brought back information.

If the fellow lived to bring back information.

Could he kill Breckonridge? Rupert's spirits rose at the thought, only to crash again. It would not be easy. He had no excuse to enter Prestwick Park again. If only he hadn't made a complete fool of himself. No, not complete, he told himself as he maneuvered the horse along a game trail. They still did not know what he was about. And he now knew he had chosen the wrong Miss Compton. Unfortunately, it was too late to seduce the spinster. Besides, she would never have believed his advances and he wouldn't have had the stomach for it anyway. Dewy young debutantes were one thing. A woman past her last prayers was something else. No, he'd have to find another way.

He reached the gamekeeper's cottage and drew his horse into the lean-to beside it. He had left his valet in London, but he seemed to be just as adept at picking up gossip. Only one night at the Barnsley tavern had gotten him a wealth of information. The locals knew of the house party at Prestwick Park. They knew how much food had been delivered, how many horses were needed for the daily rides and various trips, and how many pheasants had been flushed as Breckonridge and Prestwick went hunting. While many of the details did not matter to Rupert, one was key to any future plans.

The father of the Prestwick gamekeeper lived in Barnsley and had been ill for some time. It seemed as if the poor fellow was near death's door. The gamekeeper had requested time off to take his family to visit his ailing father, and good old Lord Prestwick had been kind enough to oblige. The empty cottage was the perfect place to hide. With a spyglass he'd borrowed from a yachting-mad friend in London before the trip, Rupert was able to watch the woods. A little hill not far away allowed him a view of the front of the house as well. He knew when Breckonridge came and went. He could also follow Miss Compton's movements. But what good did it do him if he had no plan?

There had to be some way he could finish the fellow. Nothing less than total ruin and humiliation would do. Yet, death sounded like such a neat end to the entire affair. Fitting, too, for hadn't that been how he had lost his father? What a shame Breckonridge could not also be made to commit suicide.

The idea took hold, squirming in his fevered brain. His father had committed suicide to prevent disclosure of selling state secrets, a disclosure that would have spelled ruin for his family. Rupert did not believe that his father was guilty for a moment, even though it had been his mother who had tearfully related the story. No, he was certain it had been Breckonridge who had been the culprit. If his father would sacrifice himself to hide a sin, perhaps Breckonridge would do the same.

His ability to bring that about hinged on Miss Compton. She was the only leverage, the only thing Breckonridge cared about. Rupert had to get her alone. But so far when she left the house, she had usually been with someone, and as he had been watching for Persephone, he had not paid her much mind. Now, of course, he could put all his attentions on her. Sooner or later, the elder Miss Compton would go out alone.

And then he would strike.

As for Sarah, she had begun to wonder what Malcolm was about. Although she had hoped their time in the country would bring them closer together, a part of her was afraid he would badger her endlessly about his suit. Certainly his greeting the first day had been warm beyond anything. And as time went by, she'd found only comfort in his presence. Instead of an importunate lover, she had found a true friend. As lovely as that was, however, the question of his emotions still remained. He had given her no reason to suspect he had lost his heart.

She noticed a change late in the first week of their visit. It started with, of all things, a toast. In the middle of dinner, with no apparent provocation, Malcolm had risen. Lady Prestwick did not stand on ceremony—they had not dressed for dinner since the first night. Accordingly, he wore a brown wool coat and trousers, the glint of gold buttons rivaling the shine of his dark hair in the candlelight from the brass chandelier.

"Ladies, my lord," he had proclaimed in his clear, strong voice. Immediately, all conversation ceased. All heads turned to him. The footmen near the serving board along the satin-draped wall even paused in their duties.

"I would like to make a toast," he continued, raising his fine crystal goblet high. The others reached for their glasses as if mesmerized.

"To the Incomparable Miss Compton," he declared.

Persephone blushed. Sarah's heart seemed to drop into her stomach and she scolded herself for wishing he would have chosen someone else.

"The Incomparable Miss Sarah Compton," he elaborated.

Sarah started even as Persephone blinked.

"To the Incomparable Miss Sarah Compton," Lord and Lady Prestwick chorused. Sarah looked anywhere but at Malcolm. Lord Prestwick drained his glass. Lady Prestwick took a sip and set hers down with a pleased smile. Persephone did not touch hers. But they were all looking at her and she knew she was expected to say something witty in response.

"Thank you," was all she could think of.

Lord Prestwick saved her. He popped to his feet even as one of the footmen hastened forward to refill his glass. "And to Miss Persephone Compton, the reigning bell of the ton who so graciously agreed to rusticate with us."

Persephone smiled demurely, murmuring her thanks as well, but the bright spots of color on her cheeks told Sarah she felt the first toast to be a slight.

In the next few days, however, Sarah had far more to wonder over than how her cousin might react. It was as if Malcolm had finally decided to take their courtship seriously. He was never away from her side for more than a few minutes. He escorted her to her room each night and lingered over her hand. Like as not, he was waiting in the corridor to escort her to breakfast the next morning. He rode with her and Persephone each morning and took her calling each afternoon. He bragged about her intelligence, poise, and beauty to near strangers like the charming Earl of Brentfield and his lovely wife. Lady Brentfield had even evinced an interest in painting her, an offer that Sarah had blushingly refused. The countess's other paintings were the highlight of the Brentfields' extensive art collection. Sarah could not imagine her face and form hanging next to a Rembrandt.

It was even worse when they called on Norrie. It seemed he kept in constant contact with her body. His hand cupped her elbow as they climbed the steps to the great house. His thigh grazed hers as they were seated on the sofa in the withdrawing room. He was positively possessive and completely unapologetic about it.

"It reminds me of a conversation I had with Persephone," Sarah admitted to her friend when she had at last managed to get Malcolm to discuss politics with Justinian Darby, Lord Wenworth. "She claimed that the way to know whether a gentleman was truly interested is that nothing will keep him from your side. I thought it sounded rather obsessive at the time, and now I know I was quite correct." Of course, her cousin had also mentioned that the gentleman would look at her as if she were a raspberry trifle, and Sarah couldn't admit even to Norrie that she had seen several such looks on his lordship's handsome face. Her own face burned just remembering.

"He is besotted," Norrie assured her giddily. "Sarah, I could not have asked for a better match for you. Please tell me you'll let me help you plan the wedding."

"I haven't accepted him yet," Sarah scolded her. "In fact, he has not reissued his offer."

"He will," Norrie predicted with a twinkle in her eyes. "I am so happy for you! Do not come visit the Dame School today. Only send me word when you are engaged so we can celebrate."

Sarah had only smiled. In truth, she wanted to be able to celebrate, but she knew she would only be certain of her feelings when he declared his love for her. Surely he would tell her when next he proposed. Then she could set her heart free.

She did not have long to wait. A few days after their visit to Norrie, she was listening to Persephone practice the pianoforte in the forward salon. The room, like most of the others at Prestwick Park, was graciously appointed, with twin windows facing the curving drive and the afternoon sun, and gilt sconces evenly spaced along the satin-draped walls. A quartet of wingback chairs with camel legs squatted on an Oriental carpet before a white-marble fireplace. In one corner rested the black-enameled instrument, which Persephone played for long hours.

That afternoon her choice of music was particularly melancholy, but although Sarah had suggested something lighter, the girl persisted in things consigned to funerals and affairs of state. Thank goodness her cousin had not chosen to dress the part—her ruffled pink cotton gown was all that was fashionable. Sarah, in her spruce round gown, was the one who looked severe.

Sarah focused on the mending she had brought with her, trying to stitch the patterned lace evenly onto her cousin's gown where it had gotten mysteriously torn on a recent walk. Persephone had grown more composed in the country, but somehow Sarah felt she had grown farther away as well. The girl kept her own council, rarely asking Sarah's advice on anything. Their morning rides were taken in silence. Sarah had tried to talk to her cousin, but the girl had fended off each attempt with an offhand remark. She wasn't certain how to bridge the gulf that was growing between them.

She had been working for some time when she became aware of another presence. Looking up, she saw Malcolm standing in the doorway. He had taken to wearing the attire of a country gentleman, with tweed jackets and plain brown trousers. Combined with his naturally wavy hair and heavy brows, the outfits only served to make him look larger and more intimidating.

They also made him look years younger and rather fascinating. It was as if an air of danger and excitement clung to him. She had seen any number of the local ladies turn to watch him as they rode in Lady Prestwick's open carriage through the area. Looking at him now, she could easily see why.

She was certain he had been drawn to the room by her cousin's accomplished playing, yet his gaze was for Sarah alone. The warmth and invitation in it brought a blush to her cheek, and she hurriedly refocused on her sewing.

Persephone must have realized she had an audience as well, for her playing became bolder, more impassioned. The dirges gave way to a Mozart sonata of intricate design. As always, Persephone played flawlessly. When she finished, Sarah raised her head in time to see her cousin regarding Lord Breckonridge, as if for his approval. Malcolm applauded.

"An excellent rendition, Miss Persephone," he congratulated her, moving into the room with long-legged grace. "I feel quite the cur for interrupting you with a question."

Sarah felt a shock of disappointment. So, he had come for Persephone after all. Her cousin tilted her head, letting the sunlight from the windows highlight her golden curls and making Sarah feel dowdy in comparison. "A question, my lord?" Persephone breathed.

"Yes," he replied, moving closer still. "May I borrow your cousin for a few moments?"

Sarah started, then shivered as a tingle of excitement shot through her. Her delight was tempered by the anger she saw flare immediately to life in Persephone's eyes. The girl merely smiled, however, saying, "Why of course, my lord. As long as you have her back in time to help me change for dinner."

Sarah frowned, rising. What was her cousin about now? She made it sound as if Sarah were her servant rather than a member of the family, however impoverished. Besides, none of them had changed for dinner in days.

"I'm sure Lucy will be available as always," Sarah told the girl. "If you need to change, that is."

"Do you need someone to accompany you?" Persephone persisted, rising as well. "I could ring for a footman, or perhaps I could join you myself."

"That shouldn't be necessary," Sarah told her with a frown at her sudden sense of propriety.

"We will only be in the garden," Malcolm offered. "In plain view of all the east-facing windows. We shouldn't be long."

As she accepted Malcolm's arm, Sarah rather hoped they would be long, at least long enough to erase the memory of the sour look on Persephone's face as they turned away.

"Do not let her upset you," Malcolm murmured as he led her through the rotunda to the right corridor, which held glass-paned doubledoors opening to the garden. "She is just concerned."

She noted he did not say for whom her cousin was concerned, but Sarah did not need to guess. Persephone was ever concerned about Persephone. Once, when she was a child and ill, it was understandable. Sarah had found it far less excusable for some time.

They left the manor and set off along the white-rock path that wound through the Prestwick garden. The regimented shapes of some of the larger shrubs told Sarah that once this had been a formal garden. Anne

Prestwick, however, clearly had other ideas. Daisies grew in wild abandon, hollyhocks climbed so heavy with buds that they arched over the nasturtiums below. Roses stood sentinel among the green shafts of Dutch iris. Secluded paths wound through the blossoms, revealing quiet grottos here, a stone bench there. She could not think of a better place to hear a proposal of marriage.

But he did not propose, as she was sure he meant to do. Instead, he pointed out the many varieties of roses, the families of daisies, the types of hedges. He gave such a lecture in botany that she could only stare at him in amazement. Indeed, it was one of the few times she could remember ever being bored in his company. Finally, Sarah pulled him up short.

"My lord, I was raised in the country," she reminded him. "I know the difference between a rose and a hellebore. I have gathered daisies in summer. Do you have nothing more to say to me than the names of flowers?"

He paused, looking out over the bright blossoms, which scented the air with a heady perfume. "I had something to say, but I find myself unsure whether you will like it any better now than when I asked it before."

Sarah sighed. "Neither am I sure, my lord."

"My lord," Malcolm groaned. "Have we at least graduated to Malcolm and Sarah?"

"Certainly," she agreed, "my . . . Malcolm."

"Your Malcolm." He grinned at her. "I rather like the sound of that."

"Do you?" She felt herself blushing. "Somehow I would have thought that, like my cousin, you would prefer to be the owner rather than the property."

"Property? You make me sound like a slaveowner, Sarah. I led the charge to abolish that concept. No man should be another man's property."

"Agreed," she replied. "I'm sorry. I do not mean to be offensive. I've just dreaded this moment."

He led her to a bench surrounded by roses. She sat, feeling a chill even in the sun. The hum of bees busy among the flowers should have made her drowsy but she felt taut as thread on a spindle and just as tightly wrapped. If only he would say the words that would ease her heart.

"I had hoped to make you more certain of my devotion," he murmured, rubbing the petals of a bloom between his long fingers. "I seem to have failed miserably if you dread time alone with me."

"You have been a devoted suitor," she acknowledged. "I am the one lacking." She should be silent and let him get on with it, but something in her rushed to hold him off. "I have not forgotten your first proposal. I know you did not understand my reaction to it. It is just that I am so very tired of living my life in endless gratitude. I am beholden to my aunt and uncle for food and shelter, for clothing, for companionship however feeble. I am beholden to Persephone for allowing me to take part in her Season, even as a chaperon. Aunt Belle assures me I am beholden to Lord and Lady Prestwick for inviting me to their lovely home. I suppose I shall even be beholden to Lady Wenworth for offering the position in her Dame School, although at least I know that is offered from love. Can you say the same about your proposal?"

His gaze flickered to the rose. "I'm offering you my name, a place by my side. Is that not enough?"

Her heart sank. He would not say the words after

all. "I have a name," she told him. "And I have a place at Persephone's side, until she marries or tires of me. Then I have a place at Wenworth. You will have to do better than that."

He frowned. "Do you barter yourself, madam?"

"Not in the slightest. Barter implies each has something to trade." She sighed as the pain in her chest deepened. "I'm afraid you are not ready to give me anything I want."

She had deliberately thrown down the gauntlet. He regarded her seriously with his brow furrowed. She stood, waiting for his answer, feeling as if she were waiting for a death sentence. He stepped closer, capturing her gaze with his. His dark eyes pulled her in, held her, as he brought up one hand to stroke her cheek. His touch sent an ache, hungry and demanding, to the center of her being, shaking her.

"You're wrong, Sarah," he murmured, bending closer until his lips brushed hers with fire. "I can give you something your family and friends never can."

She raised her chin, silently daring him to prove it. The light in his eyes told her he accepted the challenge. He took her in his arms and kissed her.

She thought she was prepared for his kiss. Certainly she had lived through the warmth it had stirred in her before. But this time, all her resolve was swept away. From the moment he touched her, he claimed her lips. Only her lips? Her heart, her soul, was his. This closeness, this touch, *his* touch, was what she had been longing for. This warmth, this passion, this fire! How could she have ever thought this man cool? She gloried in the feel of him next to her, the sweet urgent pressure of his mouth on hers. At that moment, there was nothing she would have denied him.

It was Malcolm who broke the kiss, lifting his head while keeping her close, as if afraid she would somehow take flight. She had no intention of doing so. Her head resting against his broad chest, she marveled that she could hear the wild beating of his heart. Or was it her own heart she heard? Heaven knew it beat just as fiercely. She felt as if she'd crossed through fairy fire and left part of herself behind.

"Marry me," he growled, arms tightening. "Can you not see how perfect we are together?"

A portion of her brain not connected with her lips warned her she was being trapped. She raised her head to answer and, as if he knew he would not like the answer, he claimed her lips again. This time it was she who pulled away, head spinning.

"Tell me yes," he commanded.

"Malcolm," she started to say, only to have him stop her with another kiss that threatened to wipe away what little reason she had left.

"Tell me yes," he persisted when she could draw a breath.

"My lord," she started, and he pulled her close yet again.

He was bullying her! She could feel it. The kiss had changed from tender to demanding. This time when he stopped, she put a hand to his chest in warning. "That is enough, sir," she said sternly, annoyed at how breathy her voice sounded. "I will own that you kiss magnificently."

"Much as I hate to argue with you over such a point," he replied with a twinkle in his eyes, "I must disagree. The magnificence is in the partnering, as I knew it would be."

"Be that as it may," Sarah continued doggedly, "your kiss is not sufficient to recommend you as husband."

He raised an eyebrow, releasing her. "After that, you would refuse me?"

The part of her brain that was evidently connected with her lips protested vehemently. Her conscience shouted it down. "Don't you understand?" she begged. "I cannot, I will not, sell my life for position or power. Nor will I sell it for passion or companionship."

His frown was more perplexed than angry. "Then what do you want from me? What more can I offer?"

She felt her heart constrict as the last of her passion died away. "You still have to ask?"

He sighed. "Love. Or rather, that fickle emotion the poets call love. Can you not see that that emotion only leads to trouble? Have Persephone and her suitors taught you nothing?"

"I do not base my concept on their sorry showing," she told him, stung by his assessment. "Have you never read the Greek myths? Shakespeare?"

"The bard at least had the good sense to make most of his romances comedy," he quipped.

"What of *Romeo and Juliet?"* she challenged.

He raised a brow again. "Would you have me die to prove my love? *That* makes for a lasting marriage."

"Do not belittle me," she cried. "If I'm such an Incomparable, am I not worthy of love? Don't I deserve to have a gentleman tell me I mean the world to him? How can I trust my heart to anything less?"

"Would you have me lay my heart at your feet, then, Sarah? Wouldn't that make me as much your slave as you complained I was trying to make you?"

"If you truly loved me," she retorted, "it wouldn't matter."

"Then I can only conclude, my dear," he said, "that you are not in love with me either. If you were, by your own definition, you wouldn't care about any of this. You'd be willing to risk anything to be with me."

His logic stopped her. Was that indeed the ultimate conclusion to her reasoning? Was it after all her own heart that was lacking as she had always suspected? Frowning, she could find no answer.

"Since neither of us is in love, perhaps we can dispense with that requirement," he suggested, with a calm that only served to infuriate her. "In every other way, we are imminently suited. Marry me, Sarah. You'd have everything you want."

"Except my self-respect," she replied. "I'm sorry, Lord Breckonridge. I will not spend my life beholden to you for an offer made without love. I thank you for that very insightful demonstration, but I must stand by my decision. I cannot marry you."

SEVENTEEN

Malcolm stormed back into the great house. The woman was impossible! Every moment in her company, every look exchanged, every touch of her body to his promised him that they would be perfect together. He'd felt her passionate response to his kiss. His body still surged from it. Did she think he wouldn't notice, wouldn't care?

He took the grand stair two steps at a time and stalked down the corridor to the bedchamber he had been assigned. Love. To think that such an old-fashioned ideal stood between him and his goal. Logic he could have fought. Misperception he could have overcome. He had too much experience dealing with people to think he could easily overpower a cherished ideal like love.

He refused to lie to her, though it would have been pathetically easy. He knew any number of gilded phrases. He could have rhapsodized about his tender feelings. He could have sworn by every false god that he was her eternal servant. Certainly he'd read the Greek myths and Shakespeare. He could have quoted her verse for bloody verse. "But soft—what light through yonder window breaks—it is the east and Sarah is the sun." More likely it was Puck's comment, "Lord, what fools these mortals be." The more fool he would be to even try such a tactic.

He could not have lost. Oh, he'd suffered a bitter set back, to be sure. She probably would be twice as wary in his company. He'd have to work hard to regain her trust. But he'd suffered worse in his career and rallied. There had to be some way he could convince her. They had four full days left of the visit. They would be forced to remain in each other's company. A great deal could happen in four days. He'd ramrodded the Income Tax Abolition Act through the Lords and Commons in less time, with three-quarters against him to start. If he could win them over, surely he could win over Sarah.

He threw open the door to his bedchamber, yanking on his cravat. Striding into the room, he loosened the buttons on his vest with one hand as he shrugged out of his coat with the other. He'd change for dinner tonight. Change his clothes, change his tactics. He'd be the consummate Corinthian, the man about town, the London gentleman. He'd show Sarah Compton just the kind of fellow she was throwing away on a simple principle. She'd beg him to reconsider. He was about to shout for Appleby when a movement caught his eye.

Someone was sleeping in his bed.

He blinked. That couldn't be right. Yet, the lump under the satin coverlet was surely not from an ill-made bed. His heart sank as he recognized the golden curls cascading across the pillow. Even as he sucked in a breath, his visitor sat up, stretching daintily. Persephone Compton met his gaze, her violet eyes wide with innocence and surprise.

"My lord Breckonridge," she murmured. "Is something wrong? Has something happened to Sarah? Why have you come to my room?"

Her room? Good God, in his frustration, had he blundered into the wrong room? Hers was but a few doors down from his own on the corridor, if memory served. Heart pounding, he strode back to the door and peered out, counting the entrances from the grand stair. Turning back to her, he noticed with a rush of relief his maple-backed brush on the dresser, his teak shaving kit near the white porcelain washstand, his Bible on the bedside table.

"This," he said to Persephone, "is my room."

Her hand flew to her mouth. "Oh, dear," he heard her murmur behind it. "I was so tired, I must not have noticed. What shall we do?"

"Nothing," Malcolm replied, striding forward. "Are you dressed?"

"Dressed?" she asked, touching the coverlet.

He paused beside the bed. *God, please let her be dressed,* he prayed. She shifted under his gaze and the pink cotton sleeve of her gown showed over the top of the coverlet. He seized her slender arm to help her from the bed, confirming with further relief that she was still wearing the pink ruffled gown he had seen earlier, even if it was hideously wrinkled. He hustled her toward the door. She resisted, her fragile body surprisingly strong, but he couldn't tell whether she was resisting her removal or merely his touch.

"What are you doing?" she piped with clear confusion. "If we are caught, if anyone finds out . . ."

Malcolm paused to peer out the door again, glancing up and down the corridor. There was no one in sight.

"We have not been caught, and no one will find out," he assured her, stepping out of her way. "I promise never to breathe a word to a soul. Go, Miss Compton."

Her lower lip trembled. "Oh, my lord, you are so noble." She stood on tiptoe and gave him a daughterly peck on the cheek. Unlike Sarah's kiss a moment ago, this one did not raise his passion. All it raised was his sense of impending doom.

"I will never forget what you did for me," she assured him, eyes glowing.

Nor would he forget it if she didn't leave. Malcolm put a hand on her shoulder to force her from the bedchamber. At that moment, Appleby stepped from the dressing room, Malcolm's coat over one arm. He stared at Persephone, and Persephone stared at him. Malcolm groaned.

He shut the door to the corridor with a snap. "Appleby," he ordered, "you saw nothing."

Appleby blinked. "Nothing, my lord?"

"Nothing," Malcolm repeated.

Persephone's lower lip was trembling again, and this time her eyes brimmed with tears. "Is he trustworthy?" she begged. "How can you be certain he'll be circumspect, Lord Breckonridge? Don't servants gossip?"

"Not Mr. Appleby," Malcolm assured her, turning to scowl his man into silence. "He finds the activity morally repugnant."

Persephone wrung her hands. "Are you certain? My reputation could be ruined. I might never find a husband. I'll be damaged goods. I don't know what my poor mother will do. This will surely send her into a decline."

Another moment would see her blubbering against his neck. This would never do. Malcolm affixed his valet with a fierce eye. "Mr. Appleby will be silent as the grave, I promise you."

Appleby had the temerity to hesitate, licking his lips. "Would that constitute another addition to my duties, my lord?"

The reprobate wanted a bribe. Malcolm stiffened,

gritting his teeth, full ready to refuse. One could only take so much of this, and Appleby was drawing perilously close to that line. But one look at Persephone Compton's puckered face stopped him. The girl would raise a fuss that would bring the entire household down upon them. Even Anne would be hard-pressed not to insist that he marry the girl. He would not be trapped into marriage. He swallowed his bile, his pride, and his temper.

"Yes, Appleby," he managed through gritted teeth, "that will be another duty, for which you will be duly compensated."

Persephone gasped as if realizing the meaning of their code. Her gaze darted between them as if she could scarcely believe they would barter over her honor.

"Well compensated?" Appleby pressed.

"I will buy you a blasted estate," Malcolm spat out. "Now let the girl be gone."

Persephone pulled herself up to her full height, barely reaching Malcolm's chin. "Mr. Appleby," she said haughtily, "I am shocked by your behavior."

Malcolm could cheerfully have wrung her neck, after he was done with Appleby's, of course. "As it is my pocket he is picking, Miss Compton, I do not think it your place to bicker. Leave, for God's sake, while you can."

"A fellow must look out for himself, miss," Appleby put in with a sniff as if Malcolm had not spoken. "It is my duty to give good service where I may."

"You call this good service?" Persephone squeaked. "You are completely untrustworthy. I have a good mind to—"

"Enough!" Malcolm thundered. "Miss Compton, you will leave my room now, or I will not be responsible for the consequences."

She gulped down whatever she had been about to say to Appleby and backed hurriedly to the door. "Yes, of course, my lord. I'm so sorry. This episode is just so upsetting to me, you see, and I . . ."

Malcolm used every weapon of intimidation known to a leader in Parliament. He stood tall, puffed out his chest, squared his shoulders, knotted his fists at his sides, glared down at her, and used the voice that could project across the Commons. "Now!"

Swallowing, she flung open the door and darted down the corridor. To make sure she didn't stop until she reached her own door, Malcolm leaned out. He had the satisfaction of seeing the pink hem of her skirt disappear into her room. There was the sound of a door slamming shut. He closed his eyes and took a deep breath, releasing his tension. Proposing to Sarah was one thing. Being forced to marry Persephone Compton was quite another. He felt as if he had just escaped a firing squad. He was lucky to be alive.

He opened his eyes to find Sarah in front of him regarding him with upraised brow. He caught his breath, heart slamming into his ribs.

"Care to explain why my cousin just left your bedchamber, my lord?" she asked coolly. He could see the icy gray in her eyes. She was furious, but with himself or Persephone he wasn't sure.

Nor did it seem to matter, for his own temper was rising again.

"No, Miss Compton," he replied. "I do not care to explain. If you're so blasted interested, go ask your cousin. Good day, madam."

And he had the momentary satisfaction of shutting the door in her open-mouthed face.

EIGHTEEN

This had to be the worst afternoon of her life, Sarah reflected as she made her way to her cousin's bedchamber. First, Malcolm had proved he could be the perfect husband, then he had refused to honor her ideals of love and proved he could never be her husband at all. She had taken a brief walk about the garden in a vain attempt to calm herself, only to return upstairs in time to see Persephone slip from his room. Her mind informed her they could not possibly have had time to do anything compromising, but the very fact that the girl was in his room was enough to set tongues wagging. Not only had Sarah lost the man she loved, but she had failed in her duty as chaperon.

She froze in the act of knocking on the door. She did feel as if she'd lost the man she loved. She had been so afraid that her heart was lacking; she had been wrong. Malcolm had accused her of having feelings as shallow as his, but he was quite wrong as well. She was capable of a deep and abiding love; she simply trusted few people enough to show it. If she were not very much mistaken, her love was now entirely bound up with that impossible Parliamentarian down the corridor. Her heart sank as quickly as it had risen. Knowing he held love so cheaply, how could she have been so stupid as to give him hers?

She wanted nothing more than to turn to her own room across the corridor and collapse on her bed to think. But she could not abandon Persephone. Inside the room before her, she heard what sounded suspiciously like crying. For all her cousin had done recently, Sarah still loved her as well. Her own emotions would have to wait. She raised a hand and tapped on the door.

"Persy, it's me," she called. At the mumbled permission to enter, she opened the door. Her cousin lay sprawled across the cream satin coverlet of the walnut four-poster bed, head buried in her arms. As Sarah crossed the Oriental carpet to her side, steeling herself to hear the worst of it, Persephone heaved herself up to sit and stare at her.

"What happened?" Sarah asked gently.

Persephone swallowed the last of her tears. "I take it you saw me."

"Yes," Sarah replied, going to sit in the rose-colored armchair near the fire so as not to appear to hover over the girl. She said no more, waiting for Persephone to speak. Her cousin merely sat staring at the white marble of the fireplace beyond Sarah.

"Well," she said at last with a terseness that surprised Sarah, "what do you intend to do about it?"

Sarah frowned. "Perhaps if you told me what 'it' is, I could tell you my plans. How did you come to be in Lord Breckonridge's bedchamber, Persy?"

Her cousin waved a hand airily. "I was tired. I came upstairs to nap before dinner and I must have chosen the wrong room."

"The wrong room?" Sarah's frown deepened. "But surely Lady Prestwick has not done all these rooms in an identical manner. My room is done in blues and greens with Sheraton furnishings, while yours is in cream and rose in the Queen Anne style. Surely Lord Breckonridge's room is another color and style as well. How could you fail to notice?"

"I told you," she snapped. "I was tired."

Sarah decided not to pursue the argument. She hated the idea that was forming in her mind. Persephone could not be so manipulative as to arrange the ruin of her own reputation, particularly with a gentleman who had shown a marked preference for Sarah. There had to be another explanation.

"Very well," she allowed. "You were so tired you failed to notice the room was not yours. I take it you fell asleep?"

Persephone nodded solemnly. "I awoke when I heard the door opening, thinking it was Lucy come to help me dress for dinner. When I saw it was Lord Breckonridge, I thought he had come to tell me something had happened to you."

"And what did Lord Breckonridge do?" Sarah prompted, almost afraid to hear. Yet, surely a gentleman of Malcolm's good sense would not take advantage of finding a lovely young woman like Persephone in his bedchamber.

"He was all that is good and kind," Persephone enthused. "He assured me of his silence, and he bribed his servant not to gossip."

"Indeed," Sarah replied, unsure how to react. Part of her was pleased Malcolm had been so levelheaded as to spot the danger to her cousin and himself. Another part frowned at the idea of a bribe. Was there something that required covering up? "What exactly did he have to pay his servant for? You were only found there by accident."

"Oh, most assuredly," Persephone agreed with enthusiasm. "But still, if people were to find out, my reputation would still be damaged, wouldn't it?"

The girl sounded positively wistful! Sarah stared at her. "Persy, you cannot want that!"

"No, of course not, silly," she replied with a giggle. "Not if I were still on the marriage mart. But Lord Breckonridge is such a gentleman. I'm certain he'll ask Papa for my hand if rumors start flying."

Sarah rose to her feet, blood firing. "If rumors fly, Persy, I'll know where they came from."

"Lord Breckonridge's valet," Persy said sagely.

"No, Persy, from you. Do you honestly think you have hidden your scheme? You are as transparent as the glass in Lady Prestwick's greenhouse."

Persephone tossed her head. "I'm sure I have no idea what you're talking about."

"Oh, yes, you do," Sarah told her, nearly trembling with the enormity of it. "You tried to ensnare Lord Breckonridge."

Persephone gave a laugh, high and bitter. "How silly! I have dozens of suitors. Why would I need to ensnare anyone?"

"Because for some unknown reason you've fixed upon him," Sarah replied, sure of herself. "From the first you wanted him for yourself, Persy. I thought you'd given that up, but it's clear that clever mind of yours just took another course. Well, I won't have it. I will not let you force him into marriage."

"I am not forcing him," Persephone declared, hopping off the bed to face her. "I was caught in a compromising situation, and he is being a gentleman."

"You have explained that nothing happened," Sarah reminded her. "He has no need to be a gentleman."

"That is for him to decide," Persephone informed her, stalking to the wardrobe. "Now, if you'll excuse me, I should change for dinner."

"I warn you, Persephone," Sarah threatened, "do not attempt to pursue this. I will stand by his side, against Aunt Belle, against Uncle Harold, against the world if need be."

"Oh!" Persephone turned and glared at her. "I believe you are jealous, Sarah! You refuse to marry him, and you can't stand anyone else to do so. You are petty and vindictive and *that* is what *I* shall tell Mother and Papa."

Sarah felt a sliver of fear, but she forced it away. It was not her concerns that mattered, but Malcolm's future. "You may tell them anything you like. I know the truth in my heart. It will sustain me."

"Oh, indeed," Persephone gibed. "Can you eat truth, I wonder? Can you put it over your head to keep off the rain when you have no other home? Think carefully, Sarah. When I am married to the most powerful man in England, I can afford to be gracious."

"You could be gracious now if you wanted," Sarah said quietly. "I don't imagine more power will improve you. What happened, Persephone? You were such a sweet child once."

"How dare you say that to me!" Persephone snarled, forcing Sarah back a step with her vehemence. "You didn't like that child. You couldn't wait to pack her off so that you could have the manor all to yourself."

Sarah stared at her. "What are you talking about?"

"You abandoned me!" Persephone accused her. "You forced Mother to send me away to that horrid school. Why would you do that if not to have her all to yourself?"

"I thought you would *like* school," Sarah told her. "I know I liked it after I grew used to it. You had to be so much by yourself growing up. You deserved a chance to be with other girls your age."

Persephone's face was puckered. "Did you really mean it for good? It was awful! No one did anything I wanted. My wishes meant nothing. They laughed when I complained. They laughed at me, Sarah!" Her lower lip trembled. Sarah took a step toward her, and the girl recoiled.

"No, do not attempt to tell me it will be all right. I will *make* it all right. I'll show them. I'm not spoiled! I'm not weak. I'm not any of those vicious names they called me. I'll have the very best husband in England. They will all have to come to me to beg for favors."

"Oh, my poor dear," Sarah murmured. "I'm truly sorry, Persephone. I had no idea. I thought you liked it at school. I can see they hurt you deeply, but dearest, do you hear yourself? You despise these girls for their cruelty, but do you plan better?"

Persephone blinked and for a moment Sarah thought she would relent. Instead, her face tightened so that she looked years older. "I knew you wouldn't understand. You have no idea what it's like to have your dreams thwarted."

Sarah felt as if she had been stabbed in the heart. "I don't know?" she cried, hand to her chest to hold in the pain. "*I* don't know? Are you blind? Think about my life, Persephone. Better, think of your threat to me a moment ago. How would you like to live your life with nothing to call your own? How would you like to live with the constant reminder of how much you owe everyone?"

Persephone stared at her, face paling. Sarah thought

she saw a new light spring to her cousin's tearful eyes. "I guess we're not so different after all, Cousin," she murmured. "All those years when I was sick, I did feel like everyone was constantly reminding me of how much I needed them. They all had to cater to me, and I hated it."

"But I suspect you grew accustomed to it," Sarah put in. "When no one would cater to you at school, I would think that must have been a very rude awakening."

"I had to prove I was somebody after all," Persephone agreed.

Sarah shook her head, feeling tears threaten. "Oh, Persy, you were always somebody. I shall always love you as the sister I never had."

"You can say that even now?" Persephone all but begged. "Sarah, I've said some awful things, done some awful things."

"Nothing that can't be fixed, I trust," Sarah encouraged her.

Persephone hung her head. "Perhaps. I am sorry for treating you like an enemy, Sarah. Maybe it's possible for us to grow closer again. But I fear I've made a mull of things. I treated my suitors abominably. It only took one of them to lose his head to see that."

Sarah felt a chill. "Who lost his head?" she demanded. "Persephone, are you all right?"

Persy nodded. "It was terrible, Sarah. I should never have encouraged him. But it's over now. I see him for what he is. I will tell you more about it another time, but right now I fear I have ruined Lord Breckonridge."

Sarah's unease only grew. "How so? You said he was the complete gentleman."

"He was," Persephone agreed. "His valet was not.

I gave him all my pin money so he would let me in the room and promise to gossip afterward."

"Oh, Persy, you didn't!"

"I did," Persephone murmured. "You were quite right to accuse me of being a conniving little tart."

"I'm sure I never said any such thing," Sarah scolded, although she knew she had been thinking it. "But Persy, you must rectify matters."

Her cousin looked thoughtful. "Perhaps if I tell the valet I've changed my mind."

Sarah shook her head. "If he was willing to be bribed the first time, he will most likely ask for more money this time."

"You are right," Persephone said in a hopeless voice. "And I have nothing more with which to pay him. And even if I do pay him, he'd no doubt come after me again expecting to blackmail me."

"I see nothing for it, love," Sarah told her. "You will have to face Lord Breckonridge with what you did."

Persephone paled. "There must be another way. You are clever, Sarah. Think of something."

Sarah regarded her with pity. "I'm sorry, love, but it appears you are out of options. You said you were tired of being beholden. Look at this as a chance to stand on your own."

"Small comfort," Persephone replied with a bitter sigh. "Might I at least do it in private?"

Sarah eyed her. "Certainly. I will look for an opportunity for you to do so. But Persy, if I find that you use that opportunity to Lord Breckonridge's disadvantage, I will not be shy about denouncing you."

Persephone reddened. "I understand. Do you love him, then?"

Sarah felt a renewed ache. "That matters not," she

said primly. "What matters is that Lord Breckonridge not be forced into marriage."

"I suppose so," Persy replied, but Sarah did not think she sounded convinced. "But, Sarah, I must know. Do you intend to accept his suit? Because if you don't, I see no reason not to continue to attempt to attract his regard. In honest ways," she hastily added.

Sarah bit her lip. Could she sit by and watch while Persephone pursued Malcolm? True, he had never shown any attraction to the girl, but that was before Sarah had rejected him yet again. And there was a very good chance that once he heard what her cousin had tried to do, he would want nothing more to do with the girl. On the other hand, there was the slight possibility that he would find her attempts flattering and be willing to enter a courtship. Could Sarah chaperon while they drove in the park, whispered endearments to each other, kissed? Her stomach knotted at the very thought. Yet, Persy was right: if Sarah was unwilling to accept him, she had to accept the fact that he would eventually find another woman to court.

But not Persephone.

"Think carefully, Cousin," she told the girl. "I see no reason you would be happy in the match. He does not believe in love. Find someone you love, Persy, not someone whose power you envy."

Persephone frowned. "Do you think I cannot love him then?"

"Oh, no," Sarah replied, hearing her own voice turn bitter. "No, he is all too easy to love, with his zeal to see his country safe and prosperous, his gilded tongue to persuade, the way his very hair glows as if with suppressed energy. He is the lightning of the storm and the thunder behind it. What woman would not love such a man?"

"You *do* love him, don't you," Persephone asked, wide-eyed.

"God help me," Sarah said, "but I do. And I have no idea what to do about it."

NINETEEN

Malcolm wasn't sure he wanted to go down to dinner that evening. On the one hand, there was a likely chance that Persephone Compton was lying in wait for him, perhaps with the local magistrate in tow. He was sure she had the banns all ready to hand to the local minister for reading. He didn't believe the girl's act of innocence for a moment. Not that he had lovely young ladies hide in his bed on a regular basis, but he did realize it was an often-used ploy to force a fellow to the altar. He had no idea why someone as popular as Persephone would want to try it, but he simply wasn't willing to play the victim.

On the other hand, he was certain he wasn't ready to face Sarah. He had had to face adversaries from Parliament many times across a dining table. He knew how to keep a smile on his face when his insides churned. He even knew how to graciously admit defeat. He simply wasn't ready to do so. Yet, he also could think of no logical next step in his campaign to win Sarah's hand.

Persephone's appearance in his room would only make matters more difficult. He was certain Sarah knew him well enough that she would not suspect him of harming her cousin in any way. On the other hand, if the girl persisted in claiming otherwise, Sarah would have no choice but to protect her cousin's reputation. Either way Malcolm looked at it, he was sunk.

But he could hardly ask for a tray to be sent to his room as if he were a doddering dowager down with dyspepsia. He would have to face them. The most he could hope for was that either Lord or Lady Prestwick would support him. And he rather thought he was done for if it were only Chas.

Appleby said little as he helped his master change. Indeed, he seemed to have taken Malcolm's orders to be silent entirely too much to heart. Malcolm had seldom seen the fellow look more Friday-faced.

"I'd think you would be pleased with yourself," he remarked as his valet finished an unsatisfactory knot in his cravat. "You managed to extract yet more money from me for your work. Or are you having second thoughts about that bribery?"

Appleby licked his lips, gaze darting everywhere but Malcolm's face. "Bribery, my lord? To what do you refer?"

"One would almost think you were accepting bribes from more than one person," Malcolm mused. He was half in jest; if he thought Appleby had so betrayed him, the fellow would not be standing in his presence.

"Certainly not, my lord," Appleby intoned, but his hands shook as he took away the two failed attempts at a cravat. "However, I beg my lord to remember that I have served him faithfully for many years. Surely I can be trusted, despite what any others might say."

"Surely you can," Malcolm replied, narrowing his eyes. "Because if you can't, you will no longer be employed."

Appleby paled, but Malcolm had no more time for

discussion. If he waited any longer, he would be late. And he didn't want to give anyone that satisfaction.

Their hosts had been having everyone gather in the forward salon before going in to dinner each evening. As he had expected, Malcolm found the Misses Compton as well as Lord and Lady Prestwick awaiting him. Standing in a group near the fireplace, they broke off conversation as he entered, heightening the sense that he had become the enemy. Anne, however, was all smiles as he approached.

"Good evening, my lord," she said as he bowed to the group. Straightening, he could not help noticing that both Persephone's and Sarah's eyes were red-rimmed. He rather hoped Persephone's tears had been caused by a fit of conscience. He didn't like to think what had caused Sarah's.

"Good evening," he replied to Anne, managing to include them all in his nod. "I hope I haven't kept you waiting."

"I'm sure none of us would be happy at dinner without you, my lord," Persephone put in. Sarah sent her a quelling glance, which made the girl color. So, some confidences had been exchanged, but what exactly he could not tell.

"Well said, Miss Persephone," Chas cheered. "Though Malcolm, you mustn't think I mind being the only gentleman surrounded by such charming ladies."

Anne smiled fondly at him, rising to take his arm, even as Persephone's color deepened. Sarah's smile at the compliment was strained. Malcolm thought Anne murmured something to her husband, for Chas turned to offer his other arm to Sarah. She hesitated only a moment before accepting it with a polite nod. Malcolm had no choice but to offer his arm to Persephone.

He wondered whether this gesture would encourage the girl, but if anything she looked more uncomfortable as they crossed the rotunda for the dining room.

"May I have a moment of your time later, my lord?" she asked so quietly he had to bend nearer to hear her. "I promise not to be impertinent."

"Very well," Malcolm agreed, thankful that he could hand the girl to her seat and escape to the other side of the table.

Unfortunately, there was no escape to be had. For all meals during the visit, Anne had seated him between Chas at the head of the table on his right and Sarah on his left. He had rather hoped he could count on Chas to keep the conversation flowing. Unfortunately, his host seemed obsessed with the conversation his wife was having with Persephone on her right. Malcolm tried concentrating on the food, which included a beef ragout that was excellent, but it seemed to him he could hear the silence on his side of the table even over the chime of his silver fork on the bone china.

He busied himself by mentally listing the acts yet to the brought to the floor next session and calculating their chances of success. He'd been to the next estate to see Brentfield and thought he knew how the fellow would vote, but Wenworth, whom they'd met last week, was still noncommittal. He'd have to see whether he could convince Prestwick to have a word with the fellow. Of course, it would be a lot easier if Sarah could talk to her friend the Countess of Wenworth. Wenworth was obviously as doting a husband as Chas. In fact, he'd have said the same about Brentfield and his charming artist wife. What was it about the Somerset countryside that bred such intimate marriages?

And why wasn't his to be one of them?

At length, he became aware that the silence had stretched. Sarah sat with head bowed, pushing her food about the plate. She was miserable, and he had caused it. Impulsively, he slid his foot until he pressed against hers under the table. She glanced up at him with a start.

"Forgive me," he murmured. "I wish I knew what to say to bridge this widening gulf between us."

She smiled ruefully, the silver misery in her eyes melting to blue. "If I've put you at a loss for words, this is indeed a gulf. But surely we are both of a mature nature and can overcome it, my lord."

"The very fact that you are back to calling me 'my lord' should prove to you the truth of the matter," Malcolm replied.

She shook her head. "Very well, Malcolm. I've been doing a great deal of thinking about this. All emotions aside, we simply have chosen to disagree. I imagine that happens fairly frequently in your vocation."

"Certainly," he acknowledged, feeling himself relax now that emotions were not part of the conversation. "But, then, several hundred of my closest friends civilly discuss the matter and vote on it, and we are bound by their decision."

She made a face. "I would not like my private life run in such a manner."

"Nor would I," he assured her. Sharing her smile, he felt something constrict in the vicinity of his heart. They shared thoughts as easily as smiles, and kisses more easily still. "I wish I knew how to change your mind," he murmured.

She reached out and touched his hand, a fleeting gesture, hastily withdrawn, yet surprisingly comforting. "Perhaps you can. You know my stance, Malcolm. And I know yours. Give me time to think. Who knows, perhaps I can change *your* mind."

She returned her gaze to her food but he found little of interest in his. She had no idea what she suggested. He had worked too hard, come too far, to place anyone or anything before his work. It was a vocation, really. He thought of the great men of history he admired—Alexander the Great, Constantine, Jesus. They had been focused on a goal, and their personal lives, whether married or not, did not distract them. If he fell in love, wouldn't he lose all? He shook his head. Sarah was right—the one thing she wanted he could not give.

Chas chose not to linger over their gentlemanly discussion following dinner, so that Malcolm was not even given that reprieve to think. They rejoined the ladies in the forward salon, listening while Persephone played a series of airs on the pianoforte. Sarah sat next to Anne on one of the chairs nearby. As Malcolm watched, Chas walked up behind his wife and placed a hand on her shoulder. His thumb tenderly grazed her ear. Anne's hand came up to rest on his, holding him against her. Malcolm felt a stab of longing. How easily could he imagine such tenderness with Sarah. How difficult it was to imagine such a scene with any other woman. He was truly trapped.

Persephone finished playing and Sarah and Anne argued good-naturedly as to who would entertain the company next. Malcolm could see the struggle in Chas. On the one hand, he clearly wanted Sarah to play so he could continue to stand beside his wife. On the other hand, he just as clearly longed to show off his wife's talents. At last, Anne agreed to play. As she went to the instrument, Persephone made her way across the room to Malcolm's side. He stiffened, but she did not turn away.

"I must apologize to you, my lord," she murmured, eyes downcast.

Malcolm crossed his arms over his chest. "About what, Miss Persephone?" he asked, even though he suspected what she was about to confess.

"I attempted to force you to ask for my hand," she replied in the same low voice. He had to admit she sounded suitably humble, but he could not be sure of her sincerity.

"And why would a young lady who is the toast of the ton need to do such a thing?" he asked.

She seemed to shrink even further into herself. "Please, my lord, do not make this more difficult for me. I had my reasons, and I realize they were wrong. The only reason to marry is for love. I knew that; I had simply forgotten."

"I would wager you have your cousin to thank for the reminder," he surmised.

"And my own heart," she assured him. "But there is something else you must know. I had help invading your privacy. Mr. Appleby accepted money from me to let me in and ensure others knew about it afterward."

Malcolm felt himself chill. So, Appleby had become greedy. Or had he? Could Malcolm believe the girl even in this? "Did he indeed?" he murmured with little conviction.

She nodded. "So you can see why I was so angry when he then asked you for more money to remain silent."

That wasn't the only thing Malcolm saw. Despite himself, he heard a ring of truth in the girl's story. Appleby's uneasiness that evening suddenly made sense. He had been afraid of just such a scene as this. He knew how Malcolm felt about treachery. Malcolm had warned him against it from the beginning. Friendly gossip was one thing. Selling his privacy was quite another.

"What will you do, my lord?" she asked, lifting her head at last to eye him solemnly.

"About you, Miss Persephone?" he returned. "Nothing. It would appear to me that your natural tendency toward goodness triumphed over your momentary lapse in good sense. Pray you do not let it happen again."

She shook her head. "Oh, no, my lord. I've learned my lesson. What about Mr. Appleby, though? How do we know he will be discreet?"

"Leave Mr. Appleby to me," Malcolm replied. "He has a comeuppance due. Now, dare I hope you will favor us with another song?"

She shook her head again, blushing. "I think I will retire, my lord. May I beg your escort to my room?"

She may have confessed, but he still did not trust her by half. He refused to allow himself to be entrapped again. "If rumors fly despite our efforts, it will do us no good to be seen alone together. I'm sure you understand."

She nodded, bidding him good night, then went to take her leave of Sarah and their hosts. Her desultory manner apparently affected everyone's mood, for it was relatively easy for Malcolm to make his excuses shortly thereafter.

His own mood was far from good when he saw that

Appleby was waiting for him in his room. The valet moved forward to help him undress, and Malcolm held up a hand to stop him.

"Is something wrong, my lord?" Appleby asked humbly.

"Yes, Appleby," Malcolm replied, "there is. You've been very helpful in relaying gossip."

Appleby cocked his head. "But, sir, that is what you asked me to do."

"It was," Malcolm agreed, moving into the room. "And for that I bear part of the blame. However, I never expected you to be so blasted good at it."

"Thank you, my lord," Appleby replied.

"That wasn't a compliment," Malcolm assured him. "However, let me return the favor. Rumor has it, Appleby, that you betrayed me. You put your monetary desires above my privacy."

Appleby's tongue flicked out to lick his lips, and Malcolm wondered why he had never noticed how much like a snake the fellow was. "I have not heard such rumors, my lord," his valet replied.

"Haven't you?" Malcolm stepped closer, arms loose. Appleby apparently recognized the boxer's stance, for he scuttled back so quickly he fetched up against the dresser with a yelp.

"Let me tell you some other rumors you will not hear," Malcolm persisted, closing the gap. "You will not hear that Persephone Compton found her way into my bedchamber. You will not hear that I refused to marry her. Above all, you will not hear anything that would cause Miss Sarah Compton any embarrassment or pain. Do you understand me?"

"Certainly, my lord," Appleby squeaked. "And may

I say that your pay is certainly sufficient to keep me from hearing or repeating any such rumors."

"No, I'm afraid it isn't," Malcolm replied. "You see, you may spend the night with the other servants here at Prestwick Park, but I want you out of the house before lunch tomorrow. You will not get another cent from me and you will not get a letter of referral. I'm afraid money can no longer be an incentive for your silence. Since loyalty never was, you will have to make do with fear."

Appleby blinked, then flinched as Malcolm leaned closer. "F . . . f . . . f . . . fear, my lord?"

"Fear, Mr. Appleby. You know the power I hold in this country. That alone should be sufficient. And if it isn't, remember that if I ever connect you with rumors about me or anyone associated with me, I will cheerfully beat you to a bloody pulp. And that, sir, is no rumor. Now, get out of my sight before I change my mind about indulging my savage streak."

White-faced, Appleby flew from the room.

Malcolm shook his head. Sarah had accused him of not being able to show his emotions. Apparently it was only the tender mercies he lacked. He managed intimidation just fine.

It was a blasted sad thing to say about a fellow.

TWENTY

Sarah didn't get much time to herself until she retired for the night. Oh, she had indulged in a brief bout of tears right before dinner, but it had not been nearly enough to ease her tensions. She thought she had acquitted herself well at dinner, however, speaking to him as if they were the friends she had hoped they'd be. She had been calm and composed, the very picture of a lady. She was quite glad to escape to her room and throw the pillows against the wood-paneled walls.

That didn't help, of course. The problem was a great deal deeper than could be fixed by a momentary fit of pique. She loved Malcolm Breckonridge, and he did not love her. Allowing herself to fall in love with him was a terrible mistake, but as she had not seen it coming, she supposed she could not have prevented it. There only remained to be seen what she could do about it now.

The choices seemed clear. Despite her calm words at dinner, she could refuse to have anything more to do with him and suffer the pain of losing his friendship. She could remain friends but continue to refuse to marry him and watch a part of her die when he turned to another woman to be his wife and the mother of his children, as he would have to do. Or she could forget the fear that held her heart closed and marry him. She thought she would make him a good wife, and she would have his companionship. It was possible he might someday grow to love her. It was also possible that he would realize his marriage was less than ideal and grow to hate her. He might even fall in love with another, but be unable to wed. In a way, wasn't marrying him without his love as much entrapment as Persephone hiding in his room?

She could not answer the question, or the others that buzzed around in her head. Consequently, she did not fall asleep until late and slept badly. She awoke with just enough time to don her riding habit for her ride with Persephone, if she missed breakfast entirely. She considered telling the girl she was unwell. Certainly she felt no better than when she had gone to bed. But a glance out the window showed the beginnings of a lovely summer's day. Surely fresh air and sunshine would improve her mood. She went to retrieve her cousin, and the two of them proceeded to the stables.

After over a week at Prestwick Park, she and her cousin were a well-known sight to the Prestwick grooms. Old Dobbs, the head groom, always managed a grin for her, assuring her again that the mare she had been riding was the sweetest-tempered mount in all the magnificent stables. Sarah didn't have the heart to tell him she had been riding since she was a child and could easily have handled the more massive thoroughbreds she could see in the various stalls. She would even have liked to try her hand at the brute of a stallion Lord Prestwick liked to ride, especially today. With her mood, she would have loved nothing better than to pelt down the drive instead of riding sedately along the wide riding path that wound its way through the oak woods surrounding the park. But Dobbs led out the dappled gray mare he had given her all week, and she could only smile politely into his grizzled face. At least she would be able to keep up with Persephone, whose roan gelding was only slightly more spirited.

They set off on the path through the woods, the trees arching overhead to form a tunnel of green and brown. A squirrel scampered away in front of them. A gentle breeze danced among the oaks, setting the leaves to chattering. But while the day was indeed splendid, Sarah soon found that the company was less than inspiring.

Persephone had apparently spent the night examining her conscience and wanted nothing more than to confess each and every one of her sins. She proceeded to tell Sarah every tiny unknown bothersome thing she had ever done. These included the time she had taken the last of the iced cakes when she'd known Aunt Minnie had wanted it and the time she had hidden the shears from her mother so she would not have to have her hair trimmed. These escapades came as no surprise to Sarah. Indeed, Sarah could have added any number of slights and unkindnesses her cousin had inflicted on the family in the last few years. What did surprise Sarah was how unwilling she was to relive them. Each story only served to push her farther into her bad mood, as if reinforcing all the things she disliked about her current life. She felt as if she wanted to scream. She could only imagine how their groom, Roberts, trailing a respectful distance behind, liked the reminiscing ride.

"Persy," she ventured after nearly a half hour of the stories, "I understand your aim. You obviously want to return to the days when you were a sweeter person. I think that's a marvelous decision. Couldn't we just forget the rest of the self-recrimination and simply resolve to do better next time?"

"I don't see how," her cousin stated blithely. "I need to see the full depth of my depravity before I can change it."

"Very well," Sarah snapped. "Accept that you are utterly lost. A full cataloging would be excessive."

Persephone was silent for a moment as if considering her words, and Sarah sighed in relief. They rode through the wood, the dappled sunlight filtering through the green of the leaves, birds calling in the distance. Sarah began to relax.

"I think I should atone," Persephone announced. "I should do some heroic act to make up for my misdeeds."

Sarah managed a polite smile. "Simply living a good life might be heroic enough," she suggested.

"No," her cousin replied, and Sarah could hear the pout in her voice. "No, I must do more. I must right the wrongs I've done."

Sarah sighed. "Very well. You may give Aunt Minnie the entire plate of iced cakes the next time she visits."

"That," Persephone told her with a sniff, "is the very least of the things for which I should atone. No, I know what I must do. Sarah, I will not rest until you are married to Lord Breckonridge."

Sarah clutched the reins so hard her very docile horse balked. Their groom pulled up short to keep from running into her. Persephone passed her and had to turn her mount in a circle to join her again.

"Persephone," Sarah scolded when her cousin drew abreast once more, "that is nonsense. There is no need for you to meddle in my affairs."

Persephone made a face. "I am not meddling, and

you are being too noble. I know your difficulties are my fault. I swear, Sarah, I did not know you loved him. Indeed, I never suspected someone like you could fall in love."

Sarah choked. "What do you mean, someone like me?"

"Someone older, more sedentary," Persephone said, obviously unaware of the havoc she wreaked with Sarah's feelings. "Mother said you never had a single admirer during your Season. As you are quite pretty and capable of being charming when you assert yourself, I assumed you simply didn't care for gentlemen."

"I had admirers," Sarah told her, hearing the pout now in her own voice but powerless to stop it. "Not as many as yours, but there were some. I was simply scared to death of them. It took me a while to become this older sedentary person, you know. I might have done all right in London if Aunt hadn't insisted on rushing home."

"To me," Persephone concluded. "Because I was sick. You see? I knew it was my fault."

"For God's sake, Persy," Sarah exclaimed, "it was no one's fault. Life simply turned out differently than any of us had planned. Do you think I expected to be an orphan? Do you think I expected to be your chaperon during your Season? Things happen. Leave it alone."

"I cannot," Persephone replied plaintively. "I must make it up to you. You were always there when I needed you, Sarah. I see that now. And I've been hideously ungrateful. But I will help you, I swear. I'll go to Lord Breckonridge and explain that you love him and—"

"You will do no such thing!" Sarah reined in her horse, forcing Persephone and Roberts to stop as well. "Do you hear me, Persephone Compton? You will say nothing to Lord Breckonridge concerning my regard for him or lack thereof. When I decide what to do about the matter, I will face him. Until then, you are to stay away from him, do you hear me?"

Persephone frowned. "But Sarah—"

"But me no buts, young lady. You are not so old that I cannot put you over my knee and paddle you!"

Persephone tossed her head. "You wouldn't dare!"

"Do not tempt me."

Her cousin glared at her. "Well, I like that. Here I am willing to sacrifice myself on your behalf and you dare to threaten me. I do not have to listen to this. I'm going back and write to Mother this instant. See if I do *you* any more favors, Miss Sarah Compton." She wheeled the horse and spurred it into a gallop.

Sarah closed her eyes. A more childish display she could not have found, and she had been the one to be the child. Sighing, she opened her eyes to find Roberts regarding her warily.

"Should I go after her, Miss Sarah?" he asked.

Sarah waved him on. "Yes, Roberts. She's liable to pitch herself from the saddle. I'll follow behind, more slowly. Perhaps that will give us both time to reflect."

Roberts touched his forelock in salute and turned to canter after Persephone. With another sigh, Sarah turned her mount as well and headed back toward the stable.

What had she come to, she wondered as the mare plodded along. She had lamented Persephone's self-centeredness. If the girl was sincere in wanting to change, Sarah should encourage her. She was evidently not as mature as her cousin named her. All it took was a mention of her own Season, when she was a frightened little girl who couldn't utter a sentence to a handsome gentleman at a London ball, and she lost all reason. Even now it hurt to admit she had not been wanted.

She had hoped it might be different with Malcolm. She had not realized how much she wanted to love and be loved until she had met him. He had indeed been a wonderful suitor. From the first he had been honest with her. It would have been easy for him to pretend he loved her merely to get her to agree with him. Certainly she would never have known the difference.

Or would she have known? What, after all, was the difference between the way a man in love treated his lover and the way Malcolm treated her? He was attentive, he was considerate, he was certainly passionate. He made her feel as if she were the most important person in his world, a fairly tall order when one considered the world in which he lived. She could not imagine a husband in love treating her better. Had she let her childhood ideals and her wounded heart color her view? How could one be loved, after all, without loving first?

The woods around her had grown as silent as her arguments. She had been a fool. In his own way, Malcolm had proved he cared for her. She had demanded something that was not in his nature to give, and so had hurt him badly. At the very least, she should apologize. Then, if he still wanted to marry her, she was ready to agree to be his bride. She urged the gray into a canter around the next bend.

Only to pull the horse to a stop when she found Lord Wells on foot in front of her.

"Miss Compton," he said, sweeping her a bow. "I've been waiting for you."

Her blood turned cold. "What is it, Lord Wells? Has something happened to Lord Breckonridge?"

He smiled sadly. "Not yet, I fear. But, with your help, it soon will."

And that was the last thing he said to her before pulling a pistol from his coat.

TWENTY-ONE

Malcolm was disappointed to find that Sarah was not at the breakfast table. He had gotten used to seeing her every morning before her ride. He too had had a difficult night, going over and over her argument, trying to find the flaw. Any argument built on emotions must have a flaw. He had reached no conclusions, but had awoken determined not to let her go. He would keep fighting until she gave in. To find no one with whom to debate had quite taken the wind out of his sails.

He had never felt so ill at ease in his life as that morning as he wandered about the great house waiting for her to return. He had debated going after her, but she would be with Persephone, and he was in no mood to share her attentions. He ended up in the library, thumbing through the books thronging the shelves, picking up one after another, seeing none of them, listening only for the front door. When it slammed a half hour later, he fairly ran into the rotunda to intercept her, only to come face to face with Persephone.

That the girl was furious, her brow knit, her mouth pouting, barely registered, so great was his disappointment not to find Sarah with her. She didn't bother to curtsy, but put her hands on her hips and glared at him.

"My Lord Breckonridge," she declared in ringing

tones, "my cousin Sarah is in love with you and I hope you tell her I told you so."

Malcolm grabbed her about the waist and spun her about. The sound of a shout echoed to the rotunda roof two stories above them, and he was amazed to realize it had come from his mouth. He set Persephone down and she staggered back, blinking in obvious amazement.

"Bless you, girl," he told her, feeling as if his heart were soaring. "You don't know what you've done for me. I'll be happy to tell anyone anything you like."

She straightened, paling. "Oh, dear. I knew I shouldn't have done that. Sarah's right. I'm utterly lost. Please forgive me, my lord, for Sarah won't."

As quickly as his hopes had soared they plummeted. "Don't tell me this is your sad idea of a prank."

"Not a prank," she vowed. "But not my right to tell you. I'm having a very difficult time turning over a new leaf, my lord. Perhaps you should talk to my cousin."

"I've been trying to do that all morning," he growled, impatience rising once again. "Where is she?"

"She should be right behind me," Persephone promised, backing toward the stair. "A few moments, no more. Be gentle. I don't think she's in a very good mood."

"It couldn't be any worse than mine," Malcolm muttered as she flew up the stairs, out of his reach.

The few moments passed even more slowly than the time after breakfast. Malcolm paced the rotunda, clasping his hands behind his back to keep from hitting something. He caught the footmen stationed on either side of the door exchanging glances. Most likely they thought him mad. He wasn't sure they were wrong. All he knew was that it was possible Sarah had fallen in love with him. That had to change the equation in his favor.

The clock in the library chimed nine, the silver bells echoing against the marble tiles below him. Malcolm paused, frowning. Had he been pacing for nearly fifteen minutes? Surely Sarah could not be that far behind her cousin. Thoroughly tired of the surreptitious looks of the footmen, he stalked to the door and let one of them scurry to open it for him.

"If I miss Miss Compton," he told the fellow, "ask her to wait for me. We must talk." So saying, he strode down the graveled path for the stables.

He did not find her there either. "Has Miss Compton ridden in yet?" he asked a tall lanky groom who was rubbing down the roan horse he had seen Persephone ride before.

"No, my lord," the groom replied. "And her man was that worried, he went back for her and left me the work."

Malcolm frowned, stepping out of the fellow's way. He was sorely tempted to go after her as well, but he'd probably be as welcome as Persephone had obviously been. Sarah likely wouldn't appreciate him waiting for her at the stable either. He reluctantly returned to the house.

When another fifteen minutes passed, he found himself back at the stables. Persephone's horse had been returned to its stall and stood contentedly munching well-earned oats. The stall next to it yawned empty.

He found Old Dobbs, the head groom, in the tack room at the end of the stable.

"She's a fine lady," he said when Malcolm asked after Sarah. "She doesn't ride neck for leather like some. You watch; she'll come prancing in like the queen of Sheba."

The thud of hooves and the jingle of harness from the stable without belied his words. No longer caring for his dignity or Sarah's temper, Malcolm dashed into the breezeway between the stalls. The Compton groom was turning his horse in agitated circles.

"I can't find her," he panted, eyes wide in obvious panic. "I rode the whole length of the path. I've lost Miss Sarah."

"Saddle me a horse," Malcolm barked to Dobbs, who hurried to comply. More grooms and stable hands gathered from their various duties.

"You there," Malcolm ordered, pointing to a lively lad with unkempt brown hair and freckles, "go tell Lord Prestwick what's happened. Ask him to gather a search party and follow us."

As the boy scampered away, Old Dobbs pulled Chas Prestwick's stallion from the stable. The brute snorted and pawed the ground, ready to run. He eyed Malcolm with thorough distrust, but Malcolm merely swung himself up into the saddle, gripping the fellow with his knees.

"He'll get you there fast enough, my lord," Dobbs assured him with a throaty chuckle. "He knows when a gentleman is aboard, don't you, my lad?"

The horse snorted again, but although his sides quivered in anticipation, he did indeed heed Malcolm's directions. Malcolm clamped heels to flanks and sent the beast flying from the stable yard. The Comptons' groom pelted after him.

As they rode, he pictured Sarah fallen, bleeding, unconscious. His heart seemed to have stopped beating. Certainly his body had stopped functioning normally.

He found he couldn't breathe, couldn't think, couldn't do anything but pray she would be found safe.

"Coming up now, my lord!" The groom had to call it twice before Malcolm slowed. They had reached a spot in the woods that looked exactly like every other spot they had passed the last few minutes. Malcolm held the stallion dancing, eying the groom.

"It was here," the fellow explained. "I left Miss Sarah here when Miss Persephone took off. She said she would go right back to the stable."

Malcolm gazed around him again. Oaks clustered on all sides, but the wide sandy track was easy to see. She had been perhaps fifteen minutes from the stable at a good trot, less if she had gone to a gallop. How could she have gotten lost?

"Sarah!" He raised his voice, booming loud enough to cross the halls of Parliament. "Sarah Compton! Can you hear me?"

Crows racketed into the blue sky, the horses shied, and something small scuttled away through the bushes. The sounds were completely unsatisfactory when all he wanted to hear was her voice saying she was alive.

"We'll ride back toward the stable," he told the groom. "Slowly, this time, calling her name. Check the undergrowth for any sign of disturbance. If she fell or went off the track, we should find some sign."

It was difficult to hold the stallion to a walk. The black was content; it was Malcolm who chaffed. They looked and they called, but they could find nothing that told Malcolm what had happened. The smaller paths that led off occasionally had clearly been made by deer or other forest denizens. None looked large enough for a horse and rider to Malcolm's eyes, and none looked particularly disturbed. If there had been tracks in the sand, he realized, the groom's first trip and their subsequent trips had obliterated them.

They met Chas and his men part of the way back to the stable. It looked to Malcolm as if the young earl had roused every male member of his household, for Malcolm was certain the tall fellow looking most uncomfortable on horseback was one of the footmen from the front door. They clustered around him and the Comptons' groom, faces expectant.

"No sign of her," Malcolm reported, feeling suddenly old. "Do you have a tracker on this estate?"

"My gamekeeper," Chas told him, reaching out from his own horse to lay a hand on Malcolm's shoulder in support. "He's the best man I have. He's in Barnsley visiting family, but he can be here in an hour or so once he gets word."

"An hour!" Malcolm all but yelped.

Chas's hand gripped his shoulder. "I know, but rest assured he'll tell us what happened. Until he gets here, perhaps we should go by foot."

Malcolm shook his head as Chas withdrew his hand. "We've already disturbed any trail. It might be best to wait."

As soon as he said it he knew it was a mistake. If he had to wait, he would go mad.

"Easy, Malcolm," Chas said for the third time after they had searched the immediate area and taken to walking the horses. "You look as if you'll explode."

"How would you look," Malcolm challenged him, "if your lady were missing?"

"Worse than you, I imagine," Chas replied calmly.

"But in this case, I know Miss Compton can't have gone far. Perhaps the horse spooked then went lame. She's as levelheaded as my Anne. She'll be fine."

Malcolm was ready to be persuaded, but there was a sudden commotion from the woods. The horses perked up their ears. The stallion neighed in challenge. The grooms who had been sitting rose to their feet.

Sarah's horse cantered onto the path. Its heaving sides glistened with sweat; it rolled its eyes and shook its head. Dobbs dashed forward and grabbed its tangled reins to pull it to a stop.

Easily parting the crowding men, Malcolm strode to his side. Chas shoved through after him.

"The saddle's in place," he commented, but Malcolm could tell he was trying to mollify him.

"She were thrown," one of the grooms guessed.

"Not from Shadow," Dobbs argued. "Docile as a lamb she is. Perfect lady's mount. That's why I chose her for Miss Compton."

Roberts snorted. "Miss Sarah was a bruising rider. She could have handled that stallion there. This horse couldn't have thrown her."

They all started muttering. Malcolm felt as if the world were closing in around him. He turned and shoved his way back to the stallion, untying the lead and swinging up into the saddle.

"I can't stay here and wait," he growled to Chas, who had followed him. "I'm going back to the stable to see whether she walked in. Send for me when the gamekeeper arrives."

Chas nodded as Malcolm took off.

He prayed he'd find her at the stable, but the place was deserted. He thought he saw a pale face looking out the window of the manor, one of the maids most likely. Otherwise it was as if he were alone in the world.

And he would be alone, he realized. Without knowing it, his world had shifted. Where once it had been completely bound up with the petty politics of Parliament, now it centered on the happiness and safety of one Sarah Compton. Despite everything he had said and done, his heart had known what he really needed.

He had fallen in love with Sarah.

He shook his head. The thought amazed him. He was in love with her. She would have been delighted. He could see her smile in his mind. The last hurdle to their marriage was overcome as easily as his realization. Nothing else mattered but Sarah. As long as she was by his side, the rest would fall into place.

He did not dare think about what would happen if she could not take her place at his side. That way lay madness. But neither could he stand about the stable waiting. There had to be something he could do, someone he could talk to.

The face appeared again, to be joined by another, and then to disappear entirely. The maids wanted to know what was happening. With a pang he realized someone else would also be wondering. Persephone Compton must be nearly as frantic as he was. He strode for the house.

No footman snatched open the door for him, but the sound of it opening brought a flurry of silk as Anne and Persephone both appeared in the rotunda. Their faces were pale, and he could tell Persephone had been crying. Indeed, he had never seen the girl in worse looks. Her eyes were haunted, her complexion was sallow, and it looked as if she had been biting the skin off her lower lip.

"How are you faring?" he asked the two of them, knowing the words sounded insipid.

Anne managed a wan smile. "Tolerably well, my lord. Do you have news for us?"

"We found her horse," he offered. "I'm sure it will only be a matter of time before she's found."

Persephone wrung her hands. "I knew it. It's all my fault. She tried to tell me she was in no mood for my problems, and I wouldn't listen. She's probably been thrown; she may be dead!"

Malcolm strode forward and grabbed the girl's shoulders. "Nonsense! You give yourself too much credit, Miss Persephone. Your cousin is a strong woman, as nearly unflappable as our hostess here."

Persephone sniffed even as Anne's smile deepened. Malcolm let go of her.

"You were right to call Sarah the Incomparable Miss Compton," the girl murmured. "I will tell her so when you return her safely to us."

"You do that," Malcolm told her. "I should go now."

"A minute, Lord Breckonridge," Anne put in. She put a hand on his arm. "I know you are concerned about Sarah, but I thought you should know what was in *The Times* this morning." Her face clouded, and he wondered what could possibly be worse than Sarah lost to him.

"There was a gathering of the reformers near Manchester," she told him, and he could see she kept her voice level with effort. "Orator Hunt and some others were to speak."

Malcolm waved a hand. "I know about the gathering. That reporter, James Wroe, asked me to join them. It would have alienated me from half of Parliament. Don't tell me the fools went ahead with it."

"Worse, my lord," she replied. Even Persephone was staring at her now. "The Manchester authorities apparently panicked over having such a crowd near their town."

"Crowd?" Malcolm frowned. "How many people could have gathered?"

"According to *The Times,* nearly fifty thousand. There were nearly two thousand soldiers and local militia present as well. Before even a word was spoken by Mr. Hunt, the magistrates ordered the soldiers to disperse the crowd." She squeezed his arm with tight fingers. "My lord, they killed over a hundred civilians and wounded nearly four hundred more, some women and children."

"My God!" Malcolm cried, staring at her. "What idiot authorized that?"

"Apparently both Lord Liverpool and Lord Sidmouth agreed to the use of force," Anne replied softly, though her gray eyes were stormy.

Malcolm shook his head. "Madness! There will be hell to pay."

"There is talk of a special session," Anne went on. "In just a few months. Lord Sidmouth promised an act that would stop the dissenters."

"Over my dead body," Malcolm swore. "Why can't they understand? It is their irrational fear of peaceable demonstrations and rational reform that caused this tragedy. I must return to the capital, form a coalition. We cannot sit by while people are killed over this nonsense!"

Persephone bit her lip. Anne took a deep breath and nodded. "Of course, my lord. I'll have your carriage brought round. I'm sure Lord Prestwick can handle the search for Miss Compton."

Malcolm froze. Sarah. How could he leave with her potentially lost? Yet if he stayed the government might well be lost. He knew his struggle must be showing on his face, for both Persephone and Anne were watching him as if fascinated. But in the end, there was only one choice to be made. He stood straighter.

"No need for haste, my dear," he told her. "I'm sure it can wait until Sarah has been safely brought home."

Persephone smiled tearfully at him, and Anne beamed. Then she blinked. "Oh, in all the worries I nearly forgot." She reached into the pocket of her gown and extracted a sealed note. "Your valet left before lunch, as I understand you requested."

Persephone's eyes widened.

"We had a difference of opinion," Malcolm explained.

"I take it it wasn't concerning matters of dress," Anne said wisely. She handed him the note. "He asked me to give you this."

Malcolm waved it away. "I have no time for his apologies."

"Normally I would agree," Anne told him. "But he seemed to think it urgent that you read it as soon as possible. He said he had gotten it from a friend."

A friend? What nonsense was this? Appleby had no friends in Somerset that Malcolm knew of. But then, what did he know of Appleby after all but that the man could tie a credible cravat and take wine stains out of silk? Besides, it was possible it had something to do with the massacre in Manchester.

He took the note and broke the seal. He could not recall ever seeing Appleby's hand, but somehow the tight, left-canting writing did not seem to belong to his valet. Neither did the unsigned contents. He felt as if someone had stuck a fist in his gut and yanked out his intestines.

"My lord, what is it?" Anne cried, putting a hand on his arm.

"Lord Breckonridge, you are white as a ghost," Persephone chimed in. "Is the government going to fall?"

They mustn't know. He could barely think, yet he knew that was true. He could not tell them that someone held Sarah captive, that this someone was even now watching the house, that this maddeningly unknown creature demanded he come alone to a secluded corner of the estate by teatime or Sarah would be killed. He could not let them suffer the fears that wracked him, and he could not risk Sarah's life. He shoved the note in his pocket.

"The government will be fine," he told them. "I must go after all, but not to London. Lady Prestwick, you might send someone with word to your husband that if they do not find Sarah, be sure to check the eastern woods."

"But my lord," she started to protest.

"No time," he clipped, even as the clock chimed two. "Just send Chas word." For all he knew, the bells sounded his own death, and Sarah's. He pulled Anne into his arms for a quick hug. She stared at him wordlessly as he released her, face pale, and he wondered whether he would at last see that remarkable reserve crack.

"Safe journey, my lord," was all she murmured.

He bowed to her and Persephone and ran for the door.

TWENTY-TWO

Sarah lay on the floor of the loft in the gamekeeper's cottage, hands trussed behind her back, face against the rough-hewn planking. The planks were so rough, in fact, that shafts of light from the room below slanted like golden rods between the floorboards and disappeared into the darkness of the thatched roof above. By their light, she had been able to recognize the musty smell as coming from the furs hanging above her to cure. She could also make out the pile of bedding in the far corner that was probably where the gamekeeper's family slept, and the stone of a chimney rising to her right. She knew behind her lay the trapdoor and open stairs down to the main room. That was how Lord Wells had pushed her up here before tying her hands.

"What a pity you got in the middle of this," he had told her without a trace of sorrow in his voice. "I'm afraid you're simply a casualty of war. I promise to make it as painless as possible, providing Lord Breckonridge cooperates, of course."

She had tried to still her rising panic. "Lord Wells, I don't understand. What war am I in the middle of? What has this to do with Lord Breckonridge?"

"It's a shame, really," was all he would say before shoving her to the floor and placing his knee in her back to truss her up like a calf about to be slaughtered. "You should never have gotten involved with him."

She had fought the bonds and cried after him, but he had simply closed the trapdoor and left her in the darkness of the windowless loft.

She had no idea how long she'd been there, no idea why he waited. And he was waiting. If she put her eye to the nearest gap in the floorboards, she could see a sliver of the room below. Lord Prestwick at least took care of his gamekeeper. There was glass in the windows of the cottage; she had seen their sparkle as Lord Wells had brought her here. From the sunshine coming through them, she knew it was still day. She could see a part of the table and chairs the room held, and once in a while a hand with a frilled cuff moved across her sight as well.

He kept rearranging the things on the table. She could hear the scrape below as well as see the changes. First she saw a piece of parchment, then an inkstand and quill, then a brace of pistols, and finally the parchment again. When he wasn't rearranging the table setting, he paced. She could hear the boards creak under his shifting weight. Why did he wait?

Ignoring the pain, she strained at the bonds again until the warm dampness on her back told her she was bleeding. She tried to wiggle back to the trapdoor, but her dress caught on the uneven flooring. Squirming, she managed to tear it free.

Exhausted, she forced her mind to think. From her brief glimpse of the door, she knew it opened by use of a rope handle. She could hardly swing it open with her hands tied behind her. Even if she did, how was she supposed to get past Wells? The stairs down into the main room were open along the whitewashed cottage wall, in plain view of the simple room. She was trapped.

She lay listening to her captor pace. There had to be something she could do. He meant to kill her; he had said as much. He was either quite mad or completely wicked or both. She was lost unless she found some way to escape.

She was considering whether she could scrape against the chimney to loosen her bonds when there was a crash from the room below. Fastening her eye to the gap in floorboards, she could see that the room had brightened. Had someone thrown open the door?

"Good afternoon, Lord Breckonridge," Wells's voice drawled. "Won't you come in?"

Malcolm, here? She nearly cried out in relief, then clamped her mouth shut. He would need no distractions if he were to deal with that maw worm downstairs.

"Wells?" Malcolm barked. "What the hell do you think you're doing?"

To Sarah's mind he had never sounded more in command, or more dear. She could hear the thud of his boots as he strode into the room.

"Saving my father's name," Wells replied, all ice to Malcolm's fire. "You maligned him, you know. I think history will prove he was no traitor."

Malcolm's voice, when it came, was quieter. "Put the guns away, Wells, and we'll talk. I explained all this to your mother ten years ago, but you were away at school. I assumed she told you."

"Save us both the time," Wells quipped. "I heard what my mother had to say. I know the story. The great Malcolm Breckonridge, a rising star in the Parliamentary firmament, caught the lowly Winston Wells selling secrets to the French. You gave the old man the opportunity to turn himself in. He committed suicide instead, the coward's way out."

"That is history," Malcolm said. "It has nothing to do with your life, or Miss Compton's."

"Oh, but it has," Wells replied. "History is about to change. And Miss Compton is going to help it along. You see that parchment on the table? You will sit and write what I tell you or Sarah Compton dies."

There was a pause, and she could imagine Malcolm glancing about the room, weighing his options. *God, please let him think of something,* she prayed. *He's so clever. Surely You can make him think of something to save us.*

"How do I know you haven't killed her already?" he asked.

Wells raised his voice. "Do you hear that, Miss Compton? Be a good girl and tell Lord Breckonridge you are fine."

She refused to help him hurt the man she loved. Sarah grit her teeth and said nothing.

"Curse you, Wells, if this is a joke," Malcolm began.

"Miss Compton," Wells said again. "I have two rounds. One is reserved for his lordship. If you don't speak up, I'm going to fire the other into the loft. I know where I left you, Miss Compton. These boards are old. Do you want to take the chance that I hit you? Now, answer me please."

"Sarah," Malcolm's voice was raw. "For God's sake, if you are here, tell me."

She had no choice. "I'm here, Malcolm," she called. "But don't you dare indulge this dastard!"

"Such a way you have with the ladies, Wells," Malcolm quipped, though she thought she heard relief in his voice. "Now let her go and we'll talk."

"I'm afraid it won't be as easy as that, my lord," Wells replied. "There is only one way to remove the cloud hanging over my family. That is for you to take my father's place."

"What are you talking about?" Malcolm demanded, even as Sarah frowned.

"A sacrifice, my lord," Wells sneered. "Someone who takes the place of another, in exchange for a life. Your life, to be precise. You deprived me of my father. You have no idea what it was like growing up the son of a traitor."

"I knew what you'd have to face," Malcolm told him. "I did everything I could to help you. I opened doors in Parliament for you. You saw how I tried to convince Lady Prestwick to accept you."

Surely he spoke the truth. Sarah remembered the time he had gone out of his way to speak to Wells when she and Persephone were walking in the park.

Wells obviously thought otherwise. "Oh, yes, so good of you to defend me, after you'd obviously poisoned Lady Prestwick's mind," he declared. "You were always conspiring against me. Oh, I'll not deny you occasionally had your uses. But I knew you were only helping me to assuage your conscience. You cared nothing for me."

"I considered you a friend," Malcolm said quietly.

"A friend?" Wells laughed derisively. "You have no friends, Breckonridge. Haven't you figured that out? You have opponents, you have followers like that idiot Prestwick, and you have admirers. You let no one get close enough to you to be a true friend. That caused me no end of problems. How was I to find anything with which to bargain when you cared for no one? You live like a monk, like a saint!"

"How very disappointing for you, I'm sure," Sarah heard Malcolm quip.

"Disappointing and time-consuming. Do you know how long it took to plot this event? No matter which way I looked, no matter what I tried, it was clear you cared for nothing else. Until her."

Sarah heard Wells laugh. "Do you know," he continued, "I was as fooled as the rest of the ton. I was certain you were after the younger Miss Compton. Who would have thought you'd prefer her plain and penniless older cousin?"

"You can't see the truth, can you?" Malcolm said. "She's worth ten of her cousin, and a hundred of you."

"Love must be blind, as they say," Wells jeered even as Sarah's breath caught in her throat. "I was almost taken with the young Miss Compton myself. Yes, I courted her, in secret. Told the girl her family wouldn't approve. She found it quite romantic."

Sarah blinked. Of course—that explained Persephone's sudden interest in quiet walks by herself! She so easily talked Lucy into doing her bidding; she probably had sworn the maid to silence as well.

"For a time I thought I had her," Wells was saying. "What better way to bring about your ruin than to take the woman you loved? But she proved fickle even before I showed my hand. She refused to give me favors. She even slapped me when I attempted to do more than kiss her. You were all so blind. You never even noticed."

The ripped dress, Sarah realized. He must have been the suitor whom Persy had claimed had lost his head. He was right—Sarah had been blind. Thank God

Persephone had had enough sense to defend herself against the miscreant.

"Then," Wells complained, "you told me you were after the other Miss Compton. I knew what I had to do. It was only a matter of studying the estate and biding my time. I knew I had to make my move soon or risk facing you next session. And today, at last, it all came together. Now, sit and write or I fire."

What did he want from them? Sarah still did not understand. She heard the scrape of chair legs against the floor and at last saw Malcolm's dark head bending over the paper. Tears blurred her vision, and she blinked them away.

"What would you have me write?" he growled.

"A confession," Wells gloated. "You will confess that you were the traitor all along. My father caught you, and you killed him, making it look like a suicide. But your conscience weighs heavy and you must confess."

Sarah bit her lip. If that so-called confession became known, he would lose everything—power, position, reputation. "Malcolm, don't!" she cried. "I'm not worth it."

"Shut up!" Wells shouted.

The chair scraped back, and Malcolm disappeared from her view. She could picture him towering over Wells. "Leave her alone," he demanded. "Sarah, you are worth anything I can do. None of this matters without you beside me. Blast him, but he's right. You're my world, Sarah. Do you understand what I'm saying?"

The tears slid down her cheeks, splashing on the floor. "I understand," she said. "I love you too, Malcolm."

"How touching," Wells drawled. "Now sit down,

my lord. I'm afraid you cannot intimidate me by glowering. I'm used to your tricks."

"Think, Wells," Malcolm urged. "You cannot succeed. No one will believe this confession. If I got away with being a traitor all these years, why would I confess now?"

"Ah," Wells replied, "but now you have an added weight to your guilt. You see, poor Miss Compton found out about your little history, and you had to kill her as well. Such a shame. I fear it unhinged your mind. I was forced to kill you to save myself."

"You bastard," Malcolm swore.

"No bastard," Wells replied. "But nearly an orphan, thanks to you. Now, if you want to add a few minutes to your pathetic life, sit down!"

Sarah blinked against the floor, watching as the chair was moved away again, but Malcolm did not sit.

"You call me pathetic," he said in obvious disgust. "What about you, spending the last ten years of your life obsessed? What a waste was that? And the best you could come up with was a coerced confession that will convince no one?"

What was he doing? Did he think by keeping the fellow talking help would arrive? Or did he hope she might provide him with help? Sarah squirmed to angle herself over another board and only succeeded in getting a glimpse of his shoulder. Her movements must have alerted Wells, for he called to her.

"You can stop struggling, Miss Compton. I tied those bonds tightly. You won't be getting away. You won't even be breathing much longer if his lordship doesn't do as I say."

"Do you think writing a confession is easy?" Malcolm countered. "I'm an orator, man. I craft my words well. You want people to believe this, don't you? Then give me some quiet to think."

Quiet? Why did he want quiet? Why was he even humoring the fellow? He could only be sending her a message, but her panic-addled brain could not perceive it. "Think, Sarah," she muttered, trying herself to block out the blustering Wells was uttering below. The man was entirely too noisy.

Noise! That was it! Surely Malcolm was asking her to make a distraction. Her hands might be tied, but there was nothing wrong with her feet, or her mouth. She took a deep breath and braced herself.

Then she screamed as long and loud as she could, hammering her feet against the planking of the floor.

TWENTY-THREE

She'd done it! He knew she'd understand him. Wells's head jerked up, and on reflex he aimed the left pistol at the ceiling. Malcolm kicked the chair into his midsection and dived over it to slam the fellow into the floor.

With a roar, the left pistol discharged, the shot disappearing through the open door. *One down, one to go,* Malcolm thought grimly. He wrestled Wells as flat as he could get him, straining for the still-loaded pistol in his right hand. Wells was pounds lighter than Malcolm, his reach far shorter. It should have been easy to take the weapon from him. But to Malcolm's surprise, a manic light appeared in the baron's startled eyes. He brought up the empty pistol and smashed it against the side of Malcolm's face with savage intensity. Pain exploded in Malcolm's temple, but he shook off the threat of darkness it brought. Straddling Wells, he leaned on both arms below the elbow, pinning the man to the floor. Wells thrashed, but he could not get up. Nor could he do more than point the still-loaded gun away from Malcolm, upward at an angle.

"Drop the pistol," Malcolm gritted out, feeling blood running down his cheek.

"Go to hell," Wells replied. With a laugh of pure

madness, he aimed the pistol at the ceiling and fired. Sarah cried out and was silent.

Malcolm felt as if it were his own life that had been snuffed out. "No!" he cried. Leaning to the left so far that he heard the audible snap of Wells's arm breaking, he wrenched the now useless pistol from the man's right hand. Though he had to be in pain, Wells only laughed again.

"I still won, my lord," he jeered. "If I aimed correctly, she is dead, the only person you had the courage to love. May you die along with her!"

"You first," Malcolm replied, slamming his fist into the contorted face. Wells went limp.

Malcolm struggled to his feet. His numbed brain informed him that he was hurt. Glancing down at Wells, he noticed a puddle of blood pooling on the planking floor. Frowning, he touched his face. Had he broken a vein? His head protested the touch, but his fingers came back sticky with congealed blood. With eyes widening in horror, he realized the blood was dripping from the ceiling. He staggered for the stairs and heaved open the trapdoor.

She lay still on the floor. His heart broke at the sight. With a strangled cry, he scrambled across the low-ceilinged room to her side.

"Sarah," he moaned, kneeling beside her and carefully rolling her over. A wooden sliver as long and sharp as a hunting knife protruded from her shoulder. Looking past her, he could see where the ball had splintered the dry wood. With hands that shook, he wrenched the spike from her shoulder, praying she would not feel the pain. Fresh blood gushed from the wound. He yanked off his cravat and used it to stem the flow. Her eyelids flickered and flew open. Malcolm caught his breath.

"Easy," he cautioned, wanting only to hug her close in thanksgiving. "I'm here. Everything will be all right."

She nodded, apparently satisfied, and laid a pale hand on his. As always, her touch was curiously comforting, especially when he had intended to be the comforter.

"Wells?" she murmured.

"Unconscious for the moment," Malcolm explained. "I have his weapons. Rest a moment, and we'll try to get you out of here."

"Malcolm," she whispered, and his name was surprisingly sweet on her lips. "Malcolm, whatever happens, I love you, and I will marry you if you still want me."

"If I want you?" The question was so ridiculous that it wrung a laugh from him. "Madam, I could not think it possible for any man to want a woman more than I want you. Sarah, you are everything to me. I realized that as soon as I knew you might be in danger. You are my world, my lifeblood. If you want me to spend the rest of my life proving that to you, I will gladly do so. I love you."

"We can discuss the rest of our lives later," she murmured. "Right now all I care about are the next few minutes. Please, my lord, will you kiss me?"

He should deny her, tell her now was hardly the time, but his own heart demanded he do as she asked. He bent to kiss her gently on the mouth, savoring the sweet taste of her lips.

Sarah sighed. Her shoulder and arm throbbed with pain, but it was nothing to the joy and delight spreading through her. He loved her! She could feel it in his touch, hear it in his voice. She could taste it in his kiss. His love whispered in the way he held her, sang in the way he murmured her name against her lips. He had said she was everything to him. She knew that he was her world as well.

Gradually she became aware of noises below. Malcolm raised his head.

"My God, it's Wells," came Lord Prestwick's voice. "Malcolm? Miss Compton? Are you here?"

"Here!" Malcolm called. "In the loft. Miss Compton has been hurt. Have someone bind Wells, and none too gently. I'll explain later."

He gazed down at Sarah while voices and boots echoed below and up the stairs.

"Can you move, my love?" he asked.

"With you beside me, I can do anything," she promised.

Sarah lay with a bandaged shoulder on a chaise lounge in the forward salon of Prestwick Park. The local physician had assured her that while she would be stiff and sore for some time, no permanent damage should be noticeable. That was simply one thing more for which to be thankful. She smiled at Malcolm, who sat beside her like a medieval knight guarding some fabled treasure. His smile in return was warm, but she could sense his weariness. Still, there were so many questions in her mind.

She was obviously not the only one.

"I cannot believe Lord Wells was such a deceiver," Persephone was saying from the armchair one of Lord

Prestwick's servants had pulled up for her. "He was wicked beyond words."

"He was mad," Malcolm put in, voice solemn. "I don't know whether it was a gradual thing since his father died, or caused by some event in his life. I wish I could have helped him."

Sarah reached out and took his hand. "I'm sure you would have tried if you'd known," she comforted him. His mouth quirked in a smile for her, but there was no depth to it. She was certain he would be hurting from the events of today for some time. She only prayed she could help him through.

"But what I truly don't understand," he went on, turning to Lady Prestwick, who sat across from Sarah in an armchair matching Persephone's, "is how you knew he was up to something. I've come to respect your judgment, my dear, and your good sense. What did you see that the rest of us missed?"

"Not a great deal, actually," she replied, eyes clouding. "I had a hint to his true character, but I had no idea he was as troubled as this."

"You saw us that day," Persephone guessed next to her. "When he met me in the garden here at Prestwick Park."

Anne nodded. "I'm afraid so, my dear. As Lord Breckonridge learned, it's difficult to keep anything secret. I saw Lord Wells with you. I regret to say I was close enough to hear how he attempted to compromise you. I was about ready to call for help when you ran from him. You were quite right to slap him."

"That was the day I caught you crying, I suppose," Malcolm mused.

Persephone nodded, coloring. "He was so dashing. A love with him would have been forbidden, as he hadn't a feather to fly with. I suppose I thought it was rather romantic sneaking around. But I guess I really wasn't thinking at all. Of course, that was before I reformed. I swear I didn't know he was such a dastard either, my lord."

"I shouldn't have left you so much alone," Sarah lamented. "If anything had happened to you, Persy, I don't know what I would have done."

Persy's lower lip trembled. "I feel the same way about you, Cousin. I'm just glad nothing worse happened."

"He took us all in," Chas said from where he perched on the arm of Anne's chair. "You're lucky to be alive, Malcolm."

"I'm lucky, all right," Malcolm agreed, giving Sarah's hand a squeeze.

Although she relished the touch, Sarah was still confused. "But where was the gamekeeper?" she asked. "From what we saw, it appeared as if Lord Wells had been hiding in his cabin from nearly the start of our visit. Please don't tell me he did the poor fellow in."

Chas snorted. "Not Robbles. He's the size of a bear and nearly as friendly. His father, who lives in Barnsley, has been ill for some time. He had my permission to visit. Wells had originally intended to camp in the woods if he had to; he confessed as much to the magistrate when he was led off. Robbles's leaving was simply luck."

"Either way, I'm certainly glad you took Lord Breckonridge's advice to search the eastern woods, my love," Anne put in.

"Truth be told," Chas replied, "I didn't think about Robbles's cottage. We were actually some ways away when we heard Miss Compton screaming. You have quite a voice, my dear."

Sarah blushed. "As I've said, I can make my opinion known when need be, my lord."

"And so you can." Chas nudged his wife. "In fact, I'd say Miss Compton is fairly close to perfect, according to the demands of a certain gentleman. Let me see, what were those characteristics again? Can you manage a home efficiently, Miss Compton?"

"Prestwick," Malcolm growled in warning. Sarah felt a smile forming.

"She manages our home," Persephone put in. "Our servants adore her."

"Oh, really," Sarah said, while Malcolm muttered, "So I've heard."

"Thank you, Miss Persephone," Chas said as if they had not spoken. "I believe we can take that on good authority." He turned to Anne. "What else was there, my dear?"

"Can she listen to Lord Breckonridge's position and find the flaw in his logic?" Anne replied. "I can answer that. She found a decided flaw, one I believe Lord Breckonridge is at last quite willing to acknowledge."

"Agreed," Malcolm snapped, as Sarah's smile widened. "Now, perhaps we can stop this nonsense?"

"Ah, but can she correct his turn of phrase?" Chas persisted, that unholy twinkle in his emerald-green eyes. "Can she warn him when he is about to make an ass of himself?"

Malcolm surged to his feet. Sarah caught his arm with her good hand. "Malcolm," she said quietly, "you are about to make an ass of yourself."

Chas threw back his head and laughed. Sheepishly, Malcolm returned to his seat.

"Very well," he grumbled, although Sarah could hear the laughter behind his gruff tone. "If you insist on checking off each item on the list, allow me to finish it for you. I quite agree that Miss Compton is neat and dresses simply. She is also generally sensible, although I wonder that she is willing to be found in present company."

Chas chuckled even as Persephone squeaked a joking protest. "I think, then," his friend said, "that you are well and truly caught, my good man."

"You have your bride, do you not, my lord?" Anne added.

Malcolm's gaze met Sarah's. In it, he saw the answer to his hopes, his dreams, and his prayers. "I believe I have, Lady Prestwick."

"Even if all London thought you were courting the Incomparable Miss Compton," Chas teased.

Persephone blushed.

"I *was* courting the Incomparable Miss Compton," Malcolm replied, returning his hand to Sarah's. His touch was so warm and tender, Sarah felt it to the tips of her toes. "The Incomparable Miss *Sarah* Compton. You once said, my dear, that you would only marry a fellow if he were so in love with you that nothing else mattered. I am ready to declare myself that fellow. Before this company I ask you, will you marry me, Sarah?"

Gazing into his eyes, she could see herself the way he saw her—beautiful, competent, and thoroughly loved. When he was near her, she felt that way. He had broken through the wall she had built around her heart and she knew she would never want to rebuild it. His love was all she would need.

"Oh, yes, I'll marry you, Malcolm," she declared. "For I feel the same way about you."

As Chas cheered, Anne smiled, and Persephone clapped her hands with glee, Malcolm bent to seal the agreement with a kiss. It needed no act of Parliament, but merely the quiet certainty of their own hearts to tell them they had come home at last.

Dear Reader,

I hope you enjoyed the story of Malcolm and Sarah. I like to think we are all Incomparables in our own ways. Certainly we each deserve to be loved for who we are.

You may have noticed cameo appearances in this book by characters from my other stories. Sarah's friend Norrie, the Countess of Wenworth, found her true love Justinian again in "A Place by the Fire," in the anthology *Mistletoe Kittens.* Lord and Lady Prestwick had their scandalous courtship in *The Unflappable Miss Fairchild.* Lord and Lady DeGuis, whom Malcolm tried to convince to support Parliamentary reform, fell in love in *The Marquis's Kiss.* And that radical American Lord Brentfield and his artist wife would never have married if it hadn't been for *A Dangerous Dalliance.*

By the by, Malcolm's desire for reform had to be tempered for some time. That November, as a result of the massacre in Manchester, Lord Sidmouth introduced The Six Acts. These measures severely limited free speech and freedom of the press, rights Americans take for granted. But reformers did prevail, leading to the ultimate change in British government that increased the power of the House of Commons to what it holds today.

I love to hear from readers. Please visit my Web site at www.reginascott.com or e-mail me at regina@reginascott.com. If you send me a letter via Zebra, please enclose a self-addressed, stamped envelope if you would like a reply.

Happy reading!
Regina Scott